Ray Dennis

The

Uncertain

Trumpet

ROY DENIAL

ISBN 0-7414-3745-7

Published by:

PUBLISHING.COM

1094 New DeHaven Street, Suite 100
West Conshohocken, PA 19428-2713
Info@buybooksontheweb.com
www.buybooksontheweb.com
Toll-free (877) BUY BOOK
Local Phone (610) 941-9999
Fax (610) 941-9959

Printed in the United States of America

Printed on Recycled Paper

Published March 2007

Acknowledgments

While the author participated in many battle scenes similar to those depicted in this book, THE UNCERTAIN TRUMPET remains a work of fiction. Admittedly the dates and locations referred to are somewhat specific, but all actions and characters described are purely imaginary.

For guidance in chronology of the story I found the history of the Seventh Infantry Regiment compiled by Nathan William White to be an invaluable tool.

Also I am grateful to Sam Mabry and Carroll Evans, both of Benton, Kentucky, for their considerable assistance with research and with certain technical aspects involved in the production of this work.

For the accuracy of detail regarding treatment for the injury suffered by Chad I must thank Thane DeWeese, M.D., of Lone Oak, Kentucky.

Lastly, I am indebted to Rev. Don Wilson, of First Baptist Church, Benton, Kentucky, for his counsel in matters regarding scripture references that appear in this work.

Roy Denial
Benton, Kentucky
February, 2007

To LaVerne, my wife

Her unwavering support and encouragement throughout
our many years together helped inspire this work.

"For if the trumpet give an uncertain sound, who shall prepare himself for the battle? So likewise ye, except ye utter by the tongue words easy to be understood, how shall it be known what is spoken?"

I Cor. 14: 8-9
(King James)

I

God, how I dread making this call. But the wedding is off. I don't want it off. Matty doesn't want it off. But it's OFF! And I've got to let Matty know right away! So what do I tell her?

I cupped my hand over one ear and closed my eyes, trying to block out the steamy cacophony of the Post Exchange. *Hey, I don't need to be reminded about the noisy crowd of GI's behind me. I swear the line must go the whole length of the PX, out the door and halfway to Columbus, Ohio. Especially I don't need this tall, uncoordinated next-in-line garlic-breathing corporal on my neck, pushing me to finish my call.*

At the clinking sound of coins dropping into the pay phone, I glanced at my watch. *Seven p.m. – not the best hour to try reaching Matty on a Saturday night. She's probably getting ready to go out with her gal friends. Saturday night was always our –*

"Hello."

I recognized the gravel voice of Matty's father and shifted to the other ear. *Haven't really talked to him since he chewed me out that time for bringing his daughter home at 2 a.m. Even after I told him the concert had run late. Hey, Beethoven's Seventh is a s-l-o-w symphony. I guess he didn't appreciate me blaming everything on Beethoven.*

"Mr. Seagrave? This is Chad." My voice faltered a little. "Matty there?" *No response. This guy's a little gruff. Maybe after I've known his daughter for about twenty years –*

1

"Chad?" Alarm in her voice. "Everything alright?"

"Could be better, sweetheart." I paused, my throat running dry. "I hate to tell you this, but our unit's moving out in the morning. So I guess there'll be a slight change in our wedding plans." Her reaction, like fingernails scraping a blackboard – then a deep, guttural groan.

"But you said – "

"Yes, I know." I could almost see her – *blond hair in curlers, those cute, dark red Betty Boop lips pursed, mascara beginning to streak.* I glanced at the corporal behind me. *Maybe it would help if I spoke louder. Hate to have him miss any of this.* "The CO just gave us the scoop at formation. We're to be packed and ready to go by reveille."

"So soon? I'm picking up my train tickets tomorrow. Why didn't you warn me?"

"Blame it on General Eisenhower, my dear. He should have called me, but I guess he forgot, seeing as I'm only a private. Look, when we get to the next stop, I'll probably be able to arrange something."

"Probably? You mean – "

The sound of her sobbing. *It's tearing me up.*

" – then Mom's dream – it was right!"

"Her dream?"

"Yes," she said. "The Lord told her in a dream that your unit leaves for overseas right away. Chad, it was all so strange, this dream. You and all the other soldiers, standing there in formation alongside a large ship. In her dream I called out, but you didn't respond. Then suddenly you and the other soldiers started to march aboard the ship."

"The *Lord* told her? " I loosened my collar against the heat, my shirt sticking to me. "Does Hitler know about this?"

"No, silly. But tell me, does this mean that now there's no chance you'll get another leave?" Matty resumed her sobbing. "We had such plans! Surely, you're not going directly overseas – are you?"

"Afraid I better not answer that question, my dear. For all I know, Adolph's probably sitting up in bed right now listening to every word we say." I paused for her response.

Not a word. Finally I said: "Lighten up sweetheart. We'll figure out something."

"But Chad, Mom wouldn't joke about something like this. She said everything in her dream was so real!"

"My dear Miss Muffet, I don't care what her dream said, or what Simple Simon said. When I hear you talk like this, I come apart at the seams. So please do not get upset about a dream. Keep in mind that you and I are merely putting Plan A on hold. When I get to the new camp, we'll just go ahead with Plan B. Meanwhile, promise me you won't cry any more – okay? Now, I've got to get off the line before the corporal behind me has a heart attack. I suspect he's trying to reach Supreme Headquarters with an important message and I may be holding up the war."

Once more Matty's voice drifted back to normal. "Darling, I'm sorry," she said. "Perhaps it's all for the best. Maybe we've been rushing things too much. Maybe God wants us to – "

"I can barely hear you, Matty, but it sounds like you're back again trying to hassle God with a bunch of minor matters. Remember, God has plenty on his mind these days. The fighting in the Mediterranean, the battles in the south Pacific – "

"I can't help it, Chad. I want to see you so much."

"Sweetheart, my throat's growing dryer by the minute. Do not wear yourself out worrying about me. Once I get away from Corporal Garlic-Breath – "

"Chad, I'm praying for you – are you making fun of me?"

"Sorry. I know you think prayer will help, so don't let me get in the way." I paused for a brief moment to glare at the corporal, now leaning over my shoulder. "I better hang up before this guy goes into convulsions. But first, move a little closer to the mouthpiece on your phone." Then I touched my lips to the mouthpiece in front of me. "Not much of a kiss, my dear, but the best I can do from this far away. Once we reach our next camp I'll probably get a pass. Then we'll just activate Plan B."

"You mean I can come down there and we'll get married?"

Now how can I answer a question like that? If I tell her the truth, she'll have a hemorrhage. All this is so much like the discussion we had about her problem with her Biology professor back in her freshman year...

Since I'd had the same prof in my first year at Wellington, I tried to explain how 19th century scientists gave names to the various stages of Man's growth, how guys with a lot more smarts than me figured Man developed from simple-celled ancestors to ape-like tree-dwellers to our present stage of "perfection". When I'd finished my explanation, she about had a fit.

"Do you believe all that heathen talk?" she asked.

"Of course not, my dear"

So now as I contemplated her asking if she should catch a train and come down to the next Army camp so that we could get married...

"Yes, Miss Muffet," I said. "Hurry on down and let your dream come true."

When a beauty like Matty asks, you tell her anything to keep her happy. That's something us heathens learned a long time ago.

II

Plymouth, Michigan
August, 1943

Leaning forward in her wire-back chair, Matty flipped the switch at the side of her dressing room mirror.

Darn! All this light and I still can't get these curlers right! And everything's so blurry! How will I ever get ready for church tomorrow? How can I possibly even go to church tomorrow?

She snatched another tissue and dabbed at her eyes just as her mother leaned in the door.

"That phone call, Matty." Eva said. "Your dad passed it along before he realized who it was on the line. Don't tell me that guy's changed his mind."

"Mom, please don't refer to him as 'that guy'. His name is Chad."

"I know."

Matty made a face at the mirror and rolled the last curler in place. As Eva Seagrave entered the room, Matty gave her a frosty look. "If you already know so much, there's no need to tell you – "

"Now, now Matty. You're upset. All the fuss about wedding arrangements, train tickets and Lord knows what else. I can understand how you feel." Eva bent over and gave Matty a kiss on the cheek. She examined her reflection in the mirror, then looked down at the counter. "What are all these tissues doing here?" Her expression changed. "Matty, you've been crying. Don't do that, baby! I know it's been difficult for you making plans for a wedding so far from home. But just remember, when you go down to the station tomorrow, we can – "

"For your information, Mom, I won't be going down to any station tomorrow! There won't be any tomorrow!"

"Now what kind of talk is that?"

"Straight talk, Mom. Straight talk. He doesn't want me to come."

"What?" Eva exclaimed, her face ashen. "I don't understand. You mean Chad's breaking up with you?"

"Not exactly. He claims the Army's moving him to another camp!"

Eva pulled up a chair next to Matty. "You poor dear!"

"Don't 'poor dear' me! I should have known that sooner or later – Remember what you told me about your dream?" She began removing her curlers.

'Now, now. This isn't the end of the world – and leave those curlers alone!" Eva leaned over and kissed Matty's cheek again. "Just calm down Matty and tell me what Chad had to say."

Matty grabbed another tissue, and in between sobs, managed to explain the extent of Chad's call, all the while trying to keep her mascara from running any more. "...and I've been thinking more about that phone call. It could be God's plan, part of my punishment."

"Don't talk like that! You're not being punished for anything. I'm sure Chad will call back."

Matty shook her head. "All of a sudden, you're an expert on Chad?"

"I just believe that being a serious young man, he'll do what he promises."

"Oh, he's serious alright. I tell him I've been asking the Lord to protect him. I let him know what the Lord has been saying to me – and to him it's all a big joke!"

Eva placed her hand on Matty's shoulder and swiveled her around. "I thought you told me that Chad was saved."

"Believe me, Mom. I've witnessed to him several times – and he said he'd accepted the Lord, but – " her eyes rolled upward. "I don't know. Remember how I even tried getting him involved with the fellowship group at the university? He came to a couple meetings, then kept complaining that no one ever explained any of the terms to him. Finally, he just said that his schedule at the college paper was getting so heavy that he wouldn't be able to attend any more meetings." Matty looked away. "Fact is, I just don't understand him."

"You mustn't come down so hard on Chad. He's been such a faithful young man." Eva put her arm around Matty. "Let's go downstairs. I'll brew a pot of tea and we'll talk."

"Okay, maybe that'll help."

Matty and her mother shuffled through the hall toward the staircase. Suddenly back at the far end of the hall, a door opened and Leonard Seagrave leaned out. Matty and her mother stopped and looked back.

"You coming to bed, Eva? Don't forget, I've got an important meeting at the plant early tomorrow, so I won't be able to go with you to the train station." He focused his eyes on Matty. "*Now*, what's the matter?" he asked, shaking his head. "Don't tell me this new boyfriend's giving you a problem!"

"Dad! Please leave me – "

Leonard Seagrave nodded. "Okay, you guys handle it. I never got to know this new boyfriend very well, but I thought he was better than – "

Matty began to cry.

Eva held one finger to her lips. "Leonard, please! Let's not revive all that – "

The door slammed.

Later, as Matty and her mother sat at the kitchen table savoring their tea, Matty leaned toward Eva. "I'm sorry, Mom. I know this has been a long week for you and I'm afraid I've made matters worse by shouting at Dad. I can't seem to convince him that this time things are different."

"I know, but keep in mind that as the war effort keeps increasing, your father's job at Ford gets tougher. And I know at times he can become more cantankerous." Eva rose to set the dishes in the sink. "Come on, baby. We'd better get to bed." She took Matty's hand and they started up the stairs. "By the way, whatever happened to those on-campus sessions where you and Chad were going to study the Scriptures together?"

Matty shrugged. "Same deal. He met me in an empty study room a few times. But that lasted only a few weeks. Then he left for the Army."

Eva halted as they reached Matty's bedroom. "Might be a good idea to write Chad a nice, long letter. Explain what you've been through." She kissed Matty on the cheek. "I believe he'll understand."

As Matty kissed her mother goodnight and closed the bedroom door behind her, she contemplated the clothes strewn across the bed, the empty suitcase on the chair, the confusion of her desk and the hushed emptiness of her bedroom. She leaned back against the door. *How can I get Chad to understand something like that? I'm having trouble understanding it myself.*

*   *   *

"Sorry I'm late." Matty said, pulling her chair over to the small table her mother had secured next to the window in the 14th floor Restaurant of Peterson's Department Store. "My Summer lecture class ran a little long." She loosened the collar on her blouse. "It's a relief to have lunch someplace where they have air conditioning!"

"No problem, baby. Dad had to leave early for his meeting at Ford, so he dropped me off at the boulevard. I caught a bus downtown and managed to do a little shopping. Anything to get in out of the heat." She eyed her daughter critically. "Have you thought over what Dad and I said about you staying in school?"

Matty gazed out the window at the busy traffic along Woodward far below, then shifted her attention back to her mother. "I told you before how I feel about staying in college instead of contributing something to the war efl Now there's a new problem."

"Don't tell me!" Eva said. She paused while the waitress took their order. "Something that'll keep you from running for class president?"

"No. Nothing like that. It's the college paper. They ran an item about me in the gossip column: 'congratulating me on looking so good after the ordeal I went through in the hospital last year'."

Eva's hand went to her mouth. "I didn't think anyone knew about it – and I can't imagine you said anything to your friends."

"Of course not."

"Then where did the story come from?"

"I don't know, but that's just another reason why I should drop out of school for now, get a defense job and – I'm sure Dad will be furious when he learns."

"Yes, and I'm the one who would have to tell him." Eva focused her small blue eyes on her salad. "You remember how much trouble I had calming him down before. He was so embarrassed about the whole – "

She broke off suddenly, both mother and daughter avoiding one another's eyes, Eva poking at the shrimp, Matty spooning up her casserole, the only sound the clashing of dishes as the busboy cleared the next table. Finally Matty said: "I hope now that Dad's satisfied. I told him then that I didn't want the operation."

Eva leaned across the table. "Now, now, baby. We've been through all that. It's over and done with."

"Maybe for you it is," Matty said, a coldness washing over her voice. "But for me, it'll never be over. I need to get out in the world, to get a job."

"But you have a job."

"That's just a part-time job Stella got for me in the Administration Office. I'm thinking about working in one of the war plants, something full-time."

"My dear, you should be getting your education *now*, so you'll be ready to go into teaching when Chad comes back."

"But Mom, I'm only thinking about an interim job, just for the duration. Then when Chad returns – then, well, we'll see what happens."

Eva turned her attention back to her salad, enduring the awkward gap of silence that followed. Finally, she spoke: "I noticed that you had a letter from Chad yesterday. What did he say?"

Matty smiled. "It was so sweet. He told me again how much he loved me, reminding me of all great times we had going to the theatre together, how happy he was to find someone like me who enjoyed the classics."

"Chad's an unusual young man. I thought you said he didn't have much of an upbringing."

"As a little kid he lost his father to alcohol, so his mother had to get a job. Which meant that Chad spent a good deal of time alone at home."

""Not exactly a scholarly environment."

"I guess he just made the best of a bad situation. Chad told me that when he was a youngster, his mother got stuck with a set of encyclopedias. So he spent a lot of time reading through them."

"I can't imagine that did much for his social life."

"True, but don't put him down, Mom. Chad has a knack for developing friends wherever he finds himself."

"That's all very fine, baby, but what has he ever told you about his friends, the men in his outfit, for instance?"

"Mom, for goodness sakes! This is beginning to sound like the Inquisition! Remember, Chad's in the Army, so he doesn't get to pick and choose his friends."

"Frankly, some of the Army types I've heard of – "

"I do remember him mentioning a couple of his buddies. One of them's a Bible College student named Prescott." Matty paused to focus on her mother's face. "And he mentioned one other."

"Who was that?"

"Garret."

"Garret?"

Matty fell silent, her eyes locked with those of her mother. "But Chad doesn't say much about him."

III

Leaving the confusion of the Post Exchange, I zipped up my jacket against the blackness and the chill night air and headed down the company street toward the barracks, my thoughts in a jumble. I kicked at a small stone that lay in my path. *Damn this war! Why must I leave college, sail off to some God-forsaken country and begin shooting at people I've never seen before? Whatever happened to those simple, early days last year when I first encountered that cute little blond on the fifth floor of St. Francis Hospital. . .*

I was hurrying toward the elevator after visiting Thelma, my favorite cousin, when I noticed this gal with a walker trying to make her way down the hall, but with little success.

"Let me give you a hand," I said.

She merely shook her blond curls without looking up and continued to wrestle with the walker. When she tried a few more steps and nearly fell, I grabbed her arm and held it firmly until she had regained her balance.

"Better let me help," I said. "Another step like that and you'll be on the floor." This time, after pulling her blue silk robe tighter, she managed a smile. Then, with me at her side, she began the long, slow trek back to her room at the far end of the corridor. All the while I kept scanning the hallway, but the few nurses I saw were hurrying past us on other errands. By the time we reached her room, I had managed to learn (1) that her name was Matty, (2) that she was hospitalized briefly because of some "female" problems and (3) that next month she planned to enter Wellington U. as a freshman.

A freshman at Wellington?

When I heard this news, I could hardly control my voice! I told her that I'd be finishing up my senior year there as well. "Maybe we could – "

I stopped in mid-sentence when I saw that Matty had a visitor – a tall, attractive, middle-aged woman standing by the window. I hastily excused myself. "Hope to see you again, Matty, either at Wellington, or here at St. Francis – next time I come by to see my cousin."

Then I headed for the elevator.

During my ride back to the first floor my thoughts raced on ahead. *What a dream!! Compared to the frothy coeds I've encountered here at Wellington, Matty sends the needle right off the scale! And to think that in less than a month, she'll be right on campus – Holy Cow!*

Suddenly I became conscious of a middle-aged man waiting in the corner of the elevator. He motioned with his cane. "Main floor, sonny. Are you gittin' off?"

I nodded and resumed walking through the lobby toward the main entrance, still in a cloud. *Hey, if I expect to visit her again here at St. Francis, I'll need some sort of an excuse.* I unlocked the door to my car and then stood there staring at it. *What reason would I have for coming back every day? How about Thelma? Yeah, good old Thelma! That's it, Thelma, I'll come back to see you every day – and even after you're discharged, Good Cousin that I am, I'll still come back to St. Francis every day.*

As matters developed, I did manage to visit Matty for several days in a row. And I'm pretty certain she saw through the flimsy excuses I used to explain how frequently I showed up. Nonetheless, each time I returned, Matty made it clear that she enjoyed my impromptu visits.

However, on my fourth visit I found no Matty – only that same statuesque, silver-gray beauty (apparently her mother) seated by the window engrossed in a book.

She looked up, smiling. "Matty's out for tests," she said. "So it may be a while." She rose to shake my hand. "If I'm

13

not mistaken, you must be the young man who helped Matty with her walker the other day."

I nodded.

"At the time I thought my daughter was out for tests. There I was waiting in her room, never dreaming that she would venture out alone with a walker. Thank you so much for coming to her rescue."

"Lucky I came along when I did," I said.

Mrs. Seagrave shook her head slowly. "Sometimes, Matty's a little headstrong."

I glanced at my watch. "It looks like I missed seeing your daughter today and since I'm due back at the University in a few hours; would you join me for a quick cup of coffee?"

To my surprise, Mrs. Seagrave readily agreed.

As we settled down in one corner of the hospital cafeteria, it felt good to trade the medicinal odors of the Fifth floor for whatever fragrances Matty's mother was wearing. And I soon discovered why she had accepted my invitation for coffee so quickly.

"Matty has mentioned several times how much she appreciates all your visits," she said. "Especially your help when she was trying to walk. Naturally, I was anxious to meet the person who had had such a profound effect on my daughter."

"Frankly Mrs. Seagrave, I think she was pretty remarkable to begin with."

"Call me Eva."

"Okay, Eva it is."

"Unfortunately, Matty's not been well this year. So Leonard and I have – "

Abruptly Eva's demeanor underwent a rapid change. She rose from the table, nearly spilling her coffee. "Please excuse me," she said, "but I must get back upstairs again. I'll let Matty know you were in to see her."

With a mixture of dismay and puzzlement I watched Eva Seagrave disappear into the luncheon crowd.

Still troubled by Eva's abrupt departure, I had just joined the cashier's line to pay my bill when someone gave me a sharp poke in the ribs. I turned to find the culprit – Garret Wald. He and I hadn't seen much of each other since joining the Enlisted Reserve Corps last year.

We had been attracted to this special Army program because it would allow us to return to Wellington to complete our senior studies before being called up for active duty.

Garret focused his slate-gray eyes on me. "What're you grinning about?" he asked.

"Just this gal I met here at the hospital. She's a patient – and an absolute knockout!"

"Be careful, my friend," he nodded, "These young gals can play tricks with your better judgment. You don't want to be robbing the cradle."

"The cradle? What makes you think she's so young?"

My question seemed to catch Garret off-guard. "Well – uh," he shrugged. "I can't imagine anyone your age giving you a second look."

"Thanks a lot, buddy," I grinned.

During the next several weeks after Matty had left the hospital and we began dating, I discovered that her folks were "church people". So I anticipated the next inevitable step: Matty invited me to come to church with her. Naturally, I wasn't too excited about going. *Not when it would involve crawling out of bed early on a Sunday morning. And then listening to all those fairy tales about Jesus. Come on.*

"Thanks for the invitation," I said, "but unfortunately I'm pulling the night shift Saturday."

As the weeks passed and I gradually ran out of excuses, Matty managed to drag me to a few meetings of her Campus Fellowship Group. There I met a few students fresh out of Dull 101 and heard a few speakers repeatedly using terms like "salvation", "born again", "holy spirit" – and never bothered to explain anything. Finally, after a few meetings, I begged off.

Not one to give up easily, Matty soon came back at me with another invitation to church. "This one's special," she said. "I can't give you too many details. That would ruin the surprise, but I'm sure you'll love it."

Easy for her to say. I'm the one who'll be working the midnight shift this Saturday. So I'm not too excited about going anywhere Sunday morning... Then again...I can't keep turning down chances to see Matty.

"Okay," I said finally, summoning a smile." Count me in."

Making good on her promise, the very next Sunday Matty met me at the door of her church, led me through the cloakroom, past the ushers and down the center aisle beneath a spectacular vaulted ceiling to the pew where her parents were waiting. Then, to my surprise, she excused herself and disappeared through a door to the right of the pulpit. Somewhat embarrassed at this sudden turn of events, I forced a weak grin, hoping the Seagraves would offer some explanation. They merely smiled back.

I was still in the process of studying the church bulletin when Matty reentered the sanctuary through a side door opening onto the rostrum. She took her place behind the pulpit, her small, cherubic face assuming an other-worldly glow. The Director then signalled the choir to rise, and before I could grasp what was happening, I heard Matty's clear, bell-like tones soaring above the counterpoint of the choir. For several minutes the lofty, ethereal quality of her voice held me in its gentle grip, transporting me to a more peaceable realm where a bright horizon beckoned with the promise of lands unmarred by war. I knew then that I must cleave to this angel.

IV

North Haven-on-the-Bay, Michigan
August, 1942

Spurred on by the fresh scent of early morning, I pushed aside the thick brush surrounding the lone birch tree and struggled to reach an opening in the woods and a clear view of the beach far below.

To my left the white sandy shore extended for a vacant half-mile before reaching the Big Ditch where, hip-deep in the sun-sparkled waters, several fishermen in waders were casting their lines after the lake trout. To my right I could see more than a mile of pristine white sand all the way to the Arenac County line – undisturbed but for several large boulders and a lone figure moving steadily in my direction, frequently stopping to select a seashell, sometimes darting to one side whenever a sizable Lake Huron wave came crashing ashore.

That must be her!

Slowly I began to pick my way down the slope, careful to use the brush along the slope to screen my descent, halting at times when my jogging shorts or my sweatshirt became entangled.

When I reached the bottom of the cliff, I could see with greater clarity the lone walker I had glimpsed before. Barefoot, she wore a bright yellow jacket over her swimsuit and had stopped alongside one of the large boulders, her head bowed. Waving and calling her name, I began jogging in her direction.

She's still too far away to recognize me.

As I drew closer, she suddenly looked up, shock in her face, then puzzlement. She waved frantically, shouting "Chad! Chad!"

Once I reached her and we embraced, she pushed me away, pretending to frown. "I don't understand," she said. " I thought you were back in Detroit. What're you doing up here? How did you – "

"One question at a time, my dear," I said, still puffing from my run and clasping her two hands in mine. "I wanted to surprise you. At the cottage they told me that you were down walking the beach."

"How *ever* did you get up here?" she asked. "I figured that on a Saturday morning you'd be hard at work turning out Ford automobiles."

"When I talked to you on the phone a couple days ago," I paused again to catch my breath. "I'd just learned that I had the weekend off."

"But why didn't you tell me you were coming up here?"

"That would have spoiled all the fun. Once I had word from cousin Thelma that your folks had rented one of the cottages at North Haven for the week, I thought I'd try hitch-hiking up here and surprise you."

"Well, I must say, you certainly accomplished your mission!"

I fell in step alongside her and we continued slowly jogging back toward the North Haven cottages, frequently passing inlets dominated by the fetid smell of dying seaweed and stagnant water. We maintained our easy pace until we reached a point in front of the North Haven property. Here the bluff stood back a good fifty yards from the water. A plain wooden stairway led from the beach up the slope to the cottages above.

As we paused to get our breath, I could see a cluster of vacationers watching us from the top of the stairs.

"Lucky I was able to snag a couple of good rides last night," I said. "Got me here by midnight."

"Did your cousin know you were coming?"

"Thelma and Aunt Hazel know me pretty well. They're always ready to put me up for a couple nights. This trip is special because they both want me to see the new little one."

Matty suddenly put her hand to her face. "Oh, you mean Thelma has a baby?"

"Yeah, it's high time that Thelma's little punker meets his uncle and – what's the matter?"

Matty had stopped and was rubbing her forehead. "Nothing," she said. "Guess I got a little winded."

"You look pretty pale. Sure you're okay?"

"Don't be such a worry-wart." She broke into a grin.

"By the way, when you were standing by that boulder back there, I noticed you had your head down. You're not ill, are you?"

"Nothing like that, Chad." Color flooded across her face. "I was praying."

"Praying? Are you kid – " I stopped abruptly. "What were you praying about?"

"The boulder."

"The boulder?"

"I know it may sound strange to you, Chad, but at that moment I just felt the Lord was speaking to me–about the rock, about all the fierce winds and rough waves that have crashed against that rock over the years. Yet it still stands."

"You mean that God is that interested in rocks?"

"No, silly. But at that moment a strange feeling came over me. Suddenly I could see that the Lord was reminding me that *I* could have that kind of strength – if only I would ask Him."

Matty's eyes sought mine, as though searching for understanding. I looked away.

"So that's what you were doing – praying for strength?"

Matty's eyes filled as she spoke. "Yes. I was praying." Then she smiled.

"Fine –" I stammered, "whatever works for you." I decided to wait while Matty regained her composure.

The plaintive call of a seagull drifted on the wind. I watched, fascinated, as two gulls swooped into a wave and

19

suddenly dropped onto the water, one with a perch hanging from his bill. When the other gull attempted to snatch the perch away, he swam off.

Finally I motioned for Matty to follow and we drew even with the stairway that led up from the beach to the cottages above. I stopped alongside the bench at the foot of the stairs. "Come along, Matty" I called out. "I see Thelma's at the top waiting for us. You'll want to hold the baby." I waited while Matty caught up, but as soon as she reached the stairs, she slumped onto the bench.

"You go along," she said. "I'm still a little out of breath. Maybe I'll get a chance to see the little guy later."

What can I say? She looks so pale. Finally I said: "Sure, you take it easy for a while. I'll stop over at the cottage after breakfast."

I have to admit that at the time I was a little concerned about Matty's health. I soon learned, however, that she was built of sterner stuff. I guess incidents like that only helped me realize how much Matty had come to mean to me.

So one warm and clear October day I found an opportunity to give her something special.

Seated with me on the ground beneath one of the few large maple trees on Wellington's small campus grounds, Matty set her bag lunch on one of the sparse patches of green grass. I selected a cigarette from my pack while Matty began to pull apart my clumsy attempt at gift wrapping a book.

"Wordsworth!" she exclaimed. "One of my favorites! How did you know?"

"You forget. I'm in your World Lit class. I hear all those questions you ask about the English poets."

"Not just the English poets. You should see our library at home. We've got collections of French poetry, German poetry, Italian – you name it. Whenever Dad returned from one of his business trips, he frequently brought me some little volume that he'd picked up in a used bookstore." Matty hugged the book I had given her, then asked: "How about all those questions *you* ask the prof? Sometimes I feel sorry for the guy. You challenge about every other statement he makes."

I cupped my hand over the cigarette to protect it from the slight breeze that had come up. "That, my dear, is what we call the educational process."

"Okay, Mr. Smartypants. But I thank you just the same." She brought the book up to her lips. "A truly thoughtful gift."

"And a truly unthoughtful act, young lady."

"Unthoughtful?"

"After all the time the doctors spent on you in the hospital, now you're back kissing books?"

Matty's smile disappeared. "I wasn't in the hospital for kissing a book."

"Well, whatever the reason, please do not waste precious time kissing books while in the presence of an eligible alternate, such as myself."

At that Matty's smile returned. "Chad," she grinned, "you're an absolute nut." Then she leaned over and kissed me as the Chapel clock chimed the hour. *Time to head for class.*

*   *   *

That little episode about the Wordsworth book only confirmed my early impression that Matty and I shared many interests. And it wasn't long before she suggested we go see an upcoming performance of Gilbert & Sullivan. Although I must admit that "HMS Pinafore" didn't hold the attraction for me that it did for Matty, I readily agreed to go.

"And don't worry about getting good seats," she cautioned. "My neighbor, Stella, has a student assistant friend in the Theatre Department. And if you've never seen a Gilbert & Sullivan operetta, then you're in for a treat. Between the comic libretto and what passes for dancing, you'll be laughing until it hurts!"

*   *   *

As the curtain fell on Act One, I had to admit that Matty was right. "You've convinced me," I said "Gilbert & Solomon have certainly put together one hilarious play."

Matty poked me in the ribs. "Chad, if I can arrange seats five rows from the orchestra, surely you can learn the names of the playwrights."

"Okay. How about 'Gilman & Sullivan'?"

"Did I ever tell you that you're a nut?"

"The last time that happened, you gave me a kiss."

"Well, don't expect one in front of all these – Look, there's Stella! She and Norm in the second row." Matty beckoned them to come and join us.

I nodded and we rose from our aisle seats to greet them. As Matty took care of the introductions, I could see that Stella was accustomed to being leader of the pack.

"That First Act – absolutely perfect!" she said, then turned to her escort. "Would you believe, Norm didn't even like it!"

"Not true, Stella," Norm retorted. "I just never – "

"Stop it, you two!" Matty said "That's no way to act when I'm trying to introduce you to my date."

I shook hands with Norm. "Don't listen to Stella," he said. "She's never happy unless she's putting me down."

"Don't give me that, oh you of generous proportions." Stella nudged Matty. "Norm may talk like Jack Sprat, but believe me, he can't wait to get to the lobby and those little cream puffs they always carry."

"Blabbermouth!" Norm grunted, pretending to scan the aisle behind us. "Now everyone knows my secret."

"Maybe we better get moving before the next act begins," I suggested, then nodded to Matty. "Do you want to head for the lobby, the Ladies Room, or some other point of interest?"

She grinned. "I just might try out one of those little confections Norm's so excited about." She turned to

22

Stella."By the way, 'thank you' for lining up such fantastic seats!"

"*C'est rien*. My friends at the Ticket Office always help me whenever the University lines up one of these road shows. Just look at this crowd!"

Matty turned to scan the seats behind us. "What I'm actually looking at are rows and rows of beautiful gowns, plus a few I wouldn't – " She gasped.

A few moments passed before Matty realized that I was calling her. Then she looked up at me, her creamy complexion now a chalky white.

"Matty!" I said. "Are you all right?"

"Yes, yes!" she whispered. "Just feel a little tired. Maybe I'd better skip Norm's little pastries."

"Okay, my dear, but I don't want you sitting here all by yourself."

Stella shook her head. "Not to worry, Chad. I'll stand guard here with her." She patted Matty on the shoulder. "Unlike some mortals, we don't need any of those little cakes."

"That's right, Matty," Norm said. "You just stay right where you are and listen to your Uncle Stella."

*   *   *

"I hope this rail is strong enough to hold me," Norm said. He leaned back against the balustrade as he balanced a paper dish holding his small, chocolate-covered pastry. Then, startled, he looked at me. "Chad, you're not eating!"

"You're doing enough eating for the two of us." The saccharine smell of little pastries pervaded the atmosphere. "Coffee and a cigarette are all I need. Got a long night ahead of me."

"I heard you're back on the graveyard shift. Don't know how you do it. Hours like that and I'd be a zombie."

I nodded in agreement. "That sounds so much like my mother – right up to the day last year when she passed away."

"That was a compliment, I trust." Norm took another bite. "Now that Registration's over and we're well into the fall term, you going to keep at it all through the year?"

"Not on your life! I'm planning to leave Ford's the end of this month. The small salary I'm getting as Editor of the Wellington student newspaper will help some, but it'll be a tough year for – " I stopped to wave at someone short and muscular emerging from the serving line. "Hey Garret! Over here!"

Dressed in a white crew neck, plus a brown sport jacket and slacks, Garret waved in an overtly casual response. Cup in hand, he maneuvered his way through the crowd and joined us at the railing.

"I tried to reach you last week," I said. "Been out of town?"

"Just for a couple days," Garret replied, sipping his coffee and eyeing Norm, now preoccupied with the remnants of his cake.

I looked first at Norm, then back at Garret. "Hey, I thought you guys knew each other."

Both men nodded. "Sure, "said Norm, "we used to work together."

Finally, after an awkward silence, I spoke up. "Don't tell me Garret Wald came to this affair all alone."

"Hardly," he shrugged. "I brought one of those cute freshmen who usually show up on campus at Registration time, not looking for an education, but maybe a little excitement. Right now she's in the powder room, as they say." He turned to Norm. "I bet I can guess the dame you brought."

Norm wiped his chin with a napkin. "You know me – Handy Andy." Then he managed a wry grin. "But we get along fine. Stella's the easy-going sort."

"You could have fooled me," Garret snorted.

I prodded Garret, nearly spilling my coffee. "Can we talk about something besides Stella?" I asked.

"Okay, how about this." Garret gestured toward me. "Are you packed and primed for action? Now that we're officially in the reserves, we better be ready to move out at a moment's notice."

"You trying to scare me?" I asked. "You know very well that the recruiter promised we'd have time to finish our undergrad work before we leave."

That drew a half-smile from Garret. "Sure, and ol' man Roosevelt will just hold up the war till we get there."

"Wait a minute you two civilian heroes! " Norm said. "Let it be known that I too have tried to do my duty. I volunteered to serve in the Navy."

"Was that *our* Navy?" Garret asked.

"No, dear friend, it was the Hungarian Navy!" Norm glowered briefly, contemplating the remains of his pastry that had fallen to the floor. "Regardless, I was rejected. Flat feet." He shifted his gaze to me. "By the way, neither one of you Sad Sacks appears to be very enthusiastic about your future in the Army."

"If you're looking for an optimist, Garret's your man," I said. "He's the perennial optimist. Every week he's working on a new skirt." I elbowed Garret. "Which one is it this week?"

"A tall, thin brunette," he replied. "Not like that last little blond. She really screwed me up."

"Garret, you're getting busier all the time," I laughed. "That's one you never even told me about."

A buzzer sounded. Norm looked at his watch. "Hate to interrupt this enlightening conversation, but since I don't have time for another pastry, we better get back to our seats."

As we hurried down the aisle, Garret nudged me, pointing to a rather tall, but gorgeous brunette seated five rows back of ours. "That's the babe I was telling you about. I expect I'll have fun with her."

Knowing Garret, I could well imagine.

When I reached Matty, Stella had already left for her seat.

"Whatever did you two talk about?" I asked Matty. "You look like you've just lost your best friend."

"Do I? You'll have to forgive me. Sometimes I get a little moody."

As the orchestra began the overture to the Second Act, I couldn't help but grin in anticipation of what the play would bring. I glanced at Matty. "Everything okay?"

"Sure, sure," she said, summoning a smile.

But something in her voice and the watery glint in her eyes spoke otherwise.

Then suddenly the curtain arose and once more we fell under the spell of "Pinafore".

*   *   *

Though initially I attributed Matty's moodiness to the loneliness she had experienced in the hospital, but when it persisted even to the time of the Senior Dance, I began to suspect that she was battling quite another demon.

We had settled at a small table at one end of the dance floor. Hands folded, Matty appeared ill at ease.

"So I've got two left feet, my parents were Baptists and Arthur Murray taught me in too big a hurry, " I grinned, reaching across the table to cover her hands.

Matty shook her head, blond curls glistening under the dim light. "You know it's not that. I'm just a – a little chilly."

"Let me get your wrap."

"No. I'll be alright."

I removed my sport jacket and slipped it over her shoulders. "There. Tan looks great on you. Now get comfortable because I've got an important question to ask."

Again that uneasy look. I watched as she folded and refolded her program. "A plate of black-eyed peas and a Japanese eggplant if you can guess what I'm about to ask you."

Her smile returned. "Chad, we've been going together for such a short time."

"It's been almost three months now."

"True, but – "

"No buts, young lady. It's been long enough."

"Marriage is a big step," she said. "With a war on and our careers to think about, marriage seems so …I know that if I intend teach music, I'd better knuckle down for the next three years or more. And you – "

"By next June I should have my Bachelors"

"But what about your enlistment?"

"Like I told you before, the sergeant at the enlistment center told Garret and me – "

Her head came up." Who?"

"Garret. We joined up together. Don't you remember? I told you about him. He's been my buddy since our freshman days. You'll have to meet him."

Matty looked away toward the dance floor, apparently for Stella and Norm. They were to join us after this dance. "Now I remember" she said, without looking at me. "The sergeant promised that you'd be able to finish your degree work before being called up for active duty."

I noted a quavering in her voice, something I couldn't quite interpret. "Okay," she continued, "so you get your degree next June, after that – what?" A pause, then: "Chad, you must know how much I love you, but – well, this marriage business…" Her voice trailed off. "It's just something I'll have to talk over with my folks."

I tilted her face toward me and kissed her.

Matty squeezed my hand. "Mom probably won't object, but my dad – "

"Yep, he's the one alright." I looked into her eyes, probing those emerald depths, trying to understand the anxiety I saw there. "But you will talk to your mom and dad about it this weekend?"

"Yes."

"Wonderful!" I rose and took her hand. "Hey, the band's getting ready for a break and the band leader's sobered up. So let's show'em we still know how to cut a rug."

27

V

Hey, they say the sound and feel of a train clickety-clacking its way to somewhere – that's supposed to be relaxing – right? Are you kidding? I haven't been able to relax since our troop train pulled out of Shenango this morning.

"Where you been?" Garret asked as I slumped down in the seat beside him.

"Waiting in line at the john," I replied.

"Man, you're lucky to have any kind of a seat in this car. You wouldn't believe how many GI's I had to fight off to save this seat for you."

"Thanks, but I'm not surprised. You should take a look at the seats in the other cars. Some wicker, some wooden. Try sitting on one of those for two or three days. Nothing like we have. I bet some of those older cars go back to the turn of the – "

"For God's sakes, Chad, forget the museum lecture." Garret paused while I lit a cigarette. "Do you realize, we almost ended up riding an open-air hand car? Thanks for calling me over just when I was about to board the train this morning."

"Don't get your shorts in an uproar. I just wanted you to meet my gal friend's parents."

"My God! Is that all?"

"Well, I didn't call you over because you were some hopped- up movie star leaving to serve his country. I wanted you to meet the Seagraves so you could give me your

28

impression of them. But you were in such a damn hurry, you never gave yourself a chance to size them up."

"Frankly, I didn't need much of a chance. I could read them like a label on a beer can. They're a bunch of religious stuck-ups. Didn't you say they were church-going folks? You're probably lucky your wedding was postponed. If I were you, I'd avoid your galfriend's parents like the plague."

Just then our train swept past Main Street in a small Pennsylvania town, the crossing gate flashing, the bell ringing and a line of autos dutifully waiting their turn.

I gave Garret a dirty look. "Stop it little man, you're breaking my heart! "

"Okay lover-boy, enough about her folks. You've traveled the train while I've been trapped here, saving your seat. So tell me, what does the rest of the train look like?"

"Not much. We have only four cars in our train – three for personnel plus a baggage car. The Mess Sergeant controls the baggage car, but does that mean we're gonna have a hot meal with all the trimmings? Not on your life! Sgt. McLeod has taken a good old khaki Army blanket and spread it out on the floor. And to show what a fair-minded egalitarian he is, anyone with a few bucks will be allowed to kneel down and roll the dice. While the rest of us have the privilege of dining on a wonderful, cold can of C-rations."

Garret's face lit up. "Yeah, I know McLeod and the way he works, but that part about the Army blanket sounds interesting. Guess I'll have to pay a visit to the baggage car later." He glanced out the window past a small farm and the forested hills in the distance. "When I get back, I'll take over guarding these precious seats so that you can go."

"Right now, you'd better count me out. I've got some serious thinking to do."

"Serious thinking?" Garret grinned. "You still worried about what's-her-name?"

"Yeah, what's-her-name. Would you believe, when we get to our next camp, Matty wants to come down so we can get married?"

Garret's expression clouded over and his voice dropped its playful tone. "You know the scuttlebutt," he said through his teeth. "We're heading for Newport News, port of embarkation. This Matty better wake up to the facts."

"Garret, I told you before, Matty and I had these plans to get married. Granted, you and I know Uncle Sam's shipping orders have knocked those plans for a loop. But she doesn't realize it yet – and so far I haven't had the heart to tell her." I let out a long sigh. "When we get to Newport News, I'll just have to phone her with the latest scoop."

Garret unbuttoned his Eisenhower jacket. "My friend, you're hopeless! Have you already forgotten what the colonel said: 'No passes, No visitors. No phone calls?' "

"Okay, so I'll write her."

Garret's eyes narrowed. "You know why you run into so many complications? Let me tell you something. Most of these young girls don't know what the hell they want. And this Matty is no exception. You'd be far better off if you followed my policy: Love 'em. Leave 'em. That way, no problems." Garret rose and stretched his arms. "But I've dispensed enough of this advice to the lovelorn. I hear a couple of little white cubes calling to me. So I'm off to the baggage car."

With mixed feelings I watched him disappear down the aisle past the other members of our company, some playing cards, some reading, others sleeping. *For a guy who fools around so much, Garret's really down on women. I can't think of Matty that way. Not a decent girl like Matty.*

VI

"Listen to me, Prescott! You're better off if you stay up here on deck!" I grabbed his shoulders and backed him up against the bulkhead.

The slim, young GI slowly slid down into a spread-eagled sitting position on the deck. "Y'all lemme be!" he mumbled. "This here sea is killin' me!" His face pallid, chin sagging against his chest, he reached for the helmet liner I had retrieved from the deck.

Kneeling, I shouted in his ear to make myself heard above the roar of the sea. "Just sit here and take in more of the fresh air and whatever sunshine comes along. You don't need to breathe in any more of those damn diesel fumes down in the hold." I got back on my feet, keeping them far apart to compensate for the pitch and roll of the ship. "I'll be back in about a half hour."

I opened my mess kit and I staggered back toward the galley, squinting at the sun dancing off the waves, frequently turning my head to avoid the spray. *From the rust around the bulwarks and scuppers, it sure looks like this Limey tub has seen its better days. Sure hard to figure. Is the U.S. hurting for equipment already? If not, why are we GI's being shipped across the ocean on a British ship?*

Outside the galley entrance the noon meal line was shorter than usual, thanks to the rough seas. Not recognizing anyone in line, I decided to eat my chow seated on the floor in one of the passageways.

31

Fish and tomatoes again? Plus crushed pineapple? For breakfast? This is the third time since we left Newport News. Are you Limeys trying to poison us? Somebody better warn His Honor, Winston Churchill, that if us GI's get fish, tomatoes and pineapple for one more breakfast, there's gonna be mutiny aboard one of His Majesty's ships. Hey, I've been able to avoid the heaves so far, so there's no point in pushing my luck. I'll just avoid the misery by tossing the whole damn meal overboard—now, rather than later.

Before I could get to my feet, however, Garret squeezed down beside me.

"Whew!" he exclaimed, "That last wave got me. I'm soaked!"

"Better get your jacket off. In that wind you'll freeze!"

Without rising I helped him pull free of his jacket. Then I gave him a swig of my coffee. "The Limey's don't know how to make coffee, but at least it's hot." I looked out the passageway door at the darkening sky. "It's been eight days now. Where do you think we'll land?"

"The latest scuttlebutt is Africa. If we were heading for England, the weather would be even worse." He studied the contents of my mess kit. "You want that pineapple?"

I dumped it in his mess kit. "The guys in mortars are lucky," I said. "They get bunks and we get hammocks. How'd you make out last night when the sea started to roll? I nearly fell out of mine."

"No reason to gripe, my friend. In these heavy seas the German subs will probably leave us alone. Too hard to get off an accurate torpedo."

I scrambled back to my feet. "I better check on Prescott. He's out on deck sick as a dog."

"That dumb hillbilly is lucky to have a nursemaid like you," Garret said without looking up.

I found Prescott where I'd left him. Replacing his canteen, I could see that he had already taken the pills that the medic had given him before dinner. I suggested it was time he went back to the hold. Then I steadied him as we slowly descended the ladder to our level amidships. Helping him into his hammock, I could hear him mumbling. Each time the same phrase over and over again: "Please God, please help me! Please God!"

I shook my head in disbelief, stowed my messkit and started back topside. *Prescott's out of his mind. With all the killing that's going on in Europe and the Pacific right now, how does he figure that this god of his has time to deal with little stuff like a case of seasickness?*

Due to the constant lurching of the ship, Regiment had canceled calisthenics on deck. This left me free to explore the ship. Before long, I discovered an unsecured door to a large stateroom that in peacetime must have served as a casino. Except for a group of GI's gambling at the far end of the room, I was free to select a booth with reasonable light where I could reread Matty's last letter. Fortunately, it had reached me at the final mail call before we boarded ship.

*   *   *

August, 1943

My dear, sweet Chad:

It's been so hard to accept the fact that you'll be leaving the country before I get a chance to say 'Goodbye'. But I must. You'll be glad to hear that I've returned to campus for the fall semester. And it just won't be the same without you. I'm seriously considering whether to drop out of school after finals in January. Dad's working such long hours now that Ford has begun producing aircraft engines. Mom has been trying to do more canning and I know she needs help. By staying out of school until the war's over, I could take a defense job and help cover my own expenses at home. I've asked the Lord to help me, but so far he hasn't chosen to give me any hints.

Rationing is getting to be a real pain – not just food rationing, but gasoline as well. Even with

Dad's priority status because of his important war work, our ration of gas doesn't permit us to visit many of our friends.

It all goes to show how events in this crazy world radically change the course of our lives. Why, this time last year I didn't pay much attention to rationing. And last year I hardly knew you. Then we were able to share that wonderful weekend at your aunt's resort on Lake Huron. That's when I really got to know you. Chad, it's terrible for me, not knowing where you are and what you're doing.

Each day when I come home from classes at Wellington, I look for your letter. Maybe someday soon one will come. Amidst all the turmoil in the world today, may Jesus give you peace.

MATTY

*   *   *

Well, there's a puzzler for you. Now Matty claims that the weekend we spent at my aunt's resort on Lake Huron was "wonderful". Wonderful? If I remember that weekend, Matty was pretty miserable. Hey, – women, will I ever understand 'em? And how about her closing words. 'Peace'. Right now that might be too tall an order for you, Mr. Jesus. But while you're on the line, maybe you could drop me a little hint about where this crazy Limey tub is going. As I refolded Matty's letter to tuck it away, I noticed the imprint of her lips in a bold red on the flap of the envelope. I closed my eyes and there was Matty right before me. *Her blond hair so neatly coiffed, her green eyes sparkling.* I pressed the envelope to my lips. Then she was gone – *and here I am seated in a lonely booth aboard a ship plying the seas headed for god knows where, the only sounds are waves battering the hull and the raucous laughter of some GI's gambling at the far end of the cabin.* All of which reminds me that I should finish the letter to Matty I had started almost a week ago:

*   *   *

Darling,

I hope you remember Prescott. He's in that last batch of snapshots I sent you from Ft. McClellan. The guy who gets up before reveille to read his Bible. The one so shy about undressing in front of the other GI's in our barracks. And upset whenever any of the guys passes around a bottle, or some dirty pictures. He's one of the few who gets up early on a 'free' Sunday morning so that he can attend chapel.

Well, you don't have to bother your pretty little head about what kind of company I keep aboard ship. Since I began training, our unit has been shifted around, rearranged, scrambled, realigned, shuffled, reorganized and generally screwed up so much that Prescott and Garret are about the only familiar faces I see. You might know that of all the guys formerly in my basic training platoon, Prescott's the one I had the least in common with. And now we're bunkmates, his hammock next to mine in our section of the hold.

Come to think of it, Prescott must be one of those "saved" people you talk about. I hear him saying his prayers at night while we're swinging back and forth in our hammocks. But I don't think his god has been paying much attention to Prescott. He's been seasick almost from the day we left port.

When Prescott's not feeling too bad, or we don't have KP or calisthenics, he and I sometimes pass the hours sitting on deck gazing at the iridescent, blue water, trying to spot sea turtles or porpoises. Sometimes flying fish break out of a cresting wave and fly through the air like little birds testing their wings. Quite a thrill to see huge waves climb skyward, then spill over on themselves, leaving the backwash smooth as freshly combed hair. And those colors! All the way from deep azure to a delicate greenish hue.

Incidentally, I've been awakened several nights by the sound of some GI falling out of his hammock. The noise of a human body striking the steel floor down here in the hold can put your teeth on edge. It's a sound usually followed by a stream of profanity strong enough to burn a hole right through the hull.

I'll write you again as soon as we land. Who knows, maybe the censors will let me identify what hemisphere we're in. I love you, sweetheart – more than you'll ever know.

CHAD

*   *   *

Early the next morning I felt someone poking me. "Wake up you SOB! Wake up!"

As I came around, I recognized the voice. It was Garret.

"We're dead in the water," he said.

Slowly, carefully I rolled out of my hammock, pulled on my pants and grimaced as my bare feet touched the cold steel deck. I listened. *No sound at all! This ship has stopped its engines!* Too sleepy to say much, I slipped into my boots and followed Garret up the ladder to the main deck. There several GI's were already crowding the rail, staring through heavy mist at what appeared to be a shoreline. Gradually as the warming sun burned through from the East, the dim outline of a city startled me with its brilliance. The GI's around me stood there, apparently mesmerized.

Land! After eight days of peering at an empty horizon, we've at last found land!

Then someone at the rail murmured a name: "Casablanca." It was quickly picked up by another "Casablanca" and repeated. "Casablanca!" And repeated "Casablanca!"

Soon Garret and I found ourselves in the midst of a raucous throng of GI's in various stages of undress – excitedly shouting, swearing and punching one another, hailing this spectacular landfall, this fabled North African city, this exhilarating mirage floating on the horizon.

Captivated by the clean profile, the whiteness of the buildings, I found it hard to turn my eyes away. Glancing about, I found Garret already guzzling from someone's bottle. I joined the celebration, trying not to think of the war ahead of us, struggling to push aside the prospect of the dangers that lay before us. Yet, as though by a magnet, my thoughts were drawn to Matty and those lines from her last letter: "…It's terrible for me not knowing where you are and what you are doing."

And without warning, two questions seared my brain: *Will I ever see Matty again? Will her god make that possible?*

VII

Shortly after arriving in our new camp, the training officer reorganized our unit into five-man squads, to simplify the training process. Our squad would be made up of Garret, Prescott and me, plus Benicek, a hefty Pennsylvania steel worker, and Romano, a former New York cab driver.

While all of us were only too glad to be back on *terra firma,* it soon became apparent that the high chain-link fence surrounding our camp served a double purpose. Obviously designed to keep us in, we soon learned that the fence also had the much more important function of keeping the Arabs out.

Initially Garret and I wondered whether the short-statured Romano would be able to keep up with the rest of us. A wiry little guy, he soon demonstrated that his greater energy level more than made up for his size.

One evening right after chow while I was trying to eliminate the fetid smell emanating from my barracks bag by drying out a few items of clothing, Romano returned to our tent, a conspiratorial gleam in his eye.

"Soon as it gets dark," he whispered, "the guys in the squad are going over the fence. Wanna come along?"

"You guys going AWOL?"

"Not exactly. Garret found out that a bunch of Arabs gathers every night on a hill about a half mile away."

"So?"

"So they bring along some of their best-looking daughters – you know, a chance to do a little business with us rich, lusty American soldiers."

"I'm not sure I want to get that chummy with any of these camel jockeys."

"Wait a minute," Romano said, rubbing his finger along his pencil-thin mustache. "I'm not planning to lay any of their broads either. They probably got every disease this side of the pyramids. But I'm not against making me some money. A carton of American cigarettes brings a good price. Even a pack is worth – "

"Well I'm not selling any of mine, but – what about a mattress cover?"

"Bring one along."

As I watched Romano go through his barracks bag looking for items to sell, doubts began to arise. "Did you forget about the MP's?" I asked. "If we try going over the fence, they'll be all over us."

"They won't give us no trouble. Except for the main gate, there's only the two of 'em on motorcycles. Right about sundown they come through our area and head for the other end of camp. That's when we go over the fence."

"Those are wicked looking whips they carry."

"Keep your voice down!" Romano held his finger to his lips. "Remember that those MP's mainly get their jollies using the whips on any Arabs they catch inside the fence. But they don't bother GI's." Abruptly he rose to leave. "Come to think of it, I'm gonna check with Prescott. Maybe he'll be interested."

"Just tell him it's his big chance to convert a bunch of ignorant Arabs. He'll come."

"Okay Fletcher, let's not be too hard on the poor guy. He means well." Romano adjusted his helmet liner. "Garret wants us ready to leave as soon as the sun goes down."

From the bottom of my bag I drew a clean, damp, white mattress cover and held it up to the light. *I know the Supply Sergeant wants this thing used as a mattress cover, or, if necessary, as a body bag. But to these dirt-poor Arabs that precious piece of cloth represents a new suit of clothes.*

* * *

Later, as the sun abruptly dipped below the horizon and a jet-black mantle took its place, Garret led Benicek, Romano and me to a spot in the far end of camp where the remains of a small, dead olive tree covered a burrow. In short order the four of us squeezed under the fence and found ourselves outside the camp, but unable to see very far because of the darkness. As our eyes gradually became adjusted to the dark, we were able to discern a few barren hillocks and a few olive trees ahead of us. When we halted at the crest of a slight rise, Garret whispered a few words to Romano, then faded into the gloom ahead. Whereupon Romano pointed to our left where the hillside was teeming with white-sheeted Arabs.

Nudging me, Romano indicated a small depression to the right of the hill. At first it appeared to be vacant, but I soon noted that a darker area in the depression was punctuated with the recognizable red gleam of cigarettes at fairly regular intervals. While Benicek and Romano proceeded toward the hilltop, I veered off to the right in order to check out the depression a little more. As I drew closer to the glowing cigarettes and began to hear spasmodic groaning, everything became clear. The glowing cigarettes were actually "warning lights", each held by an Arab woman, on her back on the ground, her legs curled over the back of a soldier who was energetically keeping his emotions in motion. I quickly decided that I was not enough of a voyeur to stand and watch the U.S. Army fornicate its way across North Africa.

It took me several minutes to rejoin my comrades in the milling crowd of soldiers and Arabs, but as I joined them, Benicek indicated someone heading down the hillside toward the depression. It was Garret with a small Arab girl in tow.

Nonetheless, I quickly became caught up in the atmosphere of the bargaining area, fascinated by the babble on every side, trying to disregard the fulsome odors that pervaded everything, Arabs bargaining for items such as razors, chocolate, underwear, and socks, GI's trading for camel skin purses, small rugs and knives with exquisitely carved handles. Eventually I encountered a tall, thin Arab who appeared to be a Bedouin chief. Dressed in a flowing robe and a wide turban, he was accompanied by two other Arabs, apparently servants, or family members. The Bedouin pointed to the mattress cover under my arm.

"GI – to sell?"

"Oui. Vous parlez Francais?"

He nodded and again pointed to the mattress cover. *"Combien?"*

At a signal from one of his men, the four of us seated ourselves on the ground and began to negotiate a price for the merchandise I had to offer. After about a quarter hour of back and forth, it became plain to the Arabs that my price was firm. Then as suddenly as the bargaining had begun, it was over. The "Chief" watched stolidly as one of his men counted out the Francs and thus he became the proud owner of a genuine U.S. Government-issue mattress cover.

By midnight everyone in our group had had enough bargaining for trinkets.

"Let's head back for camp before it gets any later," Romano said.

"Okay by me," Benicek said, looking around. "But where's Garret?"

"Probably still working out over in the depression," I replied.

Benicek smiled and slowly shook his head.

"Okay, if you guys are ready, let's go!" Romano buttoned his jacket. "Garret can take care of himself."

Our return trip proved to be slower and considerably more difficult, thanks to the heavy cloud cover that had moved in. By the time we reached camp, clouds had so obscured the moon that we were unable to locate the scooped-out area where we had crawled under the fence.

Benicek turned to Romano, his bushy brows knitted. "Okay, great leader, what do we do now?"

"I guess we climb the fence," Romano said, a sheepish grin on his face, He looked up at the fence. "I figure it to be about eight feet high."

An awkward silence followed.

Finally I spoke. "Hold my helmet liner. I'll give it a try."

With that I grabbed the chain-link fencing, dug in the toes of my boots and began to pull myself up. One hand-hold at a time, it proved to be an arduous task. When I had nearly reached the top, a bright, blinding light exploded in my face!

Oh my God, the MP! Complete silence, then a rustling. *What's that? Probably Romano and Benicek taking off.* Again no sound. I grasped frantically for the top bar, of the fence, slipping, then grabbing again – and holding! *That noise? A click. Is he going to shoot?* I pulled up, gripping the top bar till my knuckles showed white, then swung my legs over and dropped to the ground inside the camp, ready to run. But before I could turn, the MP cut off his spotlight, gunned his motorcycle and with a hearty "Yow!" sped away on his rounds. *Whew!*

*　　　*　　　*

It had been a grueling day of calisthenics, marching formations and weapons training under the hot North African sun. By evening I was bushed, but fought off the temptation to hit the sack early. Instead I flopped on my cot and after another quick reading of the only letter I had had from Matty since leaving the States, I began one of my own:

*　　　*　　　*

Dear Matty:

I'm in a new camp located on a plain where every morning we're put through all sorts of marching drills that raise huge clouds of dust. At this point I fail to understand how all this marching back and forth contributes much to winning the war. In fact, all that tramping around and around only stirs up huge clouds of dust that give the Germans a good idea of where we're located. However, since the fighting front has now moved to southern Italy, I doubt if the enemy's too concerned about our whereabouts.

On many afternoons I'm engaged in field training, which often involves taking my rifle apart, then quickly reassembling it. An exercise intended to develop our ability to break down and reassemble our weapons blindfolded. Thus far, I haven't done too well, even when I'm not blindfolded.

However, all this weapons training is a cinch for Prescott. When it comes to breaking down and reassembling his rifle, this skinny kid has managed to beat everyone in our squad. Apparently his skill with weapons comes from his background in the rural south where he was taught how to hunt deer, rabbits and wild turkeys. While I have a grudging admiration for him, he's a hard one to figure. The other day when I complimented him on his ability with weapons, he grunted something about our weapons not being so important as "taking on the whole armor of God that we may be able to withstand in the evil day. "Whew! That guy's body may be in the Twentieth Century, but I swear his mind's back in the Middle Ages.

As I write this letter I am seated on a cool hillside in the shade of an olive tree during a break in our training schedule. I can see for miles across the valley where a large lake sparkles under the bright sun. On the far side of the lake a sizable mountain rises thousands of feet. Far to my right a smaller mountain sits at the southern end of the valley. I can see a herd of cattle grazing in a cultivated area just below me, apparently the property of neighboring Arabs. A dusty road snakes its way across the landscape, skirting one hill after another.

Yet in the midst of this peaceful scene there are reminders that a war's still going on. From time to time from behind a hill to my right I hear the crack of artillery shells being fired. Then along the broad shoulder of that mountain across the valley puffs of white smoke suddenly appear. These indicate where practice rounds of artillery shells have landed, fired by a battery of cannon located behind a small hill well off to my right. (I thank my lucky stars that once I get through all this routine training, I'll be moving to a safe clerical job well away from any danger zone.)

During all the confusion resulting from my being constantly on the move during the past months I've neglected to ask about your mother. (Incidentally, she's a real beauty!) I hope she's in good health and still looks on me as her future son-in-law. Just assure her that our nuptialation ceremony has merely been postponed until the war's over. Then it's back to the States for me and wedding bells for both of us.

It's a shame that I never got to know either of your parents very well. About the only time I spent alone with your mother was the first time I met her in your room in the hospital. While you were away for tests that day, she and I went down to the cafeteria for coffee. As we talked, at first she seemed so open and willing to tell me about you. Then, with hardly any warning, your mother's mood abruptly changed. And she left in such a hurry that I felt that I must have said something to offend her.

Has your mother ever mentioned the incident? Maybe you can clear up the mystery. As for your Dad, he certainly seems like a generous person, but because of our conflicting work schedules, I haven't had a chance to spend much time with him.

By the way, this may be the longest letter I'll be able to write you – for a couple of reasons. I don't have much paper left to write on – and it's hard to obtain any stationery around here. Maybe when I get to my clerical post, things will be different. Also, there's less and less that I'm allowed to say. I'll try to send you some kind of a letter whenever possible, even if it means writing on cardboard. Meanwhile, though we're thousands of miles apart, there isn't any place so far away that I could forget you.

Love, CHAD

* * *

Even now I hate to end this letter. Because it's the only way I have to talk with Matty.

Far below me I could see GI's forming a line along the company street, reminding me that it was time for evening chow. Slipping my letter into the envelope I had addressed, I started down the trail leading to my company's bivouac area, still unhappy with myself.

Here I am lying to Matty– someone I love so much. But then, what else can I do? From all the talk around camp, it looks like we'll soon be heading for the front line in Italy. But I can't tell that to Matty. Sure, I want her to think of me, but I don't want her to put her through the wringer worrying about me.

As I stopped along the trail to gaze across the plain, the distant hills took on a purple hue. Entranced, I stood frozen to the spot, watching the blurring outline of the hills slowly segue into the shadows. *I can't let that happen to Matty, no matter how many oceans and mountains rise between us. Yet I have no idea how much farther I'll have to travel in this crazy war. And as the days and the miles begin to pile up, can I be sure that Matty's memory of me will not fade into night?*

"Garret, even from the few stories you've told me, I wonder how you ever avoided a breach of promise suit, or something worse."

"Hold on there, Sir Lancelot. Don't tell me you've never made a move like that when the opportunity came along."

"You make it sound like some sort of a game."

"That's it, exactly." Garret finished opening his can of beans. "But just remember, it's a game requiring a high degree of skill."

"And, of course, 'Garret the Magnificent' never makes any mistakes."

"Oh, I've had my share of close calls," he mumbled between mouthfuls of cold rations. "One time the gal ended up pregnant."

"Well, well. This is news. So you became 'Garret the Magnificent *Father*'?"

"Not on your life!" His brown eyes flashed. "I didn't want to *become* a father. And I certainly didn't have time to *be* a father."

"So what happened?"

"Chad, if you're not careful, you're gonna turn into a nosy S.O.B."

I looked him in the eye. "So what happened?"

Without flinching, Garret took another spoonful of beans, then made a face. "Figure it out for yoursel – "

A sudden lurch and the train screeched to a halt. Garret's beans spilled onto the floor.

Likewise Benicek's spaghetti. By grabbing a rag, however, he was able to keep the firepot from tipping over. Jolted awake, Prescott got up ready to take a latrine break before the train moved again. And a chorus of curses exploded at both ends of the railcar until the door was finally opened by the sergeant. As several GI's piled off the train into a light shower, the sergeant leaned in the door to explain why the train had come to a sudden halt. A young second lieutenant had been killed in a fall from the train. The sergeant revealed no details of the accident, but in the discussion that followed, we concluded that the young

49

officer must have pulled rank on the wrong man and someone had shoved him off the train.

During the stop Benicek and several others were able to clean up the spilled rations, the railcar door was again slammed shut, and the train resumed its odyssey through the night. The noise of iron wheels rolling over iron rails increased as the train picked up speed, bringing back the gentle swaying that softened my mood, a lassitude that I was helpless to resist. Slowly I spooned out the last of my cold beans, masticating my supper in a state of ennui, thankful that the latrine stops had somewhat diminished the odors that had accumulated over the course of the day's travel. Tuning out the swearing and idle conversation that were making the rounds in the group of GI's confined to our corner of the railcar, I leaned back against the wall and speculated about what lay at the end of this rail trip. I wondered at Garret's lack of remorse about his escapades, how little he appeared to care how his activity might have damaged the lives of others. *So different from the Garret I knew during our early years at Wellington.* But then, looking around at the confused mass of humanity crowded into this boxcar, I wondered: *Does any such remorse really matter any more?*

To get my mind off the 'sardine' accommodations in our railcar and the monotonous hour-by-hour clicking of the rails, I struggled to relive some of the times I had spent with Matty. But the effort proved futile as fatigue gradually took charge and I felt myself drifting...drifting...

...And suddenly I am at a party – a sorority party – and Matty, the honey-sweet pledge. A noisy party where one of the sorority sisters mistakes me for someone else – someone who had escorted Matty to a previous social off-campus event. Who was it? But Matty's expression remains blank – as though I had never asked...

...And then, half wakeful, I'm vaguely aware that someone has pulled open the door of our railcar. There in the darkness a screaming, hungry mass of Arab villagers besieges our train begging for food, each outstretched hand gripping a bowl or tin can...

...And again, I have reached the edge of a huge desert. My uniform in shreds, my limbs battered and trembling, I stand transfixed with horror at the sight of a monstrous, roiling storm approaching at lightning speed. On a bluff to my left a solitary, white-robed figure points the way I must go, urging me forward – to confront the grotesque, towering whirlwind sweeping toward me...

IX

The wind was blowing harder now, whisking snow into small drifts that made it difficult for Matty to avoid getting her feet wet. She stepped gingerly through the last mound to reach the freshly shoveled walkway leading to the gym entrance of Hoover High School.

She could feel the wetness seeping through her ankle sox. *I guess you were right, Mom. I should have worn boots over my saddle oxfords.* Once again she looked up at the dark, turbulent sky. *Why does it have to snow on the one night I absolutely have to go out? I only hope tonight doesn't turn out to be a complete disaster.*

Matty gritted her teeth as another blast of wind tore at her coat collar. She watched it clear snow away from the atrium that led to the gymnasium entrance. Even with the snow skittering around the edges, she found the art deco façade of the G.M. Strong Athletic Building a fascinating crazy quilt of brown and blue geometric designs, zigzags and diamonds. *I guess that's what I always loved about Hoover. Beautiful building, offbeat instructors – and some of them pretty funny. Mr. Abernethy, you were something else! A great school! But now it's time to move on to the next great school. Actually, I'd prefer U. of M., but Mom insists on Wellington U. Better Music Dept., she says. So tonight I check it out for myself.*

Ducking her head against the heavy snowfall, Matty stepped into the small atrium and pulled at one of the heavy doors. It didn't budge. *Don't tell me I have to drive around to the front entrance!* She tried one more time. Again nothing. As Matty paused to consider some other tactic, the door suddenly swung open, and there stood a muscular young man in slacks and crew-neck sweater, his hand on the latch.

"Sorry. I wasn't sure if I heard someone rattling the door," he smiled, running his hand through his brown crew cut. "Let's get you inside away from that snow. We've had quite a crowd here tonight but the big surge is over." As he ushered Matty into the gym and helped her shake snow from her collar, he pointed to the rather small group of young people milling about a series of booths arranged in a semicircle at the far end of the room.

Matty liked his ready smile. *And those eyes! What color are they?*

"Let me help you with your things," the young man said. He took her coat, fur hat. and scarf. Then, draping them over his arm, he gave Matty an appraising look "My name's Garret. Just sign the registration sheet here on the table and tell me if there's some aspect of Wellington University that especially interests you."

"Well, uh, yeah," Matty stammered. *Those muscles!* "Music and, um, Lit. I mean Literature."

"Music. That would be Mrs. Anderson. As for Literature, I'll introduce you to – " His brow wrinkled, drawing Matty's attention to his piebald complexion, his rugged features. "Right now, the name escapes me, but let's get over to the – " He paused. "Say! You wouldn't be Matty Seagrave?"

Matty grinned. "I wouldn't be anyone else."

"Well, what d'you know! Stella asked us to watch for you. It being kinda late, some of our help's already gone. Stella figured you weren't coming."

"Gosh, I'm sorry about that. Stella talked with me over the weekend – she's my neighbor, you know. I told her at church that I'd make a special effort to get here tonight, but that I might be a little late."

"I'd say that kind of loyalty and determination calls for some sort of reward."

Matty laughed. *He's wearing cologne.* "You mean I get some kind of a reward?"

"Not right this minute." Garret paused to smile at her. "But I'll think of something." Turning slightly, he motioned toward the booths." Let's get together with Mrs. – "

"Matty!"

That deep guttural voice instantly recognizable, Matty shifted her gaze to the row of anterooms on her right. There was no mistaking the ample figure of Stella Dombrowski hurrying toward them.

"A great gal. How long have you known her?" Garret asked.

"A couple years. She has a small house down the road from us on the outskirts of Plymouth. and – " Matty turned to greet her friend with a hug.

"Well, you finally got here!" Stella said, grinning.

"Sorry to be so late," Matty said. "You know my dad and his last-minute meetings. I left as soon as he got home with the car."

Stella glanced toward the booth area, fingering the glasses that hung by a chain over her ample breasts. "I'm afraid the crowd's thinned out in the past hour, so I don't think you'll have to wait long to see Mrs. Anderson and –"

"Just a minute, Stella," Garret interrupted. "Maybe I can save you the trouble. You probably have a ton of other things to take care of and Miss Seagrave and I have already discussed her needs." He handed Matty's coat to Stella. "Would you ask Norm to take these things to the coat room?" Then he nodded to Matty. "Now I'll see if we can find Mrs. Anderson. Follow me."

A little non-plussed, Matty felt herself blushing as she looked at Stella "I'll be back shortly so we can talk." As she turned, she was surprised by Stella's expression – lips uncharacteristically pursed, her normally placid expression marred by a look of suppressed fury.

By this time, however, Matty had shifted her focus to the broad-shouldered, sandy-haired collegian ahead of her. *Have no fear, Mr. Garret. I have your scent – and I'm ready to follow you anywhere."*

X

Despite heading for the front in the back of a 2 ½ -ton truck over the jolting, rutted back roads of southern Italy, I managed to get a few precious hours of sleep before waking to the sound of Garret and Prescott arguing.

"You're just makin' that up," Prescott said. "You don't know any more than the rest of us about where we're goin'."

"Believe what you want to believe, choir boy. I'm telling you that I was awake earlier than either of you guys and followed one of the sergeants over to the motor pool where the captain was briefing the non-coms before we got on this truck convoy. Captain said we're heading for a huge mountain where the Krauts have set up a strong line of defense. They call it 'The Gothic Line' ".

"You mean now we'll have to climb a mountain?" I asked.

"Looks like it," Garret said. "Captain said the Krauts have taken up positions on the mountaintop. Apparently we've been assigned as replacements for the Seventh Infantry Regiment. They're already up there trying to push the Germans off the mountain."

Maybe he's right. Maybe he's wrong. I dunno. What I do know is that if I don't get some more sleep, I won't be able to push anybody off nothing.

*   *   *

During the next few hours we passed through several checkpoints before our truck lumbered to a stop in the darkness. We had reached a heavily-wooded area adjacent to a small farmhouse. A corporal, standing at the tailgate, hurled instructions at us: "Throw your bedrolls down in this grove of trees and try to get some sleep. However, keep your boots on. You'll probably be moving out of here in a big hurry."

It felt good to get off that truck, so all three of us hurried to find a spot where we could spread our bedrolls. The processing at the Replacement Depot in Naples early this morning plus the truck ride over these chewed-up Italian back roads, had left me exhausted. So I wasted little time getting under my blankets and staring up through the trees at a beautiful sky awash with stars. It wasn't long before I felt my senses... one... by... one... giving... way... to... sleep ...

...And there stood Matty by the sofa, her playful expression beckoning to me, her arms pressing me ever closer against the intoxicating scent of her hair, till I was lost in the softness of her folds, and her –

"Benicek! Romano!" A rough summons jolted me awake.

"You Benicek?" I fought hard to orient myself to my new surroundings, the large, craggy features of the master sergeant hovering above me, his rotten breath, his – Then, abruptly, he turned away.

Though struggling to get back to my dream, I found it hard to ignore the sounds of Benicek and Romano gathering their gear. From their quick exchanges as they prepared to leave, I realized my two buddies would be accompanying the Master Sergeant forward to his unit. I settled back, thankful that I still had sack time left.

Once their truck pulled away, I would –

WHAM! WHAM!

The atmosphere exploded on every side!

I bolted from my blanket to find Prescott already on his feet, gripping his rifle. Garret still in his sack, raised his arm in a dismissive gesture. "Don't get too excited. Just another

Army screw-up. They've placed us in the midst of one of our artillery batteries." After a certain amount of grumbling, Prescott and I returned to our blankets. But the artillery continued to blast away throughout the remainder of the night, hurling shell after shell after shell into the blackness on their way to enemy positions atop the huge, dark, ominous mountain.

*　　*　　*

Returning from a visit to the slit trench, I discovered Garret and Prescott heating their coffee over a portable Coleman stove they had borrowed from the Message Center boys in the farmhouse. A small fire crackled with two cans of rations sitting amidst the coals of a small fire.

"I see you guys have already set up housekeeping," I remarked, glancing up at the cloud cover. "At least we've got a dry morning, but I don't imagine we'll be hanging around here very much longer."

Prescott didn't look too happy. "Every day we get further away from home," he remarked.

"Don't panic, choir boy," Garret said. "There's still a god up there, somewhere. Only he's looking out for our friend here, more than the rest of us. Haven't you noticed how this guy Chad gets all the mail —no matter how far away we go?" Garret pointed at me with his spoon. "What d'you hear from the home folks? "

"Cut it out, Garret. You know damn well that I don't have any home folks." I busied myself opening a can of hash. "Unless you count my aunt up on Lake Huron – and she's not getting any younger."

"Don't give me that orphan crap. I saw you reading a letter from somebody." He turned to Prescott, the left eye slightly askew "You should see that envelope. Some hot babe plastered her lipstick all over it."

"I expect that I'll be gittin' a letter from *my* ol' lady pretty soon." Prescott said. He fumbled in his shirt pocket, finally pulling out a snapshot.

"Huh? You – married?" Garret reached out to Prescott. "Let me see what she looks like."

After studying the photo for a few seconds Garret handed it to me. "Can you believe this? She can't be more than sixteen years old."

"She's seventeen." Prescott said, blushing.

"Well, *excuse* me!" Garret said, turning his attention in my direction. "I hope you're doing better than that. What about that girlfriend of yours – the one you almost married? What's her name – Missy?"

"Her name's Matty," I replied, testing the rim of my canteen cup. "I've only had two letters so far – and I guess I'll have to keep rereading the last one until I get another. Maybe I'll have a chance to write her today."

"When she finds out where the Army has sent her loverboy, I bet she'll have mascara streaming down her face."

With a glove on my right hand I lifted my C-rations off the fire. "I'm certainly not going to worry her with any letters about where they're sending us. For all she knows, I've got a soft job somewhere well back of the lines."

Garret nodded. "You've got the right idea, Chad. Otherwise, if she figures you probably won't make it through the war, she'll start looking around for a new boyfriend."

"Now wait a minute, Garret. You don't know Matty. She's pretty solid. When a gal like Matty tells you she'll wait for you, she'll wait, regardless. I just don't want to put her through the wringer worrying about me all the time. She says she prays for me. I can't understand it, but that can't hurt, right Prescott?"

Prescott took a few moments to finish chewing his ration. "I don't know your galfriend, mind you, but I reckon that if she's praying for you in faith, you can depend on her. Jesus hisself said faith can move a mountain."

"Okay, okay, I get the idea," Garret said, "but I bet before long her old man will throw a monkey wrench in the works."

"What makes you say that?" I asked. "You never got a chance to meet him."

Garret stared into his coffee for several seconds. "It's not difficult to spot a hardnose. Seagrave's behavior in the train station back in Detroit didn't impress me as too friendly." He took a swallow of coffee and made a face. "You're just lucky you passed muster and got that close to marrying her. I guess luck just follows you around."

"How do you figure that?"

"Well, for one thing, how does an ugly Sad Sack like you latch on to a looker like Matty?" he laughed. "Luck."

"Yeah, sure. Everywhere I go, luck just follows me around."

"Alright, how about that episode back in Tunisia – the one where the Arab got into our tent? Did you spot that knife he was flashing? A *jambiya*. I made out that much. If I hadn't stumbled into the tent when I did, that gook could've made shish kebab out of you."

"Very possible, and I thanked you at the time. But I don't imagine it registered. In your condition you couldn't have understood English, French or Swahili."

"Okay, so I'd had a little too much. But I got that camel jockey to bolt through the hole he'd carved in the back of the tent. You were so scared that I bet he'd run halfway to Cairo before you realized he'd gone."

Yes, I guess I do owe a lot to Garret's stumbling into our tent that night back in Tunisia. But why all those remarks about Matty and her dad?

Then, when Garret and Prescott went off to find the latrine, I remembered Matty's latest letter. I pulled it out of my shirt pocket.

*   *   *

60

October 1, 1943

Dear Chad

I had to spend a few days in the hospital last week. That same old "female trouble" I had last year. But don't worry, dear. The doctor has me on some medicine to build up my blood. I thank the Lord that I'm feeling better now and back at Wellington. But. you know, every time the folks and I attend church lately I keep wondering about you so far from home. Do you have a church close to where you're stationed? Does the Army let you attend every week? I certainly hope so. Chad, just let the Lord become a regular part of your life, and you'll –

*   *   *

Sure, Matty. You'll find me right up front in church every Sunday. I may even join the choir – once I learn to sing in German. That's what brought us GI's to Italy in the first place. We want to make Christians out of these nasty Huns. But first we've gotta get 'em out of those rotten holes up on the mountain. Once they fully appreciate that we're only trying to bring them the message of God's love –

"Fletcher! Wald! Prescott!" I recognized the lieutenant's voice. "On your feet!"

It took only a few minutes for his message: "Report to Sgt. Marlowe at the CP. He'll be guiding you up the mountain to where your company is positioned."

*   *   *

My muscles ached as I reached up to grip the rocky ledge above me, my hand cold and trembling. I tried not to look down at the ledge I had just left on the stark, rugged granite heights of Mt. La Difensa. Slowly I pulled myself up to the new ledge and settled back against the rock, waiting for Prescott to catch up, giving me another opportunity to curse the lieutenant who had sent us on this mission.

Apparently when the lieutenant announced that the three of us had been assigned to F Company, he must have forgotten a few things. "Sgt. Marlowe will guide you up to F Company,' he said. No mention that the trip would involve climbing a mountain. Or that each of us (including Sgt. Marlowe) would have a heavy wooden box of C rations strapped to our backs, plus a rifle, a bandolier of rifle ammunition, our backpack, and our bedroll.

In the fading light I found it difficult to see the valley thousands of feet below, but the frequent flashes of fire from the valley floor bore witness to the continuing struggle our troops were having as they tried to wrest the town of Mignano from the Germans.

Safely on the new ledge, I looked around for Garret and Sgt. Marlowe whose heavy beard had already begun showing. I discovered the two of them in the far corner of the ledge quietly unloading their ration boxes. Garret leaned his rifle against a boulder and slumped back against the wall of our ledge.

"We'll hold up here for a bit," Sgt. Marlowe whispered. "The Krauts can probably hear every damn thing we say." The sound of rustling below told me that Prescott was approaching our ledge. I kneeled down to help him reach us. Breathing heavily, his face ashen, he clung to my arm and struggled up onto the ledge.

"Never prayed so hard in my life," he said, puffing. "One slip on these slopes –!" He stood up to remove his pack.

Sgt. Marlowe reached out with one gnarled hand and yanked Prescott's arm. "Get down, you S.O.B.!" he muttered under his breath. "You want to get us all killed?"

Garret's eyes narrowed, but Prescott merely bowed his head, his lips moving. To distract Sgt. Marlowe, I asked: "You just returning to your company from the hospital?"

"Nothing like that." The sergeant rubbed his hand across his face. "Just my turn to spend a day at Regiment where I could shave and clean up a little. We been fighting solid ever since way back at the Volturno River. God, it sure felt good to get a break."

I noticed that Prescott started to say something, then stopped.

I hope he'll keep his mouth shut. We don't need this non-com making things rougher for us.

"How far to the German positions?" Garret asked.

"Probably not more than 100 yards. That's why we'll stay on this ledge till dark. Then we'll move up to your foxhole. Not much of a hole, actually. Mostly a bunch of big rocks piled up around a fairly level spot."

Garret shook his head. "Why not move up now while we can still see where we're going?"

"The Krauts would love that! ", an edge of steel in Marlowe's voice. "They already have their hole close enough that they can hear us breathe. I said: 'we only move after dark' – understand?"

"Yes sir!" said Prescott.

"Don't 'sir' me!" the sergeant whispered. "Save your 'sirs' for some chicken officer. Just pay attention and don't give me any of your hill-billy lip!"

Prescott closed his eyes tightly, as though he had been struck. Then calmly took hold of his rifle and began wiping it off.

Garret, however, seemed little fazed. "Whatever happened to those mules we used when we first started out on the trail up this mountain?"

Sgt. Marlowe slowly shook his head. "If I'm gonna play nursemaid for you guys, then you better move in closer." He paused to pull a government-issue chocolate bar from his pack. "As for the mules, Regiment doesn't want them to carry rations or ammo up this far. Not sure-footed enough. And they sure as hell would be spotted by the enemy. Besides that, if one of them gets hit, he couldn't easily be replaced and – "

Startled by a sudden loud buzzing, we all ducked, then looked up as the sergeant spoke. "Don't worry, just our Piper

Cub." He pointed to a single-wing plane now plainly visible flying slowly back and forth in front of the mountain at a level only slightly above that of our ledge. "That plane serves as forward observer for our artillery. He used to drop us supplies."

I nodded. "Not a bad idea."

"Yeah, but whenever he dropped anything for us, a lot of it would miss the drop zone and tumble down the mountainside. That only made it easier for the Krauts to pinpoint our position. Then one of their observers would call in a barrage of mortars. So Regiment told the airplane people not to drop us any more supplies.

"They sure as hell got us bracketed in," Garret said

Prescott sat up a little straighter. "How about the Chaplain? Does he get up here?"

"Don't hold your breath," Sgt. Marlowe replied. "Few of 'em ever make it any further than Regiment. Once in a while the Catholic father reaches Battalion Headquarters. Of course, he brings his bottle with him. That bottle makes him pretty popular with the guys. All of a sudden everybody's a Catholic."

I couldn't help but grin, then looked to Prescott for his reaction. He had resumed wiping off his–

WHOOSH!

All of us flattened against the rocks. I looked up in time to see the Piper Cub falling like a leaf in the wind, then recovering several hundred feet below us. Meanwhile, one of the German's Stuka fighter planes, having made a sudden swipe at the Piper Cub, swept a mile down the valley, and quickly turned to make another pass. Nonetheless, the Piper Cub continued its descent, making it difficult for the Stuka to slow down enough to get off another shot. We continued to watch, entranced, as the enemy plane tried to engage his smaller adversary – but no luck. Then within minutes the German dive-bomber broke off the action and left the scene. Before long the Piper Cub climbed back to its former position, waggled his wings and resumed observation.

Abruptly I became aware of an intermittent whispering in the air above us, so close that I felt I could reach up and touch it. I asked Sgt. Marlowe about the sound.

"Just the sound of our shells passing overhead, on their way to the Kraut positions. Our friend in the little plane directs the fire." Without further ado the sergeant began rearranging his pack and bedroll. "Now let's cut the chatter and get some shut-eye. When darkness comes, I'll wake you."

*   *   *

By now the sky had turned so black that I could hardly discern the outline of the "hole" Sgt. Marlowe has led us to. "Stay in this spot," he whispered. "I'll take my ration box up to our squad's machine gun nest. It's okay for you guys to open one of your ration boxes. We'll get the rest of the crap up to the other squads later. Just don't drink too much water. Remember, the canteen on your belt contains all the water you're likely to get until Battalion brings us a fresh ration."

Then he was gone.

"Well, my friends, we've certainly maneuvered ourselves into a rotten situation," I muttered to the others, my eye fixed on the meager horizon above us. Intermittently the mountaintop sky flashed orange-red as another chemical shell exploded on enemy positions. Otherwise, I heard little else except for that same quiet whispering of our artillery shells passing overhead on their way to the mountaintop.

Suddenly Prescott pointed to a fire burning fiercely on a shelf at least 1000 feet below. "I can barely make out a wing and part of a tail," he whispered.

"It's a plane," Garret said. "Probably our friend in the Piper Cub."

Remembering the sergeant's admonition, I dragged one of the ration cases toward me and began prying it open. Each of us selected a can of rations and used the attached key to open it.

"Let me offer the blessing," Prescott said.

"The – *what*? Garret's initial surprise segued into a half-smile. "Okay, choir boy," he said finally, "but keep your voice down. I bet God doesn't even know we're up here, so don't advertise it to the Krauts."

Garret and I watched as Prescott bowed his head.

"Dear Lord," he said," at a time like this, we realize how dependent we are on Yer grace and how much we need Yer protection. Please bless this food for our bodies and guard us through the night. Amen."

Now that Sgt. Marlowe had left, I felt pretty certain that Garret and I shared the same desire for a smoke. After we cupped our hands to hide the flash and glow, Garret spoke up again. "That prayer of yours may have sounded pretty good, my friend, but let's face facts. We've got ourselves in one hell of a desperate predicament. If along comes just one German mortar round, or just one bullet with our number on it – "

"D'y'all know what the Bible tells us? " Prescott said. "It says – "

"Who in hell cares what the Bible has to say about – "

"Keep your voice down, Garret!" I said. " Let him speak."

"The Bible tells us to stand firm, meeting our opponents without so much as a tremor."

Garret poked me. "Okay Chad. You were so hot to hear him speak. Now tell me, what in hell does that mean?"

I shook my head.

"When the going gets rough," Garret asked, "are we supposed to stand up in our hole and quote the Bible to our friends up there with the burp guns?"

But Prescott would not be put off. "I reckon prayer remains kind of a mystery us humans will never undertand," he said. "We don't always know the Lord's will, but He wants us to tell him what we're afeared of. And then, just trust him fer the future."

"Look screwball," Garret mumbled, "this ain't exactly like Sunday School. You go ahead with your damn praying. I'll watch out for my own ass."

Prescott made no reply, but merely stared at Garret.

*　　　*　　　*

The noise of Prescott stirring in his corner of the hole woke me with a start. I looked around. In the faint yellow light of dawn I could see that he had drawn a New Testament from his pack and, squinting at the text, his lips moved soundlessly. Garret still slept.

Our nearness to the enemy certainly had changed. Now I could hear the dull thud of our shells exploding on the mountaintop. Otherwise, little activity. I peered over the rocks lining our hole. *All those chalk-white rocks across the mountainside – probably hiding five to ten GI's. Yet not a sign of anyone. Creepy.*

As I reached into the box for another can of C rations, someone's head suddenly appeared at the lower rim of our hole. I grabbed my M-1, but quickly recognized the intruder – Benicek. I said nothing, waiting until he had crawled past Prescott. His arrival managed to wake Garret.

"Well, you guys finally got up here. Welcome to the party," he grinned. "Our corporal sent me over here for a few of your spare rations." He began stuffing several cans in his jacket.

As the three of us listened, Benicek explained quietly that he had discovered a sheltered path around the rocks leading to our hole. "My squad's machine gun is mounted in our hole," he said. "So I guess that's attracted a lot of attention from our worthy opponents up above. In fact we've lost several men in the past day or so." He paused to draw a deep breath. "So now the corporal has made me assistant gunner."

"That sounds like a fun job," Garret grunted.

"Thanks for the encouragement – and the rations," Benicek said. "I better be getting back." Then, touching one finger to his helmet, he slid back out the way he had come in.

Garret, meanwhile, had crawled to the edge of our hole and begun relieving himself when a series of explosions just above sent a shower of stones down on us.

"Medic!" someone shouted. "Medic!"

I prodded Prescott. "You okay?"

He nodded, picked up his rifle, gripped it tightly and pointed toward the far end of our hole. Garret scrambled to get back into the hole.

"Medic!" Again the call from somewhere above us.

"What should we do?" Prescott asked.

"Better sit tight," Garret grumbled. "No sense getting our ass shot off by being too nosey."

Now I could hear voices above and to our left, then the sound of movement. I signaled quiet. All three of us kept our heads down expecting another barrage of mortars, but nothing happened.

Suddenly I noticed someone peering over our pile of rocks. Romano, his new-grown charcoal beard a marked contrast to his eggshell skin.

"Where did you come from?" I asked.

"I'm company runner now," he replied, nodding to each of us, "and Murphy's just been hit." He paused to get his breath. "We've got hold of a litter stashed under that overhang a few yards left of your hole. Captain wants Fletcher and Wald to carry Murphy down to Battalion."

"He – what?" I asked.

"You heard me! Better snap to it! Murphy's in bad shape, so follow me."

Slowly and as quietly as possible Garret and I crawled out of our hole and, following Romano, we inched our way through a mass of scree to another pile of rocks. As the two of us struggled past them into a small depression, we came upon the aid man wrapping a bandage over Murphy's upper leg, the dressing already soaked with blood.

Then, wasting no time, the medic rose to a half-stoop. "Remember, keep your head down" he said, "and try to keep up with me." Garret and I lifted the litter and in a crouch slowly started down the extremely narrow trail toward Battalion Headquarters.

Every time we paused to level the litter as gently as possible, Murphy groaned. I expected every minute that our noise would trigger another enemy salvo. Somehow we managed to slow our pace down the slippery slope for some fifty yards before we could finally stand erect. I kept trying to maintain a pace not too fast for Garret at the other end of the litter.

When we paused to make a sharp turn on the slope, I looked back. A narrow sliver of crimson ran off the litter onto the white rocks. In the dim light Murphy's face had taken on a gray, cobalt cast, his eyes closed, his lips not moving.

Is he already dead? And how about Matty's prayers and Prescott's prayers. Do they count for anything? Are they powerful enough to get me off this mountain alive? Or will I soon be joining Murphy?

XI

Mt. La Difensa, Italy

November, 1943

Garret and I alternately slipped and slid all during our trek down the mountainside, trying to keep pace with the aid man, struggling to hold the stretcher level, fighting to maintain our footing all along the tortuous, rock-strewn trail.

By the time we reached the Battalion Aid Station (a relatively flat area cut into the side of the mountain) we were greeted by a staff sergeant who quickly confirmed that Murphy had died. He directed us to place the litter in the far corner of the Aid Station where they were temporarily holding KIA's.

After we had filled our canteens and picked up several K rations to take back with us, the sergeant told us we could rest briefly before starting back up the mountain. We took a few minutes to talk with a party of three walking wounded who were getting ready to make their way down to the base of the mountain where an ambulance waited. Then we headed for a quiet corner of the Aid Station and settled back against the granite wall of the mountain.

Lighting up, Garret blew a smoke ring in my direction. "Chad, the more war I see, the more stupidity I see."

"Meaning the Army classification system?"

"You got that right. For four years I busted my butt learning how to identify the parts of an internal combustion reciprocating engine, how to calculate an engine's cubic inch displacement – crap like that. And what did it get me? A war comes along and all of a sudden I'm classified as an ammo bearer for a heavy machine gun on some god-forsaken mountain in Italy."

"Don't forget," I said, managing a wry grin. "I put in my four years studying English Lit. Now I'm no higher in the pecking order than you are. How much luckier can we be?"

Hardly able to keep our eyes open, we had barely nodded off when the sergeant came by to remind us that it was high time we returned to our company.

Even though now we carried no wounded burden, the trip back up along the narrow trail again proved exhaustive and perilous before we got back to Prescott waiting in our squad's hole.

Romano, who was just leaving, paused to fill us in on the orders he had just explained to Prescott: "At dawn our 81mm mortars will be laying in a barrage on the German positions just above us, " he said. "When the barrage stops, all the men in our platoon are to leave their holes, begin working their way up the slope and – "

"You mean we're going out in the open?" Garret asked.

"Look Garret," Romano said. (I could see the artery throbbing in his neck.) "I don't like it any more than you do, but that's what the order says. Is that clear?"

As Romano slipped out the edge of our hole, returning to the platoon commander, I shook my head with resignation, Prescott looked the other way and Garret let loose a flood of expletives strong enough to split granite.

"Is that damn lieutenant trying to kill us off?" he asked.

I could not speak. *There's no answer to that one, Garret.*

Meanwhile, as we felt a frigid blanket settling over the mountainside, it was time to set up rotation for guard duty – two men trying to sleep, one man keeping watch.

*   *   *

Sure enough, at first light our mortar squad opened up, raining a barrage of shells on the German positions, a scant

71

200 yards above us. I moved over to a gap in the rocks lining our hole so that I could observe the –

WHAM! One shell landed close to our hole, showering us with stones, bits of ice and shrapnel. I could hear rocks falling from above.

"Keep your head down!" Garret shouted. "Those short rounds'll kill you!"

Meanwhile, Prescott had stretched himself out at the far end of our hole where he could watch for Romano's hand signal. As the *whomp-whomp* of our mortars hitting the enemy positions above gradually subsided, Garret and I each slipped a bandolier of rifle ammunition over one shoulder and took hold of an ammo box. Before long our mortar barrage halted. Prescott signaled that it was time to move out.

The three of us crawled out of our rocky haven, started up the frosty slope, but almost immediately enemy machine gun bursts tore up the scree on every side. We slid back into our hole.

Panting heavily from our near miss, I watched a GI from a hole to our left emerge from shelter and begin inching his way up the slope. He kept working across a shallow depression, seemingly oblivious of the bullets striking the rocks near his head. Tracers from another Kraut gun passed inches over his back.

I shuddered. *Slow, but sure, this guy's making it up the slope – but no one's following him!*

As the intensity of the enemy fire slackened, I scanned our immediate surroundings and spotted a small overhang slightly higher and off to my right. "Let's try it again," I shouted to my two partners. Then I rose, scrambled up the slope off to my right and dove under the protection of the overhang. Garret and Prescott followed.

Fortunately, the German machine gunners above us must have been preoccupied with other targets because they failed to traverse our paths until we had reached the comparative safety of the overhang.

By this time mortar rounds again began coming in from the German positions. Two of them struck the top of our overhang, smashing one side of it. Peering up the slope, I could see Benicek and Sgt. Marlowe trying to lead our attack. Suddenly they stood up, waving and shouting to the rest of the platoon. Although amidst the ear-splitting blasts I couldn't hear their exact words, plainly they wanted all of us to keep moving up the slope.

They've got the right idea. Keep moving. Only we're moving down, not up. The way these Kraut mortars are bracketing our outcropping, we can't stay here much longer, or we'll all be killed.

"Back this way!" Prescott shouted, then slid out along the path we had used earlier. Garret and I followed, skidding and slipping down the slope out of sight of the Germans. Soon we were back where we started – only now our hole was only half as big. During our absence it had suffered a couple of direct hits from mortar fire.

We huddled together at one end of the hole where again I could squint uphill. Still standing in the open, Benicek and Sgt. Marlowe by this time had been joined by two other GI's, who were crawling, heads down, struggling to reach the slightest depression where they might return fire. By now Benicek stood atop a small ledge that had been abandoned by German gunners earlier in the fighting.

Suddenly, in total disbelief, I watched Benicek pick up an abandoned enemy light machine gun, carry it forward to a position even more exposed and begin pouring fire at the dugout above where another German machine gun was located. Still in the open and apparently out of ammunition, Benicek discarded the machine gun he was carrying, drew his .45 and scrambled up the last twenty-five yards to the side of the enemy position. He fired directly into the pit and must have killed or wounded both gunners. I watched in awe as he wrestled the Kraut gun out of the pit and started down the slope with it in his arms. He had nearly made it back to the small ledge when a burst of fire from another enemy dugout caught him in the head. He spun around and fell backward over an escarpment.

I motioned to the others. "We better stay here. Looks like Benicek's gone."

Although the German mortars continued to pound us, the machine gun fire subsided. After about five minutes, the mortars stopped as well.

I scanned the slope above us. "Where's Marlowe?" I asked.

"He must have doubled back when Benicek made his move," Garret replied. "He sure as hell knew it was a suicide mission."

"I spotted one feller still on the slope," Prescott said. "But he hasn't moved in the past five minutes."

"He's done for," Garret grumbled. "You can bet no one's left alive on the slope now. As for our stupid attack, it's melted down into a puddle of crap!"

I glanced at my comrades: Garret, his hand cupped, shielding a smoke. Prescott, his head bowed, lips moving in a ritual-like pattern.

After a few moments I bowed my head. *God, are you up there?* I waited, but I heard no answer. I looked up at the leaden sky. And I could not find any more words.

XII

I grimaced each time the bandage stuck. Then the orderly, a balding, over-thirty corporal finally succeeded in removing my dressing. He examined the long, red gash in my upper left arm.

"You are one lucky SOB." He spoke slowly as though tasting every word. "A few inches to the left – " After applying a fresh bandage, the orderly helped me up from my cot. I stood erect, my legs unsteady. The smell of disinfectant permeated the large room. *Is that what I'm breathing?*

"You've got your shot," the orderly said." Just go to the end of the line over there and start counting backwards from 100."

I took my place with the other ambulatory wounded waiting to enter the Operating Room and began the count: "100...99...98...." I could feel the creeping effects of the injection the nurse had given me. Ever so slowly the line snaked its way through the ward past rows of badly wounded GI's, many of whom had lost an arm or a leg or had suffered severe body wounds. Almost without bidding my lips moved in a silent prayer of thanksgiving: "87...86...81...75...."

*   *   *

Awakened by the brilliant sunshine streaming through the windows at the far end of the hospital tent, I noticed someone in a khaki Eisenhower jacket standing by my cot.

"Hi, goldbricker."

75

I tried to focus my eyes. "Wha…? Who…?" I looked about the room. A blurry line of cots along each wall of a large tent. I shifted my gaze back to the foot of the bed. *Who is it standing there, slightly cockeyed with the blotchy complexion and the huge grin? Garret.*

"Gotta give you credit," he said. "Whatever it takes to get sent to the rear – that's what you do."

"Rear?" Again I looked at the dozens of other cots that filled the room. Some GI's sleeping, others writing letters, some reading, some playing cards. My gaze traversed the entire room before it once more came to rest on Garret.

"I swear, this 23rd General looks like Heaven to me," he said. "You sure as hell got it made here. You got a dry bed to sleep in, no Krauts to give you trouble and a bunch of cute nurses that reminds me of good old St. Francis."

"St Francis?" My tongue felt so thick.

"Yeah." He sat down on the empty cot next to mine. "Man, when I walked into this hospital, I couldn't believe my eyes. You've got some real lookers on the nursing staff here. That's why I hung around St. Francis so much. Whenever I needed a date, I could always find a live one at St. Fran – you okay?"

I sat up on the edge of the cot, finding it difficult to shake the confusion, puzzled by the fact I was wearing a damp-smelling, mud-caked uniform with the left sleeve torn loose. "How …how did I get here?"

"Buddy, you got yourself a million-dollar wound. You should be glad you ended up with only a scratch on your arm." Garret removed his green helmet liner and tossed it on the empty cot. "It happened about five days ago–when we were still up on the mountain. When we got news that we were being relieved that very night by the 36th Division. With all the racket we made getting our gear together for the trip down the mountain, the Krauts figured something was going on. So they lobbed a heavy barrage on us for about fifteen minutes."

"Now I remember," I sighed." Mortars dropping on every side." *I could still smell the cordite.*

"Would you believe, the Captain had us standing in line – like sitting ducks – waiting for the column to get moving, hoping the next shell didn't have our number on it. Then one round struck close to our platoon and threw you up against an outcropping. You were out cold. When a light rain began falling, the lieutenant finally told us to leave you there and to start moving. That's the last I saw of you. Prescott and I thought you were dead."

"Sure must have shaken me up. I'm just now coming to my senses." My eyes sought out the reassuring sunshine. "What – how did you get here?"

"Once we came down off that stinking mountain, they trucked us back to a bivouac area complete with pyramidal tents about ten miles north of here. After a couple days while we got settled, the CO gave everyone a one-day pass."

"How are the rest of the guys?"

"Well, you saw what happened to Benicek. Romano and Prescott are fine. In fact, the choir boy told me he'll be in to see you later today." Garret shook his head. "That guy's about as nutty as ever."

"Now what?"

"Nothing much. A couple mornings after we got ourselves set up in the bivouac area, I came back to the tent after morning chow – and there was Prescott, sitting on his bedroll mumbling to himself. Said he was praying. 'Who you praying to?' I asked. 'God,' he said.' I notice he never says much about who God is, or where God hangs out. I figure he's trying for a Section 8."

"Why so damn hard on the guy?" I asked. "Maybe you just don't understand what he's talking about. After all, he keeps up with the rest of us, doesn't hurt anybody."

Garret's eyebrows arched. "Don't tell me you're falling for his line of crap?"

"Not exactly," but I hesitated. *How could I explain my feelings about Prescott?*

When Garret met my gaze, I shifted my attention to the blond nurse who had just reentered the building, her perfume floating toward us. "What have they got you guys doing now?" I asked.

"Next week we're supposed to start training for some 'big move', whatever that means. So far, all we've done is pull a long hike through this deep Italian mud – with full equipment, mind you. So don't be in a hurry to get back to the outfit. We'll probably have more heavy training in the weeks ahead."

"Hey, I'm sure glad the rest of you guys came through in good – " I couldn't help myself when a nice looking brunet in nurse's cap and heavily starched blue apron entered the tent carrying a tray of medicine. She stopped at an empty cot and set her tray down. When she bent over to pick up her dosage list, exposing her white stockings, the surrounding GI patients let go with a chorus of shrill whistles – which she ignored.

"That reminds me," Garret said, managing a twisted smile, "If nothing turns up here, I think I'll head for the *Galleria*. The guys tell me there are plenty of those olive-skinned *signorinas* wandering around downtown looking for business. I need to find me one before my pass runs out. Maybe I'll top it off with a bottle of *vino* and a little *spaghet.*"

Same old Garret. Always looking for a dame.

I shook his hand. "Say hello to the guys in the outfit. Tell 'em I'm in no hurry to get back."

As I returned his final wave at the door, the brunet nurse proceeded to my cot and began adjusting my dressing. *Again the perfume.* I recognized the aroma. *Do they all use the same bottle?* That's when I realized something was troubling me. *Something about Garret's visit. What? We hadn't talked about much, other than St. Francis.*

I winced as the nurse tightened the tape holding my dressing and gave me a pill. Her inspection complete, she muttered a few words of comfort, patted me on the shoulder and headed for the doorway. At first I couldn't keep my eyes from following her progress down the line of cots, her skirt swishing, her buttocks alternating. With great effort I forced my eyes to look elsewhere, my thoughts to travel elsewhere – anywhere.

What had Garret and I talked about? St. Francis? St. Francis Hospital! That's where I met Matty! What I'd give to be back there now – as a patient– or even visiting my Matty. Then she'd get better, she'd get discharged and we'd get married! Sure, Fletcher. And Adolph Hitler will come to America and join the Boy Scouts.

As I struggled to steer my thoughts away from St. Francis, my gaze came to rest on a batch of unopened letters lying on the flimsy wooden crate that served as a nightstand separating my bed from the vacant cot next in line. I vaguely remembered seeing them before. Four letters from Matty. I had started opening them late yesterday, but must have fallen asleep. Picking up the letters, I noted the dates, October 30 - November 15. I opened the earliest one.

*   *   *

Dear Chad:

It was so good to get your sweet letter from Morocco – my first from you overseas! I almost cried with joy when I learned you had been assigned to a service unit stationed in Africa – far away from the fighting. Thank You Lord! Thank You! Thank You!

I see from your letter that the way my parents behave kind of bothers you. I understand. It used to bother me as well, but after a while I figured it out.

Remember the first time you asked me about Mom's strange behavior? Something that happened when I was in the hospital. You and Mom were enjoying coffee in the cafeteria while I underwent some tests Abruptly Mom expressed surprise, got up from her chair and left with a hasty explanation, leaving you sitting there alone. I can imagine how you felt. My guess: Mom probably saw someone she recognized in the cafeteria – someone she wanted to avoid. Several times I've overheard Mom talk with Dad about a few of her acquaintances who bore her to tears. And Mom sometimes can be quite abrupt. Remember, at the time she was probably very worried about my tests.

As for Dad, you must know by now that he has a short fuse. Quite often, when he's in a situation where he's likely to lose his temper, he's learned to simply walk away from the problem. That's probably what he did at the train station that day. However by now I'm sure he's reconciled himself to the fact that you and I are going to be married – maybe not sooner as it seemed at the time, but later, according to the way the Lord has worked things out. Please dear, don't worry yourself about my parents. They both love you and miss you just as much as I do.

Went to the movies with Stella last Saturday night. (Remember how you and I always went somewhere on that special "date night"?) During the newsreel we saw pictures of the troops overseas, showing how the chaplains hold services in the field, no matter what. You never mentioned your church services. Do you go to them every week?

I must say Goodbye, for now, sweetheart, thanking the Lord for giving you a safe job over there. It's such a relief to know that you're not in danger. I can't imagine what I'd do if anything happened...

* * *

I looked up at the sound of rain whipping against the canvas roof of the hospital tent, trying to figure how to break the news of my wound to Matty. *Hate to get her upset.*

Maybe it's better if I don't mention it. Her letters will still come to me in care of my unit's APO address.

Once again I looked back over her letter, trying to understand her explanation of her parents' behavior. *Still find it hard to understand. But then – what would I say if someone asked me to explain my dad's behavior – or even my mother's? Especially the time she tried to commit suicide. Hey, I have enough trouble understanding my own conduct.*

Also, why did my hackles rise when Garret made those comments about Prescott? Sure, some of that hill-billy's remarks make you wonder. But as for him pretending he's off his rocker...

At the soft sound of rain beating against the tent I began to feel sleepy again. Shoving Matty's letters under my pillow, I stretched out on the cot. Gradually the noise in the room began to fade....

...Again I am with Matty in a huge, vaulted room busy with a horde of departing soldiers. Oblivious of the movement, the shouting, the clamor on every side, I run my hand along her creamy skin and cup her face in my hands, her essence exhilarating. But before I can kiss her, she is gone. I turn to her mother, then her father. Where is Matty? They shake their heads. Her father slowly walks away...Again I find myself with Matty and her mother, introducing them to Garret. They acknowledge him, but their figures become indistinct, their smiles faint. I look to Garret, his expression smug. When I turn back to Matty and her mother, they are gone...

I jerked upright on my cot, my heart pounding.

"What the hell's wrong?" This from a GI across the aisle, his head heavily bandaged. "Cut out the damned screaming!"

* * *

I rifled the pages of my little notebook. "I know it's here somewhere."

"Fergit it," said Prescott. "Jus' somethin' I'll probably never need no-way."

I can smell his breath. Bad.

"Don't kid yourself," I said. "The way things are going in this man's army I want someone to know how to communicate with Matty, in case – "

"How 'bout one of them letters on the bed?" He brushed his straight hair away from his face.

"Of course!" I shook my head. "How stupid of me!"

Prescott carefully copied the address, then stared at the slip of paper. "Okay, I'll take care of the big one, but let's pray I never have to." He tucked the note in his breast pocket. "Remember, my friend, y'all had better take care of the small ones."

"Prescott, I'm not going to get Matty all worked up for nothing."

"You mean you're not gonna tell her 'bout yer wound?"

"Of course not. By the time she'd get my letter, I'd be back with my outfit, anyway."

"Don't y'all think you should?"

"Prescott!"

"Okay, okay." he said, retrieving his helmet liner from the empty cot next to mine.

"By the way, do they have a PX here at the hospital?"

Before I could answer, the GI on the next cot spoke up. "Would you guys bring me back a pack of cigarettes?" He explained how to find the PX.

Prescott started to zip up his jacket, then stopped, nodding to me. "Is it okay for y'all to leave the ward?"

"No problem, as long as we stay on the hospital grounds."

Outside in the chill of early evening, we turned up our collars. Prescott nudged me. "Did Garret come to see y'all, or was he too busy chasin' the ladies?"

"That sounds a little unkind, coming from you," I remarked. "Yeah, we had a nice visit." Suddenly I felt dizzy.

"Hold on, Prescott! Guess I've been on my back too much this past week."

We resumed wallking, but at a slower pace.

"Don't fret none. Be thankful fer God's will. That's why y'all are still breathin'."

"Frankly, I'd give the medics most of the credit," I said, " – but you say God did it?"

"Yep, God – the Creator of the Universe – and us humans, by the way."

"Come on, Prescott. How do you know He did anything?"

Prescott kicked at some stones on the walkway. "Okay, how do we know that Columbus discovered America?"

"Now wait a minute – "

"Y'all studied history in college – right?"

"It was my minor."

"Okay. What y'all know of history mainly comes from what's been written by folks alive at the time – long before any of us."

I nodded.

"So, to know 'bout God we pretty much have to rely on the word of folks who lived long before any of us. People like Job, who lived around the Sixth century B.C., or so.

He said: 'God removed the mountains, commanded the sun and spread out the Heavens.' Or Jeremiah, who lived 'bout the same time. He said: 'God made the heavens and the Earth.' "

Even though our conversation had nearly brought us to the door of the PX and the bright lights beckoned, I wasn't anxious to go inside yet. Not before I could challenge at least some of Prescott's statements. "Okay, so we grant that your God handled all those big jobs involved with creating everything," I said, "do you really believe He's going to bother Himself about what happens to a couple of jerks like us down here?"

Prescott nodded. "He surely does – and he even wants us to send Him messages about the problems we're havin'."

"Messages?"

"Y"all know what I mean. Prayer. It's our way of – "

At the sudden, deep-throated wail of a siren we dropped to our knees in the shrubbery. Other sirens quickly joined in, reaching a piercing crescendo within minutes. All about us lights were being extinguished, first in the PX, then in most of the hospital proper. I felt my throat going dry.

"Air raid!" Prescott mumbled, *as if I needed to be told.*

We hurried up to the shelter of an entranceway of one of the outbuildings on the grounds of the main hospital where we huddled. Despite the circumstances, I couldn't help but grin. *Prescott, you smell worse than I do!*

As we watched the sky, the drone of bomber engines filled the air. Thumping puffs of ack-ack hung white against the skies to the north. Searchlights and tracers criss-crossed the heavens. The drone of enemy aircraft soon reached a crescendo, prompting us to scramble to our feet and –

EEEYAH!

A lone plane zoomed overhead driving us back under the overhanging entranceway. We watched the aircraft disappear behind a nearby hill and erupt in a ball of orange flame.

Slowly Prescott rose to his feet. "It's okay now. Looks like they're after the Naples harbor," he said.

Over the hills to the south we could see the focus of activity shift to the waterfront area as the night sky became a maelstrom punctuated with flashes of antiaircraft fire and exploding bombs. Fascinated, the two of us watched for nearly a quarter hour. Then, as suddenly as it had erupted, the ground-air battle ended. Sirens sounded "All Clear"; hospital lights snapped back to life.

As we hurried on toward the Post Exchange where all was bright. I glanced at my watch. "Hey, it's 8:30. This place probably closes in a half-hour, so let's postpone our big discussion while we spend some *lira.*"

Some twenty minutes later, as we emerged from the PX, I sensed that Prescott was getting restless.

"It's high time I got myself a ride back to camp," he said, "but let's not fergit that tonight's bombin' is just one more example of God sparin' us. So let's be sure to thank Him."

"Yeah, sure." I could feel the cold night air chilling my arm, reminding me that I needed to get back to that pot-bellied stove. "But before you go, I've got one more question. If, as you say, this fantastic god you're always quoting – if he receives these urgent messages, do you actually believe he runs out and switches things around every time he gets a request for help?"

"Not always. But Bible scholars a lot smarter than me tell us that we oughta pray without ceasin' because the ears of the Lord are open to our prayers. That's somethin' to think 'bout alright." Prescott touched his finger to his helmet liner in a kind of salute. "Sorry, but I better git myself a ride back to camp before curfew. I'll write you more about it first chance I git."

I watched him disappear into the gloom as he headed for the Motor Pool.

*   *   *

As the days of recovery became weeks, I found myself relishing the comforts of the Red Cross lounge in the hospital's Main Building, free to write letters, read magazines, play cards, whatever. Yet I could not fight off a feeling of guilt. Guilt that I was here enjoying all the pleasures of this large hospital when I could guess what my buddies were going through at this very moment. I looked out the window at the grounds surrounding the hospital – the lawn, the bushes, the equipment shed – all of it so ordered, so tranquil.

If I were back with my outfit, that same scene would look far different. That lawn would mark an open area certain to be bracketed by Kraut shellfire. No one would be so foolish as to venture across it during daylight hours. The bushes, an obvious location for an enemy machine gun, the shed a suitable site to hide enemy mortars. What has happened to me, God? Why must I look at your world – and only see death and destruction?

The clock above the Main Desk shook me out of my reverie, the chimes warning that it was nearly time for lunch. *Noon – and I'm still having trouble finishing this letter to Matty. Why can't I bring myself to tell her that my job in the Army is not as safe as I had led her to believe? After all, you don't get hit by shrapnel at the kind of rear-echelon camp where I told her I was stationed. Maybe a few words about front-line conditions might help her understand why I don't have much of a chance to attend any kind of church service. I haven't even seen a Protestant chaplain since I joined my company. But why turn her world upside-down? Hey, now that I'm in the hospital, conditions are different. Tomorrow being Sunday, I'll plan on attending the Army church service in the Chapel. Matty should be glad to hear that.*

I turned over the envelope containing her latest letter. Once more I paused to savor the imprint of her lipstick on the back flap.

Will I ever kiss those lips again? Will I ever cup that small, angular face in my hands again? Hold her in my arms again? All that so long ago, so far away – an experience in some previous existence, one to which I could never –

A sudden stirring and movement toward the Lounge exit by several GI's reminded me that it was time for noon chow. I carefully folded my sheet of Red Cross stationery, stuffed it in my jacket pocket, and soon joined the line of soldiers outside the Cafeteria.

Though I joked with others in the line, thoughts of Matty kept dogging me. *She' such a beauty, so faithful, writing me practically every day since she got my address, even kissing the envelope – that's something new–and precious. Yet I still don't understand those explanations about her parents:*

"Dad's always been that way. Whenever he wanted to avoid losing his temper, he'd say nothing further, just walk into the next room." Sure, Matty. Just like that morning at the Michigan Central Depot– him just disappearing in the

crowd. And Mom?" She must have seen someone in the Cafeteria that day – someone she was trying to avoid."

Conscious of the aroma of food al about me, I stared at the large pan of steaming scrambled eggs. Then I stared at the GI standing behind the counter, his large spoon at the ready. *Who are these 'someones'? Or is there just one 'someone'? Would it be – could it be – Garret?* I felt my blood rising.

"Wake up, soldier! You want some eggs – or not?" I nodded to the server in the hospital chow line.

Sure, I can ask Matty for a better explanation. But Garret's closer at hand. That's all I need. Back to my squad, back to the lousy war, back to –

CRASH! I looked down at the mess on the floor. I had dropped my tray.

As I fell to my knees in an effort to clean up the slippery, congealed mess of eggs, potatoes, coffee, etc. another GI bent down to help me. "If you're trying to get yourself sent to the Psycho Ward," he grinned, "next time try doing this in front of one of the doctors."

I couldn't help but smile. "You're right." But my thoughts had already roamed far afield. *You don't know the half of it, soldier. Now I see a mess that I've got to clean up. And it's a hell of a lot bigger than this one.*

XIII

Her legs rubbery, Matty grasped the hospital's hallway rail tightly and held on till the surging stopped. *Please Lord, don't let me fall!* White-faced and momentarily overcome by the pervasive antiseptic smell of her surroundings, she smiled vacantly at a passing nurse who, eyes focused on her clipboard, hardly gave Matty a second glance. *If you've forgiven me Lord, then please don't let something like this hold me back. Give me the strength I need!*

"Whoa, there!"

The abrupt intrusion of a man's voice brought a rush of color to Matty's cheeks. Still gripping the rail tightly, she turned to discover someone supporting her arm, a look of concern clouding his tanned features.

Matty managed a weak grin. "I'm okay. I merely – "

"Look here young lady, I've been watching you from across the hall. Another step like that last one and you'll be on the floor."

"Don't worry. Just let me – "

"Nurse!"

*   *   *

The bright morning sun streaming through the hospital window slanted across Matty's face. She twisted from side to side, tangling the bed sheets, then gradually opened her eyes. Her surroundings slowly came into focus. *I'm back in my room, but who is that standing at the foot of my bed? Is it that fellow from across the hall?*

"What happened?" she began.

"Happened? I don't know. I came back again today to see how you're doing. Hey, you and your blond curls nearly keeled over on me yesterday."

Matty struggled to come up with a half-smile, her eyes traversing the short-cropped dark hair, the ready smile, the light-brown slacks and matching T-shirt. "Sorry, I must look a mess! Maybe I just tried too hard yesterday." She looked toward the door. "My nurse – that old grouch – she wasn't too happy with me."

"I don't imagine any of the nurses want you climbing out of bed on your own." He shook his head. "I'm surprised no one stopped you beforehand. They're probably short-handed here, what with the war and all."

Matty studied her visitor more intently, her brow furrowed even further. "I'm afraid I don't – "

The young man managed a red-faced grin. "Oh I'm sorry. I never – The name's Chad, Chad Fletcher." He touched his hand to his forehead in a brief mock salute.

"You must – " She paused as a loud voice came over the public address system. "You must already know my name – Matty – "

"Matty Seagrave. It's on the door."

"And you came back to Ann Arbor again – just to see me? Now I *am* flattered."

"Not a bad reason, I must say. Actually, my favorite cousin's on this floor. She gave birth about a month ago and had a few complications."

"Complications?" Matty felt another surge of pain sweep her midriff. She closed her eyes until the surge had passed. Then she sat up in bed and patted her curls. "Is she alright?"

Chad moved a chair next to her bed. "Lee's a pretty healthy country gal. Already has one little guy. She and her husband own a home on Lake Huron and – " He looked at his watch. "Holy Toledo! I better get on my way. I'm supposed to meet a fellow on campus in about an hour."

"You're in school?"

Again a pause for an announcement over the public address system.

"Oh yes. This is my final year at Wellington. I have a chance to get a textbook for my French Lit class at a bargain price."

"Did you say 'Wellington'? That's wonderful! I mean – " Matty blushed again. "I'll be enrolling there in September. And you're almost ready to graduate? That's quite an accomplishment – at a time when the draft is taking away so many."

"Hey, I'm a senior, but don't move me along so fast. I still have a tough year ahead of me. If things go as planned, I'll miss the draft. My buddy and I are scheduled to join the Enlisted Reserve Corps this summer. That'll allow me to finish college before I have to leave for the service."

Matty smiled wanly. "If it helps you finish college, I'm all for – " At the sound of voices she shifted her attention to the doorway. "Why Stella! Come on in!"

Attired in white shorts, a colorful top and carrying a light jacket, Stella proceeded directly to Matty's bedside and gave her a kiss. "Would you believe," she said," first thing this morning Norm got me out of bed to go canoeing on the lake?" She brushed her straight black hair away from her face. "Of course, he wanted to make sure I packed a picnic lunch." She shook her head. "That sun was plenty hot, so that canoe trip turned out to be an exhausting experience. I think I did most of the paddling."

Matty laughed. "That's Norm alright! Is he coming back for you?"

"He'd better. Norm has an appointment in Ann Arbor. Should be back in about a – "

"Oh!" Matty slapped her forehead lightly. She turned to Chad. "I'm sorry. Stella, here's someone I'd like you to meet."

She watched as the two exchanged greetings, Stella beaming. Somewhat embarrassed, Chad rose to shake Stella's hand. "I've seen you down at Wellington and – " He glanced at his watch. "Look, I'd love to talk more, but I'm running late. So if you two will forgive me, I better be getting out of here." With that he nodded to each of them and left.

Matty watched him leave and her eyes lingered at the door. *You're out of here for now, but maybe not out of my life.*

When Matty turned her attention back to Stella, she avoided eye contact. "Say, you and Norm picnicking and canoeing on the lake? Does that mean you two are finally a couple?"

"Yes and no," Stella replied. "We work together in Admissions, but as I told you before, we're not exactly a couple." She sat down and gave Matty an appraising look. "I'm really sorry to hear about all the trouble you've had but– " She stopped briefly as a nurse came in to check Matty's vital signs. "you're far better off in a big hospital like this. They'll give you a thorough going over."

"The doctors have pretty much done that already," Matty said, " but the way they keep poking me with a needle, I'm beginning to feel like a pin cushion. One or two more tests and I should be discharged." She shifted her eyes to the window and the golf course adjacent to the hospital grounds. "You know, of course, that my dad had to pull a few strings to get me in here. Nevertheless, it's been an ordeal, including the food. But I hope all that's behind me now." She paused as tears welled up. "One more thing, Stella – " Again she had to look down. "Please don't forget your promise."

"Matty, no one's going to hear it from me. Haven't I been your friend ever since your grade school days? As far as others are concerned, you just had an upset stomach." Stella squeezed Matty's hand, waiting for her to regain her composure.

Matty managed a smile. "By the way, lifetime friend, are you still holding that part-time job open for me?"

"Yes," Stella said, "but a lot depends on how soon you're back on your feet. Keep in mind that we've had some budget cuts this year, so it's been necessary to let a few people go – and that included a *certain person.* So now with a smaller staff we'll have to get underway much sooner than usual."

Matty blushed. "Yes, I heard that you let him go." She shifted her gaze back to the window. "I guess I should be grateful about all this, about how well I'm doing. But you know, I'm still upset."

"About what? Afraid you won't be ready when I need you?"

"No, not that. Give me a little time and I'll be back on my feet. What bothers me is *his* reaction. My mom and dad were the ones who decided to go ahead with the procedure, not me. Yet from that moment on, he cut me off. Haven't heard one word from him since."

"Matty, don't go on expecting to hear from him." There was steel in Stella's voice. "It just won't happen. Not from his kind. And it's certainly not worth your shedding any more tears." Stella grinned. "But then it doesn't look like you've wasted any time finding someone new."

Again Matty blushed. "Him? Now wait a minute! Don't go jumping to any conclusions. I just met this guy!"

"Sure you did."

An awkward silence followed.

"Oh he's good-looking alright," Stella said. "I've seen him around campus a number of times, but don't you worry, honey. I won't give you any competition. He's too young for me. Norm may not win any blue ribbons, but at least he's dependable." Before Matty could respond, a rattling in the hall heralded the arrival of a nurse and an aide.

"Sorry, ladies," the nurse said as the aide maneuvered a gurney over to Matty's bed. "It's time for more testing."

"Already?" Matty said. "My folks were coming down this morning."

"Don't worry," the nurse said. "This won't take long. When you come back, the sun will be shining and your folks will be waiting."

"Guess I'd better wait for Norm in the Lobby," Stella said. "If your new friend returns, I'll tell him where you are."

As the aide wheeled Matty from the room, Stella bent over and kissed her on the cheek.

Matty turned her head away to hide the tears. *Lord, you brought him into my life, so it must have been for a reason. Please bring him back. Let me find the reason.*

XIV

Unsure of my footing, I dropped my water-can and box of ammo at the head of the ramp. The sound broke through the eerie, murky quiet of the morning as I squinted toward shore, trying to make out the contours of the Italian coastline.

Securely wedged onto the sandbar, the LCI (Landing Craft, Infantry) bobbed slowly in the swells.

I turned to Garret and Prescott in line behind me. "Why are they holding us up?" My voice the only discord in the hush that lay over the beach. "Are we making this beach landing, or not?"

Prescott spoke up. "The lieutenant's on shore with our gunners trying to make sure we landed at the right spot."

"I bet right now the Krauts are laying back in the bushes, sighting their guns," Garret grunted, "waiting for the rest of us to come ashore. We'll be sitting ducks."

Suddenly a muffled command from Geoffrey, our squad leader, standing knee deep at the shoreline. "Okay Fletcher, come on down."

I scooped up my load and cautiously proceeded down the ramp that led into the water, the fetid odor of dying seaweed assaulting my nostrils. At the sight of wavelets lapping over the end of the ramp, I paused.

Again, more urgently: "Fletcher, for God's sake, keep moving!"

Stepping off the end of the ramp, I immediately sank over my head! I thrashed about, losing the ammo box, struggling to secure a footing, frantically trying to reach upwards through the watery blackness that had closed in above me.

All at once a strong arm gripped my ammo belt and dragged me into a shallower area. Stumbling forward onto the beach, I fell to my knees, choking and spitting out the salty water. Right away I saw Garret standing in the reeds up ahead wiping off his rifle.

Prescott knelt down beside me, coughing up water as well. "Y'all must have stepped into a hole," he gasped. "I guess Garret got hold of you."

"Yeah" I said, still choking, and moved to catch up with Garret and thank him. Then I stopped. I couldn't bring myself to do it.

"Damn you guys!" It was the squad leader again. "Get up here!"

Slowly the three of us gathered with the rest of the squad, including Lt. Watson and watched as the remainder of the section came ashore, the pervading quiet more ominous than ever. At a signal from the lieutenant our machine gun section marched up from the beach in a column. I shivered uncontrollably, trying to sweep my hair away from my face, my uniform completely soaked.

During the next several hours, in a series of starts and stops our column moved steadily inland, still with no sign of the enemy. As the light of dawn peeled away the forbidding darkness, it became clear that we were moving through open country along a paved road. Finally Sgt. Geoffrey halted us by a darkened farmhouse. Garret and I were ordered to begin digging an emplacement for our machine gun.

Meanwhile the gunners, Hensley and Kilgore, waited expectantly while Lt. Watson kneeled next to a tree stump poring over a map with the captain of E Company.

"This ground's full of roots," I grumbled as Garret and I began using our entrenching tools to begin gouging out a hole in the farmer's front yard. With the sun beginning to heat things up, it proved to be slow, backbreaking work, made more difficult by an abundance of tree roots. From time to time I glanced at Garret who had removed his jacket. He chopped and tugged at the roots, hardly looking up, even when an Italian civilian emerged from the farmhouse. In shirtsleeves and rumpled slacks, the guinea's light build was topped off with a dark beret.

"Voi Inglese?" he asked.

Garret, already perspiring profusely, ignored his question. I stopped digging and pointed to the American flag emblem on my jacket.

"Americani? Bene!" The farmer's face immediately brightened. *"Tedesci!"* He pointed down the road. *"Tedesci no good!"*

At this point Geoffrey approached the farmer, and with a few exaggerated gestures conveyed our need for better implements. Although not too enthusiastic about our digging a big hole in his front yard, the Italian nodded his understanding, went back to his barn and returned in a few minutes with two shovels.

Quickly appropriating our new implements, Garret and I went back to our task with renewed hope for an early finish. Meanwhile Lt. Watson returned from his conference with the E Company officers and began talking with the farmer, gesturing frequently toward the house. Finally, as he began to understand the lieutenant's gestures, the farmer frowned and went back inside.

Lt. Watson then motioned to Prescott who had been standing by to spell us digging the emplacement. Promptly Prescott gathered up his gear and tagged after the lieutenant, then halted while Kilgore and Hensley waited with the machine gun. Within a few minutes a squad from E Company formed up with them and the patrol started down the road with an E Company lieutenant in the lead.

Since the rising sun had begun to burn off the mist, I could see the patrol follow the road for several hundred yards, then abruptly veer to the right into a misty area approaching a woods. Then I lost sight of them.

Meanwhile, I continued to experience difficulty cutting through the root system plaguing our gun pit. I could see that

Garret was struggling just as much. But through it all, he said nothing. Finally when Lt. Watson returned to the area where E Company had gathered, I tossed my entrenching tool aside and slumped down on the edge of the emplacement. *Why all this work? We don't even know if there are enemy troops anywhere near here.*

I reached over and pulled my rifle into the pit so as to examine it a little more closely.

"Sure was a big break getting these carbines issued to us," I said, glancing at Garret who was still digging away at his end of the pit. I hefted my rifle a few times. "They're one hell of a lot lighter than those M-1's we dragged around in the mountains." I opened the breech, then snapped it shut. Garret continued digging, as though he had not heard.

I shrugged, settled back against my pack and lit a cigarette. *I know what's bothering him. He's still ticked off about the argument we had coming up from Naples on the LCI...*

...I had been sitting on my bunk wiping out my mess kit when Garret returned from a smoke topside. Immediately he screwed up his face. "This place stinks!" he grunted, looking around the hold at the other members of the squad. "Which one of you guys is guilty?"

"These bunks didn't smell half so bad till you came back," Hensley grinned. Prescott and the rest of the squad erupted in laughter.

Even Garret managed a smile as he sat down on the bunk opposite me, the single light bulb above us casting long shadows. "There's no rain topside," he said. "So the latest scuttlebutt says we'll be getting off this tub sometime during the night." He nodded to me. "What do you think?"

His query caught me miles away in thought. The more I mulled over questions about Matty and her past, the more I cursed myself for not having had the guts to ask Garret about his relationship with her. "Who knows?" I replied, lowering my voice and avoiding those gray eyes. "But here's something you might be able to clear up. Did you know Matty before I met her?"

As Garret straightened up, he struck his head on the metal bar that secured the bunk above him. "Damn!" he said, rubbing his head. Then, his face red, he seemed to refocus his eyes and scrutinize me more closely. "Now where in the world did that come from?"

"What difference does it make? Answer the question!"

"Go to hell! I can't believe you're still mooning over that broad!"

"Don't you call her a broad!" I jammed my mess kit back into its canvas cover. "But then, that's the way you talk about every woman you've ever known."

Garret continued to stare at me, his expression implacable. "Get this straight, Chad. I'm not responsible to you. So like I said, before: GO TO HELL!"

I slid off my bunk and doubled my fist. Whereupon Hensley stepped between us and pushed me back. "That's enough! Save your fighting for the Germans!"

A long silence ensued. Then Hensley turned to Garret. "Okay soldier, go back topside, find the lieutenant and ask him when we're going ashore. Then come back and enlighten the rest of us…"

…Now as I sat on the edge of our gun emplacement thinking about that incident, I felt the dampness of the earth creeping up my leg. I stood up and stretched. Garret was still finishing his smoke. "Thanks for saving my bacon back there in the water," I said, forcing a grin, but averting my face.

Garret nodded, but never looked up. At that point I caught sight of the lieutenant on his way back. I resumed digging.

About an hour later, with our gun pit nearly complete and rivers of perspiration coursing down my back, I decided it was time for a break.

Looking down the road, I could see our patrol slowly making its way toward us. As the column of GI's drew closer, I noted that two of our men wore bandages. Once they reached our position, it was evident that Prescott, his tan face pale, now had a small dressing on one hand; a rifleman had his right arm swathed in bloody gauze. Kilgore, Hensley and Prescott stopped off at our dugout while the rest proceeded to rejoin their comrades in E Company. Kilgore and Hensley promptly reassembled the tripod and gun barrel in position and sighted it down the road. With a long sigh, Prescott sat down beside me on the steps of the farmhouse. I looked at his bandaged left hand.

"A mite painful, but jest a scratch," he said. "Probably git me a Purple Heart, but not enough to send me to the rear for treatment." He unsnapped his canteen and took a long drink.

"What happened?" I asked.

Hensley spoke up. "We met a tank and about fifteen Krauts digging in about a mile from here."

"The tank fired on us," Prescott added, "so we pulled back."

Before long a medic came over to our emplacement, rewrapped Prescott's hand and wrote up a ticket for the wound.

"You mean the Germans caught you guys in the open?" Garret asked.

"Sure did, but we made it back," Prescott replied.

Garret shrugged. "You can thank the Fickle Finger of Fate for that."

Everyone nodded, except Prescott. "I thank God," he grinned. "He's my refuge and strength." He looked around at the other squad members seated on the grass. "Jus' where d'y'all figger the Fickle Finger gits his instructions?"

His demeanor reflected a calmness that surprised me. I nodded agreement. "You better hope that God hangs around here for a while. This is a mighty small beachhead." (I felt my heart beginning to thump.) "And I'm afraid we've stirred up a hornet's nest."

I glanced at Garret for some show of support, but he turned his head away. *Now he won't even look at me.*

At a nod from Hensley, I began stacking ammo boxes next to the machine gun. While Kilgore checked the gun's magazine, Hensley peered down the road with his binoculars. "There's movement up ahead. Looks like more than one tank and some enemy troops, well dispersed, heading this way."

Geoffrey motioned to Prescott. "Better get the lieutenant over here right away." He directed the rest of us to spread out on either side of the gun and dig in.

"Where's our FO?" Garret asked. "We can call in artillery on 'em."

"Not much chance of that" Geoffrey slid into the pit alongside the two gunners. "Our artillery hasn't even come ashore yet."

"Probably still back in Naples drinking *vino.*" Garret said.

But Geoffrey would have none of it. "Okay fellas, let's cut the crap and get busy digging."

Koo-WHACK!

A flat-trajectory shell from the enemy tank rocketed by, exploding about 100 feet back of us. As we hugged the damp ground, my fingers dug into the dirt. Geoffrey shouted for us to keep dispersed. But all I could think of was the smell of the earth around me. *Where is the lowest–the very lowest – part of the ground? How can I melt into it?* As I waited, my heart pounding, I could almost picture the German tank crew adjusting their gun sights, preparing for the next shot.

Yet in the midst of all this, I could not keep my thoughts from straying back to Garret and Matty. *How could she mess with a womanizer like him? And why? But then –who can say why we do anything? Who – or what – determines our actions? Will Matty make a mistake like that again? Will the German crew fire another shot?*

Is it up to the Fickle Finger – or God?

XV

"When do y'all figger we'll have to head down the hill into them buildin's?" Prescott asked Garret, his voice low, his teeth chattering from the chill of the wee hours. Like him and Garret, I shivered from the dank of the earth. From our position at the edge of a steep escarpment I could barely make out the line of stark white buildings at the bottom of the hill. No sign of the enemy. I scanned the dark hillside, grimacing at the jumble of grape arbors that we'd have to work through and the railroad track that we'd have to cross before we reached the first of the buildings. "Not too encouraging a prospect," I said, "and the timing's still something of a secret." I nudged Garret. "Why don't you enlighten us, Garret? You know so many secrets."

"The sooner we go after them the better," he said, ignoring my insinuation. "Keep in mind, the longer we wait, the stronger they get. "

"I sure hope we ain't fixin' to do it in the dark," Prescott said.

"Not much chance of that," Garret murmured. "Anyone with any brains knows that taking a town this size calls for street fighting – and we sure as hell aren't going to do that in the dark. It'll be tough, but we'll lick 'em."

Well, well. Finally some encouraging words from General Garret himself! I ought to bring him up short, but that would only lead to a fight and get me in more trouble with Geoffrey. But what does he mean – saying 'anyone with any brains'? Hey Garret, you're no smarter than the rest of us. We're just a bunch of foul-smelling dogfaces up against some pretty tough, highly skilled enemy soldiers who have already beaten several other armies. So Garret, where do you come off, thinking you're so smart?

I poked Prescott again. "Ain't we lucky to have such a brilliant military analyst right here in our squad?"

Garret turned to me, his face livid. "You starting in again? I've heard just about enough outa you!"

"Well. I certainly haven't heard much from you. At least, not about you and Matty. Guess I was right in the first place. The two of you were shacking up before Chad the Dummy came along, right?"

Garret only shook his head.

"What does it take for you to tell the truth?" I asked. "Admit it, my friend. You and Matty were lovers!"

"Hey you two!" Prescott murmured. "Keep it down!"

CRACK!

A flare launched from the Kraut position. I watched as an incandescent pencil-line arched into the blackness overhead, then burst, suddenly flooding the hillside in a ghostly light. Like my two comrades, I held my stance, every nerve taut, watching for the slightest sign of movement, yet fascinated by the sight of the flare drifting slowly downward – and the stark landscape it revealed. I struggled to keep myself from becoming overly distracted by the naked beauty of the scene.

Keep your mind on the job, Fletcher. Remember, behind every one of those dark windows in the buildings down the hill there's a highly trained Kraut waiting to kill you.

Crackling and spuming light, the flare finally floated to the ground and expired, leaving behind its signature aroma. Once more we were confronted by the uncertain darkness.

Geoffrey's quiet voice abruptly snapped me out of my fascination with the flare. "Remember, you guys, Kilgore and Hensley have the gun set up to cover our right flank. Keep a sharp eye on the left. We don't want any Germans outflanking us."

Garret looked at me, then looked away.

"Go ahead Garret," I said, keeping my voice down, but not wanting to miss this chance. "You were about to divulge your deep, dark secret before we were so rudely interrupted."

No response.

"You and Matty were lovers, right?"

"Is that a question – or an answer?" The words barely audible through clenched teeth.

"Answer the question!"

"Okay, so I knew her. Is that a – "

Another flare burst and again we all remained transfixed until it burned out.

"Looks like them Kraut fellers are gittin' nervous," Prescott whispered.

While I kept my eyes (and my carbine) zeroed in on a dark alleyway down the hill to the left, my attention remained focused on Garret. "How about all those repeated visits to St. Francis Hospital? Those were visits to Matty – right?"

"Whatever gave you that idea?"

"Why was she in the hospital?"

"How should I know?" He turned toward me, his voice as cold as his eyes. "Damn you, Chad! Leave me out of it. She put herself in the hospital."

I leaned toward him "Why?"

"Why ask me? You're her fiancé!" His elbow jabbed my cheek, rocking me backwards. "Now stay outa my face!"

Where moments before I had been shivering from the chill of night, now I could feel perspiration running down my neck. I grabbed Garret's collar and pushed him. We tumbled into my foxhole struggling for dominance.

Then a muffled cry from Prescott. "This is crazy! Do y'all want to git us kilt?" The next I knew Prescott had me by the shoulders and pulled us apart. Garret eased out of my foxhole and began crawling back toward his hole.

By this time as Geoffrey returned, I heard a faint cough from across the tracks. *Mortars!* WHUMP! WHUMP! WHUMP! Three of them were clear misses, but the fourth – WHAM!– hit the edge of our gun position, caving it in.

As soon as the barrage subsided, Geoffrey scrambled to his feet, seething. "Cut out your damn-fool arguing or I'll have the two of you court-martialed for abandoning your posts! Now Chad, get back where you belong!"

Then he turned to Prescott. "Get back there with Garret!" he said.

I watched them crawl back over the dark landscape, gradually disappearing out of earshot in the murky gloom behind us. *I bet Geoffrey's gonna give Garret a verbal going over he won't soon forget!*

After some time had passed without further incident, I heard someone coming up behind my hole. I was surprised to see Prescott, clearly puzzled. "Where's Garret? " I asked.

"I thought he was back up here with you," he whispered

"He's not here." I said, trying to keep my voice low. "Geoffrey sent him back a while ago to give him a going over, I guess."

"Well he's not with Geoffrey. I just saw Geoffrey. He's all alone and mad as a wet hen."

"Garret's probably gone over the hill. Good riddance! "

"Mebbe so, but it's plum crazy the way Garret and y'all keep arguin'", he said.

"All I asked was for the truth about him and Matty. Then he took a poke at me. What do you expect?"

"Okay, but why not surprise all of us. Overlook it. Garret's done a lot fer y'all. Fergive him."

"Forgive him? You outa your blooming mind? Why should I do that?"

"That's one of the big lessons Jesus taught. Did y'all know that even when He was hangin' on the cross, Jesus fergave them Romans who nailed him there?"

"That doesn't make sense." I turned to peer into the darkness ahead. "And it doesn't make much sense for you to be out here. You better get back to your hole."

"Love and fergiveness don't have to make no sense." He said, his voice hushed. Then he turned about preparing to crawl back where he had come from. "But it's what a Christian would do."

I climbed back into my foxhole and watched as Prescott disappeared in the gloom.

Well, for your information, Prescott, I'm not a Christian – okay? To me that's just an easy way of covering up your –

Another flare vaulted into fading blackness and again I became a stone figure until the last light had faded.

Before long I detected the first yellow streaks of dawn emerging over the hill on our right flank, outlining the white buildings below. Then from the left I heard a slight scraping sound, a faint, methodical scraping of earth. *The Krauts! They've got a patrol moving up on our left!* My heart began to pound as I peered into the dim light, all the while fingering the trigger of my carbine. Finally a shape became distinguishable. It was Lt. Watson, our platoon leader.

He paused at the edge of my foxhole. "E Company's moving down in about ten minutes – and we are to follow them. Tell Geoffrey to watch for my hand signal." Then he was gone.

As the lieutenant moved back, Geoffrey returned. When I gave him Watson's message, he shook his head in disgust. "It'd be great if these 90-day wonders would give us dogfaces a little more notice about what's coming up."

Before long Geoffrey waved to me. Without further incident I clambered out of my hole, following Kilgore and Hensley and linking up with the rifle section further down the slope. I saw no sign of Garret so I waved to Prescott. Then we all moved toward the rail tracks, only slowing down as we muscled our way through the tangle of grape vines, and later when a splatter of machine pistol fire cut down one of the E Company riflemen up ahead. We waited while a rifle squad spread out among the surrounding buildings amid intermittent fire. By this time Prescott and two of our replacements had caught up to us. *But no sign of Garret!* We followed Kilgore and Hensley down a narrow street to a small square. Once again they set up our machine gun, aiming it down the street at the end of which towered the steeple of a Catholic church. Geoffrey positioned the three of us so that we could cover the machine gun's left flank.

Although gunfire crackled from the center of town, he cautioned us to sit tight awaiting further orders.

*   *   *

By afternoon, except for occasional rifle fire and grenade explosions, activity in our squad's sector had noticeably diminished. While Prescott and I were busy enjoying a large chunk of cheese and some dark, grainy bread taken from an enemy prisoner's pack, Lt. Watson helped one of our light tanks find an unobstructed firing position.

Suddenly Geoffrey reappeared at a hole in one wall of the building we had moved into. He nodded toward me. "I've got Private Newman outside with about thirty prisoners we rounded up in one of the tunnels. I want you and Prescott to help him take these POWs back to Regiment. Leave your ammo boxes with Kilgore."

After delivering our ammo to the machine gun position, Prescott and I shouldered our carbines, then trudged around to the back of our building. There Private Newman, a fair-skinned recruit of 18 or 19, stood holding his rifle on a sizable group of Krauts seated on the ground.

"The lieutenant told me to follow the highway south out of town," he said.

I motioned for the prisoners to get on their feet. Amid spasmodic machine pistol fire we began moving them back across the railroad tracks with Newman in the lead, Prescott and I covering the rear. Twice we had to adjust the pace of march in order to accommodate those prisoners unable to keep up.

I was scanning the hill to our right when I thought I detected movement along the ridge. But about the time I concluded that it must be a wounded GI or straggler, a shot echoed sharply and Newman's helmet went spinning. He dropped like a sack of lead and everyone hit the ground. Crouching in the open while Prescott kept the prisoners under control, I squeezed off several shots aimed at the hilltop. After a few minutes with no return fire, I rose up to see where the bullets had been coming from. I couldn't spot anything. When I turned to check with Prescott, a lone German soldier stepped out of the brush within a few feet of me. He wore a green camouflage cape and brandished a Thompson sub-machine gun. Caught off-guard, Prescott and I dropped our rifles and raised our arms in surrender.

A well-built, swarthy German with rugged features, our captor spoke to us in perfect English: "You may drop your hands. Unless you want to end up like your companion – " he motioned toward Newman who lay sprawled and bleeding profusely from a head wound – "Don't do anything foolish. Believe me, it will be your final act. I will keep my hands under the cape, but my pistol will be watching."

Though there was an immediate stirring and babble among the prisoner group, the way our captor silenced them with a few brusque commands in German, I felt certain he must be at least an *unteroffizier*.

Turning to Prescott, he said: "We are going to change direction and swing north across the shoulder of this hill. So as not to attract attention from any of your comrades we may encounter, I want you up front, as though you are leading our group. Your friend and I will bring up the rear. If we are stopped by any of your soldiers, tell them you are under orders to escort your prisoners to a special POW cage in the rear."

He motioned toward our rifles lying on the ground where we had dropped them. "Now, at my signal, I want each of you to empty the chambers of your rifles. Slowly. One at a time. Remember, I am likely to misunderstand any sudden movement."

Shaking noticeably, the two of us were careful to follow his directions to the letter. Then Prescott took his place at the head of the column and I positioned myself in the rear, next to our captor. Promptly we began moving our motley group up through the brush and across the hill toward the intersection of two roads leading to Cisterna. We picked our way through the rubble of battle, past abandoned war materiel, the wreckage of two light tanks and the bodies of several American and German soldiers, already putrid in the heat. To my surprise, we encountered no battalion or regimental headquarters personnel. Apparently all the regiment's reserves had been committed to the battle for Cisterna. Sporadic gunfire and explosions, however, could still be heard coming from Cisterna, now to our right.

As we reached the top of the hill, I could see that only a single Military Policemen stood guard at the intersection of the two Cisterna roads. Anxiously I searched our captor's face for his reaction to this development. With a slight inclination of his head and a quiet command, the *unteroffizier* indicated that we should shift direction toward the sentry.

When we reached the bottom of the hill and the MP's post, the guard approached Prescott. "Where you goin' with all these prisoners?" he asked. Slowly, carefully I moved off to one side so that I could see the guard.

Prescott made no response. He looked at me without saying a word. By this time our Kraut escort had moved into the midst of the other prisoners so as not to draw attention. Finally Prescott said: "We're headin' fer Regimint."

The MP motioned to me. "The one with the cape. Bring him up here." *Apparently the MP must have caught a glimpse of our German bodyguard before he shifted position.*

Gesturing with my rifle, I was able to get the *unteroffizier* to separate from the other prisoners. We both moved up alongside Prescott who, though exhibiting signs of nervousness, kept his eye on the prisoners behind us.

Reaching over to feel the prisoner's cape, the MP seemed puzzled. "Haven't I seen you – "

The cape billowed as a burst of fire from the Kraut raked the MP across his middle. He crumpled in a heap.

Slack-jawed as in a trance, I could only stare at the prostrate Military Policeman, who seemed to be in convulsion, innards oozing from his mouth. As I maintained a white-knuckled grip on my rifle, a feeling of revulsion and hatred washed over me. I shifted my gaze to the *unteroffizier*, his expression grim, his dark eyes mere slits.

"Let's get moving away from here before someone else comes," he said with hardly a glance at the MP. Once more I took my place at the rear of the column alongside our captor. Prescott in the lead, we resumed our journey westward.

As the Cisterna road fell further to the rear, the heat began to build up, I thought I could hear a jeep in the distance behind us. Even as the sound of the motor grew somewhat louder, I kept my gaze forward. I knew better than to turn my head, even to look at our lone German. Gradually the sound of the jeep faded and I found myself wondering what this crazy Kraut would do next. The bloody images of Newman and the MP provided answers I did not welcome.

Although I could not see Prescott, I knew what he must be doing.

But what the hell, Prescott. What happens, happens. And who cares? Not the Fickle Finger. And certainly not some kinda god, either. So no point in wasting one of your precious prayers trying to get us out of this one, Prescott. Not when the guy who once was my best friend decides to become a deserter. And the gal I almost married turns out to be a tramp.

XVI

Plymouth, Michigan
June, 1942

"But Matty, you know how the doctor cautioned you." Eva emerged from the kitchen carrying a tall vase.

"Mom, how can I forget it!"

Eva stopped at the table next to the sofa, deposited the vase and began to rearrange the flowers. "Your dad sent these – "

"...No climbing stairs for another few weeks. Stay off your feet as much as possible." Matty repeated Dr. Able's strictures in a louder sing-song pattern, then paused. She punched her pillow and lay back against the sofa. "Norm and Stella will be here in a few minutes – and I hate for them to see me like this. Way last winter Garret and I had planned to go to this dance with them – in case you've forgotten."

"Don't talk to me like that, young lady." Eva's small blue eyes narrowing. "Your father and I have tried to help you through this any way we can." Eva unfolded a blue comforter and tucked it in around Matty's feet. "Anyway, you wouldn't want to go anywhere with that individual, so don't go wasting time and tears on him. I've fixed up a bed for you in the library so you won't have to climb the stairs." Eva straightened up and brushed her dark hair out of her face. "I hate to admit it," she sighed, "but I'm afraid these past few months have been a nightmare for me."

"Tell me about it." Matty adjusted her pillow and watched, her green eyes expressionless, as her mother sank into a chair next to the phone.

"All this wouldn't be so hard to cope with if your dad were home more often."

"The war, mother. The war. Remember?"

"Yes, I do remember." The words crisp and sharp. "You might also remember that I'm your mother, not one of your college chums." Eva's frown then relaxed. "I guess we should both thank the Lord that your father was in town just when he could bring you home from the clinic."

"How long will he be gone this time?"

"I don't know exactly. Those War Production Board meetings in Washington often last several days." Her brow furrowed as she regarded Matty on the couch. "Look, it's been a tough day and I'm really washed out. I've left the door unlocked so your friends can come right in. I'm going upstairs to rest for a – "

The doorbell jangled.

Matty sat up. "They're here."

*   *   *

Stella settled down on the edge of the couch. "Don't fret yourself, Matty. So you miss a dance or two. Not the end of the world." She looked over at Norm, perspiring in his tight-fitting white jacket and dark slacks. "Why don't you go fetch us something cold to drink? Eva said she's set out some things in the kitchen."

A half-smile crossed Norm's pudgy face. "Not a bad idea." He grinned at Matty. "A beautiful evening and I know we'll miss you, but there'll be other times." He left for the kitchen.

"He's right, you know," Stella smiled. "There'll be other times."

Matty turned her head away. "Oh sure. I should live so long."

"That's no way to talk," Stella said

"How do you expect me to talk?" Matty fingered a curl, flattened it out, then let it snap back in place. "The two of us could have worked things out if my folks hadn't – "

"It's just as well." Stella's cheeks reddened."Garret wouldn't have been right for you – not with his temper. In fact, that's why we had to let him go."

Startled, Matty looked up. "You mean he's not part of the Wellington recruiting team anymore?"

"Hadn't you heard?"

"I'm afraid I haven't been that much in touch with him." Matty's hand went to her mouth. "He hasn't left school has he?"

"Oh no, nothing like that." Stella moved to an armchair and turned to face Matty. "He's planning to join the Army Reserves this summer so that he can finish his senior year at Wellington before he leaves for the service."

Matty broke into a grin. "Well, well. You really do keep tabs on him, don't you?"

Stella turned her head away and waited for several seconds before she spoke. "Matty, that was an unkind remark. You must know that Garret gets no more attention than any of our other part-time people. Incidentally, there's been a change. The offer I made before will only be open until the first week in September. If you're still interested in working with us when you enter the University this fall, I'll find a spot for you."

"Then you and Norm are back full-time?"

"Yep. Greenman confirmed it last week. Just in time, frankly. With our graduation coming up, I was beginning to wonder."

Norm returned with the tray of drinks, set it down and handed a glass to Matty. "That's some Mom you've got! Everything in perfect order. Incidentally, how's she taking all this?"

"She's upstairs resting right now. I'm afraid Mother has let this Garrct business get the best of her."

Stella and Norm exchanged glances. After an awkward silence, Stella spoke: "Matty, I do wish you and…someone were coming with us tonight. " She set down her glass. "Now, I'm afraid the clock says we'd better be on our way."

*   *   *

Matty listened to their car pulling out of the driveway. *Someone? Dear Lord, I had a someone. Then I made a terrible mistake – and you took him away. Tell me, do you have another 'someone' for me – somewhere?*

At the sound of her mother coming down the stairs, Matty buried her head in her pillow.

XVII

Anzio, Italy
May, 1944

As we plodded ahead, bypassing a wrecked tank, an abandoned jeep and other litter from yesterday's battleground (all of it under the watchful eye of our German captor), I could feel a river of sweat flowing down my back, as much the effect of our precarious circumstances as from the hot summer sun.

The next half-mile brought us to a hill from which, dead ahead, I saw a small, dense woods, and some distance beyond that, an east-west highway crowded with American military traffic. *It's a safe bet that our friendly neighborhood Kraut won't want us to get anywhere near that highway!*

Apparently Prescott must have shared my concern about the danger of our column getting any closer to the busy road up ahead. For suddenly he raised his arm signaling "Halt!", bringing the column to a sudden stop. Surprised by Prescott's abrupt signal, our German escort hurried to the front of the column, spoke heatedly to Prescott for a few minutes, then evidently satisfied with Prescott's explanation, he pointed to the nearby woods, issued some brief orders and within minutes we were again on our way, this time heading for the nearby woods with the *unteroffizier* and I bringing up the rear of the column

Once we reached the shelter of the forest, our captor shed his cape and helmet, called out several German non-coms from among the POW's for a brief conference. When the parley broke up, one by one the members of this special group took positions on the perimeter of the woods at points offering cover for observation of the road to the north as well as the terrain to the south back toward the Cisterna road.

Then I watched in awe as he made a hurried inspection of each of his "lookout" positions, then delegated another of his non-coms to collect the remaining prisoners in a group that could be mustered quickly in an emergency. His actions sent a chill down my spine. *Obviously this guy has a plan that he intends to carry out – whatever the cost.*

Meanwhile, Prescott and I were ordered to drop our rifles and packs. Then we had to sit on the ground with our backs against a large tree facing the *unteroffizier.* For the first time I noticed he carried a small pair of binoculars and that blond whiskers were difficult to distinguish against his tanned face.

"It's much cooler in the woods, so I think we'll wait here until darkness," he said, slumping down onto a fallen tree a few feet away. "Meanwhile, let's relax and see what rations you have for us."

With the noise of military traffic on the road ahead still drifting across the plain, I found it hard to concentrate on what our captor was saying and doing. Placing the Tommy Gun at his feet, he began rifling our packs. In mine he soon found two cans of C-rations and three of Matty's letters that he quickly tossed aside. When I protested, he pursed his lips and feinted toward his gun.

"It may come as a surprise to you," he said, "but I fully intend to reach the safety of our own lines. I'd like you and your comrade to come along with us. However, if necessary, I can make trip without either one of you." The fire in his eyes spoke volumes.

While I could see little to gain by arguing with our captor, I thought about asking him to share the C-rations, but decided to wait for a better opportunity. *I could almost taste the spaghetti!*

Much to my surprise, the German's statement seemed only to pique Prescott's interest. "Where did y'all learn to speak such good English?" he asked.

The Kraut smiled and opened the can of spaghetti (*Oh, the aroma!*) "Sounds like you're from Dixie. Would you believe that's where I grew up?" He pulled several packages of crackers from Prescott's pack. "I came over to America with my folks in the 30's when I was still a youngster," he said. "We settled in a little town in Alabama." Pulling a combination fork and spoon from his pocket, the German began eating the cold spaghetti.

Prescott broke into a wide grin, which I found hard to understand. "I come from a small town myself – near Dalton in northwest Georgia. My daddy has a little farm there."

Prescott! Are you nuts?

"No farming for me," the German continued. "I spent many happy years in Bavaria, so I learned to love the mountains." He stopped to swat some ants crawling on his boots. "When I was in high school here in the States, some of us teenagers used to hitchhike over to Talladega during the hot summer months" The Kraut nodded in the direction of the nearest hill. "Of course, Alabama's mountains are nothing compared to southern Bavaria, but those trips were fun." He set his C-rations down and wiped his mouth on his sleeve. Suddenly he looked at me. "You Americans make pretty good spaghetti." The he turned his attention back to Prescott. "Yes, I'd say that in high school I made many good friends."

"And I'd say y'all speak English purty good."

I tried to interrupt the conversation, but the two of them kept at it.

"*Ja,* but my school mates thought I had quite an accent," he laughed. "In fact, that's where I got my nickname. Before long they began to call me 'Alabam'."

Prescott slapped his knee. " 'Alabam' – that's a good 'un, alright. Sounds like y'all were havin' a right good time in high school." Prescott removed his helmet, wiped off his face and neck, then replaced it. "But with jobs so hard to git, how come y'all quit your job in the factory and went back to Germany?"

Prescott, that's enough! I started to say something to caution Prescott, but thought better of it However, I made the mistake of glancing at Alabam – and I caught his eye. *No doubt about it. that Kraut knows exactly what I'm thinking!*

"*Ja,* I guess I was pretty lucky. " Alabam loosened his collar."Before long, my father sent me a little newspaper he had been getting from Munich. And when I began reading that little paper and saw how Adolph Hitler had come to power, how he needed – "

Prescott's face turned red. He winced and looked at me before he spoke: "I see, but tell me more about Alabama. Where did y'all go to church?"

That's enough, screwball. That's enough! "Prescott!" I shouted.

Although Alabam kept peeling the wrapper from his crackers, he turned his attention to me. "You have something against our talking?"

I looked away.

*   *   *

From the high point in the woods where we could observe, it became clear that the volume of American military traffic on the north-south road had increased substantially, stirring up a towering cloud of dust. The column of troops on foot had long since passed. Now I could see a mixture of half-tracks, tanks, a few tank destroyers and a variety of trucks, some pulling anti-tank guns – a development that aroused a considerable amount of murmuring among the "lookouts". I could only imagine how the drivers and other GI's were trying to breathe in that billowing thunderhead of powdered earth. Granted that from my limited vantage point I wasn't able to discern the unit's insignia, I assumed it was a support unit by-passing Cisterna for a possible attack on enemy north of the town.

Since we were all nearly exhausted from marching through the torrid battle zone, I expected that the experience of watching a strong American force move to a cut-off position north of Cisterna would rattle Alabam's nerves.

At first I couldn't detect any particular reaction. Then suddenly his demeanor changed. Once again he summoned his chosen leaders from the prisoner group. Then after a brief discussion that included Prescott, the leaders began forming up all their comrades in a column as before. Obviously Alabam was preparing us to move out. Yet I was puzzled. *Why does Alabam want to move out now with so many American troops in the area? And why will we be moving further north, right into the heart of danger?*

Turning to me, the *unteroffizier* said: "We're going to resume our march. Georgia will take the lead again. You and I will watch the rear *(I felt the intensity of his eyes boring right through me)*. I expect everyone to be on their best behavior."

As I rose to retrieve my rifle and shoulder my pack, I glanced at the highway ahead, still glutted with military traffic. Immediately I saw what had prompted Alabam to move so quickly: A half-track and a two-man jeep had separated from the mainstream of traffic and were heading for our woods!

Under Alabam's close scrutiny our column filed out into the open, heading straight for the approaching jeep. We hadn't gone far before the jeep skidded to a stop and the officer in charge called out: "Where are you going with those prisoners?"

We halted immediately and while Prescott hurried out to confer with the officer, the half-track promptly shifted to one side to provide a clear field of fire in case of a problem.

What they were saying I could not hear, but I began to perspire heavily. *With several guns trained on Prescott what if Alabam makes a suspicious move?* I caught myself mumbling: "God, please help Prescott to – " I stopped abruptly. *Cut it out, Fletcher! You're beginning to sound like you-know-who!*

Apparently uneasy about the protracted length of the conference, Alabam moved out to one side of our column, continuing to watch Prescott intently. For myself, I couldn't keep my eyes off Alabam's cape. After a few more tense moments, the officer waved to our group, returned to his jeep and the entourage headed back to rejoin their unit.

Prescott then made his way back to the rear of our column and, his face flushed, waited with me for Alabam who had since hidden himself in the midst of the other prisoners. At a nod from Alabam, Prescott filled us in on his talk with the American officer.

"He said we're goin' the wrong way. To reach our Regimint we need to back track to the main highway outa Cisterna and foller it west."

As he spoke, Prescott kept glancing at Alabam, as though anxious for his approval. Like me, his eyes focused on the ragged holes in the folds of Alabam's cape, mute testimony as to what lay behind it. When Prescott had finished, much to my surprise, Alabam seemed satisfied with Prescott's brief report. Then he issued a few quiet commands and the column reversed itself, again with Prescott in the lead.

We marched off through the billowing heat, retracing our path across open country toward the bloody road intersection. Since now the pace was much slower, I was puzzled. *Why are we going so slow? Is Alabam stalling for time? What desperate plan does he have?*

As the sound of the military traffic faded into the background, I stole a glance at our captor, plodding along beside me, and I thought I heard him humming a catchy, but unfamiliar tune. He appeared to be much more relaxed, little affected by the turmoil swirling about him.

Does he have another plan? Don't be fooled by his demeanor, Fletcher. You know full well that beneath the surface a fuse is burning, slow and unrelenting.

XVIII

Anzio, Italy

May, 1944

Once we had reached a point beyond which anyone in that military convoy would likely observe our movements, Alabam called to Prescott. "Head for that grove of trees where we can wait."

Wait? What would we be waiting for?

Alabam's latest move prompted a little grumbling from some of the POWs, but a few sharp commands from Alabam quickly squelched the murmuring. I shook my head. *Typical German discipline. This kind of iron control explains why we're having so much trouble driving these lousy Germans out of Italy.*

Once we were in among the trees, Alabam again posted two of his non-coms on the northern edge of the woods. My guess was that they would signal when the heavy flow of military traffic on the road had dropped off. Prescott and I exchanged glances.

With darkness coming on, does this crazy Kraut still think he can reach his own lines?

Prescott and I settled down in a comfortable spot next to a deep shell crater. To our surprise, Alabam decided to join us. Cradling the Tommy Gun on his lap, he pulled the stub of a cigarette from his tunic. He started to light it, then –

CRACK! A rifle shot split the air. Alabam cried out, stumbled and fell into the crater grasping his knee.

I immediately snatched my carbine, slid down into the crater and managed to place one boot on the writhing

German's neck. I raised my rifle to bring the butt down on his skull, but Prescott grabbed my arm.

"Let him live!" he cried.

A quick pivot and I sent Prescott sprawling. Within seconds he was back on his feet, but not quick enough. For with a surge of hatred, I brought my rifle butt down on Alabam, crushing his face. He emitted a muffled cry, squirming to get away from the rifle butt, then suddenly collapsed. But the eyes remained open, watching.

"Why'd y'all do that?" Prescott shouted, his face crimson. "Haven't we had enough killin'?"

"That Kraut deserved everything he – "

Suddenly two GI's emerged from the brush, one of them Garret! He rushed over to the edge of the crater; the other guy hurried to the area where the POW's were congregated.

Garret, his voice trembling, exclaimed: "Damn you, Chad! I purposely wounded that creep in the knee to give Regiment a chance at interrogation." Garret contemplated the stricken Kraut whose face had become a pulsing, shapeless mass of red and gray and white. "This guy probably won't last another five minutes. Thanks for being such a big help."

"Get off my back – both of you! " I said, climbing out of the crater. Even as I did so, I felt like a set of eyes was following my movements. I shrugged it off and nudged Garret. "Okay mystery man, we've waited long enough – who is that guy with you and where – "

Garret, his shirt soaked with sweat, nodded in the direction of the POW's on the other side of the grove. They were making no move to escape. And there holding them in check with his Tommy Gun was the newcomer.

When Garret reached down to give Prescott a hand getting out of the shell hole, Prescott hesitated. "What about him?" He indicated Alabam, who was now bleeding profusely.

"Forget about him and come on up." Garret replied. "We've got more than enough live ones to worry about."

Reluctantly Prescott grabbed hold of Garret's hand and clambered out of the crater.

It wasn't until the job of lining up the prisoners had been nearly completed that Garret finally acknowledged our questioning looks.

"Okay you guys," he said, pausing with a flicker of a smile. "Meet Corporal Peabody. He's the Battalion Commander's jeep driver. He helped me track you down."

Both of us nodded to the corporal.

"Glad you were able to help us out," I said, my throat now so dry I was having trouble speaking.

"No problem," Peabody grinned. "I tell you, this is the most fun I've had since fighting those crazy Italians back in Sicily!"

I couldn't help but smile. *Garret, this is your fighter? A guy who barely comes up to my shoulder? With a woman's complexion and a face full of freckles? Sure doesn't look like he could deck anybody. Okay, maybe an Italian. But not any Krauts I'd ever seen.*

As for the German prisoners, some were so shaken by the sudden turn of events, that they still had their hands in the air. Peabody wasted no time dealing with them. *"Hande unten!"* he shouted, then turned to me. "You guys watch these Krauts while I get my jeep." He threw me a bandolier. I snapped a clip into my carbine and tossed the bandolier over to Prescott.

Before long several of the prisoners broke out in smiles, apparently relieved that Alabam's wild scheme had been short-circuited before any of them were killed or wounded.

Within minutes Peabody returned with his jeep. He lifted a half-carton of C-rations from the rear of the jeep and pointed to his water can. "I don't have much with me, but this should tide you guys over till you reach Regiment with these POW's. Meanwhile, I better head for Battalion before the CO chews me out for taking so long." He gave us a quick salute. "Nice doin' business with you lads." Then he spun his wheels and set out for the Cisterna road.

As we split up the rations and organized our column for the trip back to Regiment, I paused at the edge of the shell crater for a final glance at Alabam. His eyes were still open, but now I could hear gurgling sounds. I turned away.

"We better get moving," Garret said. Once more Prescott took his place at the head of the column and I kept to the rear. Garret, however, motioned for me to get up alongside Prescott. "I can handle this end of the column myself," he said, eyes straight ahead.

Without further comment I moved up alongside Prescott and we resumed our trek through layers of heat. I tried to forget what lay behind us. *Alabam's still back in that crater and he ain't going anywhere. But what about those eyes?*

XIX

Hey, this is crazy! We captured Rome almost two weeks ago. And I lived through the whole damn thing. Now our unit's off the line and our company commander wants us to celebrate. He's given everyone in the company a pass to go into Rome for the day. Great! Except here it is 4 p.m. and while the rest of the guys are in town whooping it up, what am I doing cooped up in this hot Regimental Library tent writing a letter?

Trouble is, I'm not actually writing *the letter. I'm* trying *to write the letter. For the life of me I can't make up my mind about what to say to Matty. She's a beautiful girl with a wonderful disposition and two bright red Betty Boop lips. She smells like a million bucks and I love her very much – I guess. But how can I love someone who hasn't leveled with me about her past hanky-panky with Garret?*

And there's the other problem – Garret. Here's a guy who's been my buddy for years and he's saved my bacon several times. So I should worship him – right? But how can I revere somebody who's been fooling around with my Matty and refuses to admit it?

I wadded up another sheet of looseleaf paper and was preparing to start over when Prescott showed up.

"Figgered I'd catch you here," he said.

"Kamerad!" I raised both arms in a gesture of surrender. "You caught me red-handed!"

"I thought y'all were on the truck going in this morning," Prescott said. "By the time we got into Rome, I realized y'all hadn't showed up. Y'all must have left the company area right after morning chow."

"I was just too tired, so an 'off' day like this gave me a chance to catch up on my correspondence. You wouldn't believe how quiet it's been in here. Did Garret make it to Rome?"

"Sure did – and he had quite a tale to tell."

"I bet. But how much of it can we believe?" I stuffed my unfinished letter into the German dispatch case I'd 'liberated' a few months ago.

" 'How much can we believe?' Prescott made a face. "Chad, when are y'all gonna start trustin' Garret a little more? That feller's gone out of his way to help and – "

"Now, now, my friend. No need to tell me what a wonderful person he is."

Prescott pushed his chair back. "Do you want to hear what he had to say – or not?"

I gave Prescott the three-fingered Boy Scout salute. "Of course I do, so don't get your shorts in an uproar. It's just that I'm very interested in where he was when all hell broke loose and we started to attack Cisterna. He was supposed to go back to Regiment and bring us our ration of fresh bread. Well, he went to the rear alright, but he didn't come back till all the shooting was over. Of course there could be a reasonable explanation. Perhaps he noticed that some of the bread smelled stale and he decided to wait around while Regiment baked a fresh batch."

Prescott made no response other than a faintly audible sigh. We left the Library tent heading for our company and evening chow.

As we followed the path that would bring us to H Company, Prescott finally mustered a grin. "Fact is, Garret never got very far on his 'bread patrol'. Some lieutenant from Battalion HQ grabbed him for an emergency assignment. It seems that F Company had captured an "important prisoner" that Battalion felt should be taken back to Regiment right away in the colonel's jeep. That prisoner was Alabam and the jeep driver was Peabody."

We stopped briefly at our tent to get our mess kits.

"That explains how Garret and Peabody got together," I said, "but how in Heaven's name did they ever allow Alabam to escape?"

"Trouble started when the two of 'em took off for Regiment with their prisoner in too big a hurry. They hadn't gone far when Peabody discovered he had left his smokes behind. He decided to stop by the road intersection south of Cisterna so that he could bum some cigarettes off the MP."

The narrration came to an abrupt halt when we reached the Cook Tent with its aroma of roasting beef and coffee. Once through the chow line, I indicated a spot under some trees where we could talk, then waved to Chaim, one of our newer squad members.

"Garret and Peabody stopping for cigarettes at a time like that sure looks like somebody made a big mistake," I said.

"Sure 'nuf," Prescott nodded. " 'cause while Peabody and Garret were jawing with the MP, this feller Alabam grabbed Peabody's Tommy gun from the floor of the jeep and ordered Garret and the MP to drop their weapons. Then he kicked their guns into a bush and before anyone knew it, he ducked into the brush and was gone."

"You mean they didn't even – "

"I reckon if either one of 'em had challenged that German feller, it would have been their *second* mistake and – Say, what is this stuff we're eatin'?" He scrutinized the white, lumpy gravy that covered his piece of toast. "Smells kinda funny."

"The GI's who've been with the outfit for a while call it 'SOS'."

" 'SOS'? What does that mean?"

I grinned even with my mouth full. " Prescott, you wouldn't want to know."

The sudden glimmer in Prescott's eyes told me had figured it out. "Well sir," he continued, "Garret and the MP scrambled through the scrub growth all along the hillside, but never could find their prisoner. I figger Alabam was desperate to get back to his unit and meant to take a passel of his friends with him."

"He certainly wasn't any ordinary *unteroffizier*," I said. "He probably rushed directly to the top of the hill, and later spotted us coming his way with all those prisoners." I set my mess kit down on the ground and took a long, slow drink of coffee. "It's too bad that Newman had to get a half-dozen slugs in the gut," I said, "so that this wild-eyed Kraut could take over our patrol. I'm glad I finished him off. "

Prescott started to say something, then paused. He stopped outside the entrance to our tent. "Fact is, he was already wounded when you hit him with your rifle butt," he said. "There was no need for a killin.'"

Though surprised by Prescott's statement, I decided not to argue the point in front of the other squad members. After nodding to Chaim and one of his buddies who were bragging about what they'd do on their next visit to Rome, we stashed our mess kits and headed back toward the Battalion Rec Tent where we could listen to some records.

But down the trail a few yards, I signaled to Prescott. "Let's stop for a minute while I light up." I took a couple drags on my cigarette, then turned to Prescott, blew a smoke ring and watched it slowly disintegrate in the stillness of the evening. "Tell me, my friend, do you actually believe there was no reason to kill Alabam? Or are you kidding?"

"No reason, except hatred," he said. "Sure 'nuf, I know there's a war goin' on. But human life is still valuable. I 'member our pastor askin' us one Sunday: 'What is the value of a human life?' He said that all the chemicals that make up our body – what are they worth? A couple dollars, mebbe? Even Jesus' life, it turns out, brought in thirty pieces of silver."

"So what's your point?"

"My point is that human life is too valuable fer any dollar sign. The value of a human life is limited only by what a person gits to become. We all know there's bin enough killin' in this war. When we git the chance, we oughta try showin' a little mercy."

"Prescott, you're getting mixed up. We're in a war. That means it's either them or us. While you're standing around figuring how to be merciful, their finger's on the trigger and you're dead. These Krauts deserve – "

"Sure 'nuf, they deserve death, just like the rest of us, but God offers to spare us. Every time I think of all the sins committed in my life, I shake in my boots. I deserve death, yet the Lord has showed me mercy."

"And I'm willing to bet that you're gonna tell me that Jesus had something to say about that."

"As a matter of fact He did. Back in the days when Jesus walked the earth, He spoke to a large group of folks who had follered him into the wilderness. One of the things He said was: "Blessed are the merciful for they shall obtain mercy.""

"You Christians sure have quite a racket." I grinned. "Sin a little bit here. Sin a little bit there. Ask for forgiveness and you're home free."

"Y'all know it's not that simple. Christians git forgiveness because they have been faithful to Christ's commands. And one of the things He wants us to do is pray for our enemies."

"Well, Alabam was faithful alright – faithful to Hitler. And one of the things he got for it was a knock on the head. So forget about him!"

Prescott's face turned red. He managed a weak smile and said: "I think I'll skip the movie tonight. I better be gittin' on my way. See y'all later." Then he left, back the way he had come.

I can see Prescott's upset. But that's his problem. He should quit nagging himself about Alabam. In this man's war you can't go around remembering everything bad that's happened. You don't see me getting all upset about Benicek, Murphy, or any of the other guys we've lost in our section. And you certainly won't see me losing sleep over a creep like Alabam. In fact, I've already forgotten about him.

XX

I picked up Matty's latest letter to read it once again, turning over the envelope to feast my eyes once more on the bold, red imprint of her lips.

*   *   *

April 3, 1944

Dearest Chad,

My calendar has been lying to me. It seems like you've been gone for over a year. Yet when I check the calendar in my room, I can count only eight months since you came home on a pass from camp and we made those plans for our wedding. All that seems like it happened oh, so long ago.

Chad, the fact is I miss you terribly! I miss the simple bag lunches we used to share at Wellington, sometimes in the cafeteria, sometimes on the steps in a quiet hall near the smelly Med Tech Lab. I miss going out with you on dates. Maybe to see Gilbert & Sullivan in the University Theater. Or sitting in the stands at a football game, the taste of a mustard-smeared hot dog on a crisp fall Saturday afternoon. Wellington seldom won a game, but it was fun just being there with you. I remember the press passes you received as Editor of the University newspaper. We had front row seats at the Cass Theater for some of the best plays I ever saw. I even miss the late-night jingle of the phone when you would call to wish me "sweet dreams" as you put the weekly issue of the Wellingtonian to bed.

It certainly seems that this war is bringing out the worst in human nature. Some people here could care less about what's happening on the fighting fronts. Their only interest is making the most money possible. Others are so consumed by bitterness that they talk of little else than wiping the Germans and the Japanese from the face of the earth.

In the midst of all this chaos, I only know that I love you, Chad. And I yearn for this nasty war to end so that we can be together again...

*   *   *

With that kind of letter in front of me, how can I start mine out asking Matty if she was Garret's lover? The truth is – I cannot. Because, despite all the suspicions about her past, I still love Matty – and I don't want to lose her. It doesn't make sense, I know, but where is it written that love has to make sense?

Maybe I could begin my letter by answering some of Matty's silly questions: "Did you get the muffler I sent you for Christmas? And my folks are wondering if that game of Chinese Checkers reached you in good condition..."

I know when I write Matty I should preface my questions with something – but what? Would she like to hear what I've been doing the past several weeks – when I wasn't playing Chinese Checkers?

How, after clearing out Cisterna, we made a quick-march toward Artena where we expected the Krauts were digging in for their next stand? How, soaked with sweat and the taste of dust on our tongues, we waited along the railroad tracks several miles from town for a procession of

Italian civilians to trudge past us – all of them heading south to get out of the battle zone. How some of the GI's were so irritated at the sight of these civilians that they swore at them. These were people carrying children and dragging carts filled with all manner of meager belongings.

"Damn you people! If you hadn't let Mussolini mess around with Hitler, we wouldn't have had to come all the way over here to straighten things out! Get the hell out of our way! We're trying to finish this damn war so we can go home!"

A few men even threw rocks at them. Not a pretty sight.

Or maybe I could explain to Matty how it feels on a coal-black night trying to sneak past an enemy outpost, then to have some GI accidentally trip a flare wire, a burst of whiteness exposing all of us to German eyes and the murderous chatter of machine gun fire. How it feels when you're lying flat on the ground seeking sparse defilade while tracers pierced the air inches above your back, how it feels to hear the groans of recruits like Jefferson and York as the bullets cut into them.

Could I bring myself to tell her about the savage tank fire we encountered when we finally attacked Artena? How those flat-trajectory shells provided no advance notice, exploding in our midst within seconds after firing?

Or maybe I should brag a little about the first enemy soldier I captured myself. How I was moving through a farmyard on the edge of Valmontone with the rest of my squad when a German soldier darted from an out-building. And before I knew it, I had dropped my equipment and tackled him. How he smelled. How it took two of us to hold him down while the Medic sifted sulfa powder into his open leg wound and –

No, I can't tell Matty stories like that. She thinks I've got some sort of cushy job well back from the front. Let's leave it that way.

In the midst of my musing, Prescott reappeared, shaking his head. "Missed y'all at chow this morning," he said. "Figgered this was the place I'd find – " He paused, his eyes

131

coming to rest on my blank sheet of paper. "Don't tell me it's another letter to Matty."

"Still the same one."

He took a chair opposite me. "I just found out that Battalion's gonna be tearing down the Rec Tent when we go back to training in a few days," he said. "We oughta go listen to some records while we still have a chance." Prescott removed his helmet liner and wiped his brow. "Phew! And we better to do it this morning before it gits any hotter!"

"Okay, but you've got to help me. I'm still having trouble figuring what to tell Matty. Everything we do is so dangerous. I don't want to worry her too much."

"Tell her 'bout Rome. I wrote my ol' lady yesterday. Told her 'bout the two of us goin' to St. Peters and how they let a couple hundred of us soldiers inside this big palace where the pope lives. Sure was amazin' the way he was carried into that huge room, on that big ol' throne, the sun shining through them big windows, him turnin' from side to side sprinklin' us with that holy water, or whatever it was. Goshamighty, I didn't have any trouble findin' stuff to tell her."

I laughed as I folded my paper and stuffed it in my breast pocket. "Did you tell your wife about the place we went for a spaghetti dinner? That was some kind of apartment – all those GI's, all that spaghetti giving off a wonderful aroma and only one fat, blond-haired Italian Mama running the whole show."

"Y'all mean – " Prescott recoiled ever so slightly, his eyes taking on a wounded look. "I don't know – "

"Prescott, your wife would just love to hear all that." I couldn't help but grin at his embarrassment. "Hey, no need to be ashamed. That spaghetti was *magnifico*. But you kept asking about those large double doors, why they were shut. Later, when Big Mama came through the doors with that skinny little private, nobody had to draw you a picture."

"Mebbe yer Matty wouldn't want to hear 'bout that neither."

"Remember, my friend, all I did was eat spaghetti. But in the middle of all that clatter of plates and GI's calling out for more *vino,* you went on quoting Bible verses about fornication, condemnation and all that other stuff."

"It was only the right thing to do."

"Sure it was, but you nearly got us thrown out. Later I could hear Big Mama banging around in the kitchen muttering a whole string of Italian words that didn't sound too friendly."

Prescott rose, stretched, adjusted his chair, and leaned closer. "These Eyetalian folks are a powerful sinnin' bunch of people. 'Member that apartment y'all told me 'bout?"

"You mean the family with the beautiful daughter?"

He squinted at me with just the hint of a smile. "Yesiree, that's the one."

"And it just shows you, ol' buddy, that sometimes this guy Chad is a little slow to catch on."

"Count it as a blessin' ".

"Blessing or not, there I was alone, walking down this narrow street in Rome not far from St. Peters. The mother and dad came out on their little balcony and called to me:

"Spaghett?"

Probably because I was all alone. So I went up to their apartment and they sat me down at a tiny table in a room all by myself. A few minutes later, the mother, a big woman – they all seem so big – the mother came through the door with a huge plate of steaming hot spaghetti. And I was left alone to eat it. But before I had hardly begun, the door opened again and out came this attractive, slim, well-dressed young Italian brunet, all perfumed up and wearing spike heels. Never said a word. Just sat down at the table with me and watched me eat."

"Didn't y'all talk to her?"

"Not much. My Italian isn't all that good. We exchanged a few words, then I went on chomping the spaghetti. I was really hungry. Meanwhile she kept sitting there looking gorgeous, radiating passion, but still kinda bored."

"And y'all didn't know why she was there?"

"Took me a while to figure it out, to start thinking about her, to start imagining things. Then I remembered Matty back home waiting for me. Finally I merely shook my head. and the young girl quietly got up and left."

"Y'all believe yer Matty would want to hear 'bout that?'"

"Not sure." I looked at my watch. "Hey, it's getting on toward noon chow. Maybe we better head for that Battalion tent now before they take it down. But if we're moving out in a few days. I'll need to get Matty's letter in the mail mighty quick, so I may need your help. Let's get going."

"Okay," he said, turning to leave, then paused at the door of the tent. "I tried to talk Garret into joining us, but I doubt if he'll show up. When I got back from morning chow, he was writing a letter."

"Garret – a letter? Hey, that jerk never writes anybody."

"That's what I figgered," Prescott grinned. "But I was surprised. He looked so guilty. You'd think I caught him in the act of stealin' somethin'. I tried to joke with him a little, but he seemed flustered. He finally wadded up the letter and tossed it aside."

"Don't look for him to join us. He'll probably head into Rome again tonight," I said. "That guy's only happy when he's chasing women."

As we walked along the trail toward Battalion, Prescott began whistling softly. *A catchy tune. One I'd heard before – but where?*

"That tune you're whistling – what is it?" I asked.

" 'Amazin' Grace'. Y'all know it?"

"Why sure I do. That's a song Matty used to sing."

"And do y'all know what's it about?"

"It's not about a girl," I said. "That much I do know."

But actually it is about a girl – Matty. I can see her now, standing on a riser behind the pulpit, her pert five-foot-two inches so relaxed, her golden hair carefully coiffed, her bell-like tones floating out over the hushed congregation. Just to think about it made my skin tingle.

Matty once told me that she had learned to sing "Amazing Grace" by playing the record over and over again. I can recall the first time I ever heard the record. On one of those Sundays after church when her folks invited me over for dinner in their fabulous home in Plymouth, Michigan. After dinner Matty and I sat alone in their library listening to her record collection. And when she brought out "Amazing Grace", I couldn't believe my ears. Matty's rendition was better than the soloist on the record!

Later on, when I started wearing a uniform, I would often hear the record played at a USO or at an Army Rec Center. Each time with that record, the past all came flooding back. I could close my eyes and see Matty up there in front of the congregation once more – her blond hair, her sweet voice – my Matty!

Yet now all that seems so long ago, so far away.

As Prescott and I approached the Battalion Rec Tent, I realized I was still somewhat puzzled about the song. "'Amazing' I understand, but 'Grace' – I don't know. What's this business about 'grace'?"

"That's a good 'un" Prescott said. "If I was takin' a test, I'd say 'grace' means God fergivin'our sins, even if we don't deserve it."

"Now come on, you mean God's going to forgive everybody's sins?"

"Yessir, He'll do it, if we become believers."

"Believers? Believers in what?"

"Believers in Jesus Christ as the Son of God. Believing that He died on a cross so that our sins *could be* fergiven. Then askin' Jesus to do the actual fergivin'."

"Whew! That's a tall order. We'll have to get together sometime and talk about that." I nodded toward the Rec tent entrance. "Right now, let's see what they've got inside."

We entered the tent, which was already very stuffy, and found only three other GI's were there, two seated on the ground and one on a folding chair next to a card table. Apparently in charge, he was going through a small file of records while the phonograph played a piece I recognized, Cesar Franck's "D Minor Symphony". Prescott and I settled down on a patch of grass in the far corner of the tent.

135

From the look on Prescott's face I could sense that he wasn't too thrilled about listening to classical music. Nonetheless, he merely grinned, leaned toward me and whispered: "Oh, I fergot to ask. How did y'all like the movie you saw the other night?"

Innocent as they were, his words stung, bringing to mind a spectral image I had been trying to expunge.

"The movie was okay, but nothing special," I replied.

But that's not true, is it, Fletcher?

Even now as I lay back listening to the opening *adagio* of the Franck symphony, I felt a growing tightness in my throat…

…as though gripped by some unseen hand, forcing me to face once more a dark, shadowy landscape strewn with the carnage of battle, the smell of cordite and a deep crater where a German soldier lay, his face a bloody mass, his eyes slowly following the movements of something, someone off camera …

XXI

Entering the Cafeteria amid the chatter of trays and dishes, Matty ignored the stares of several students. She headed for a table off in one corner, eased into a chair and reached across the table. "Wake up, neighbor", she said.

Stella looked up from the report she had been studying. "Why – why, hello Matty!" she said, a trifle embarrassed.

"Hello yourself, stranger. You know, I haven't heard too much from you in the past few weeks." Matty loosened her cardigan. "Your secretary said I might find you in the Cafeteria."

"I admit it's kinda noisy and drafty in here, but I had to finish going over this report from the University President before Norm and I leave this afternoon for a conference in Lansing."

Matty noticed that Stella's usual smile was missing. "Well, according to the forecasts, things are kinda cold and nasty up in Lansing. I hope you don't run into a storm." Stella smiled, but made no reply.

"I trust I'm not disturbing you too much." Matty said, her tone a little edgy.

"No, no. Not at all. It's just that I've been so busy. " Stella poked at her salad. "Aren't you eating?"

"Stella, the aroma from the kitchen's so great I can almost taste it. I'll grab a bite later. Right now, I've got something else on my mind." Matty reached into her purse for a copy of the University newspaper. "I thought you might be able to help me track down the source of this item in the *Wellingtonian.*"

"That's okay, as long as you don't hold me responsible for everything in the college paper. If you know anything about that crazy editor, you'd – "

Matty's demeanor sobered. She shoved the newspaper across the table. "The item I'm talking about appeared in the gossip column. You ought to read it."

"That's fine. But while I'm reading this, why don't you pick up one of these shrimp salads," Stella said. "They're delicious!"

Stella ran her hand across the page to smooth it down and read: "Campus Newcomer Matty Seagrave's looking considerably more perky now that she's recovered after …uh…let's just say a 'summer of unusual affliction.'"

Stella looked up at Matty, trying to smile. "Looks like you're a celebrity."

"Hardly." Matty fought to control her tone, keep it even. "I had hoped my hospitalization would be kept a secret." She looked squarely at Stella. "Where did this blabber-mouth columnist get her information?"

It was Stella's turn to color. She paused to address her salad. "Matty, like I promised you last summer, I never said anything to anyone about your problem."

"Well, someone did some talking." Matty's eyes filled as she looked away.

Stella moved to leave, but Matty touched her arm. "Don't leave just yet."

"There's something else?"

"Yes there is," Matty said, her lips twitching. "A few weeks ago you said your budget for this year is extremely tight. Yet when I stopped by your office this morning, who do I find back on staff? "

Again Stella's color rose. "You mean – ?"

"You know who I mean."

Stella slammed her fork down on her plate. "Now listen to me, young lady. I am not responsible to you for decisions made in our department." Stella paused. "Garret was let go last spring when we weren't certain of our full budget for fall semester. Once I learned that we'd have full funding, I felt obligated to bring him back on board."

As Stella rose, Matty stared at her. "I don't see how you could – "

"Cheer up, my dear," Stella said, placing her hand on Matty's shoulder. "Why don't we get together at my place this weekend? Do you realize that I never heard the details about your trip to Lake Huron to see your boyfriend's cousin."

Matty shrugged. "Not much to tell, really. The weather was fine, but the way everyone kept going on about his cousin's newborn kinda turned me off."

"Matty, for Heaven's sake! We've gotta do something about this black cloud that's hanging over your head. This is not the Matty I've always known." She patted Matty on the shoulder. "I'll call you Saturday morning."

Matty stood up, feeling a little light-headed. And all at once the rattling sound of trays coming and going, the buzz of multiple conversations – all of it faded from Matty's consciousness as she watched Stella make her way through the crowd toward the exit. *And you're not the Stella I've always known either.*

XXII

Cavalaire sur Mer, France

August, 1944

The sea spray vaulted over the ramp of our LCVP (Landing Craft, Vehicular & Personnel) as we headed toward the German-held shores of southern France. Again and again cold, brackish seawater smashed against my face and washed over my helmet, chilling me all the way down to my combat boots.

This sure isn't anything like Anzio. All we had there were those lousy LCI's (Landing Craft, Infantry). I nearly drowned when I stepped off the ramp into deep water. Now with these LCVP's we'll be getting off in much shallower water. This time it's a bigger operation with all kinds of naval craft (including battleships) bombarding the beaches. Great. Nothing like notifying the Germans that we're coming so that they'll be wide awake and ready to greet us.

Along with the rest of my squad I stood huddled and shivering as the landing craft surged toward our designated landing site still more than half a mile ahead, hardly visible through the smoke. On either side similar craft bounced through the waves, the advance units of a sizable flotilla of naval vessels ready to –

BWOM!

A huge shell from one of the battleships cut through the air high above us, heading for an enemy emplacement guarding the beach. Now nearly a mile behind us, the battleship was fulfilling its part of the mission to pound the beaches and interdict all roads leading to the surrounding rocky headlands. Crowded shoulder to shoulder with the rest of my squad on our small craft, it was easy for me to feel the tension mounting among my buddies. It had been building all morning.

Matters got off to a fast start in the dark, pre-dawn hours when we infantry elements were routed out of our fetid bunks deep in the dank bowels of the ship. Then, with our gear assembled, we sat down to a bracing meal of steak and eggs, the first to be fed.

Of course we'd have steak and eggs. Just like any condemned prisoner and his last meal. For many in our unit this would indeed be the last meal. I paused to dip my toast into the yolk of my egg. *Would I be in that group?*

Once we had hurried through breakfast and visited the head, we scrambled to our assigned posts at the ship's rail, clambered down the cargo net with full pack and, timing our move with the rise and fall of the sea, dropped several feet into our landing craft. Then it headed for shore.

As our LCVP bounced through the surf, I had a chance to take a look at the seaman who had the dicey job of piloting our crowded boat through this maelstrom. *Hey, look at the way he keeps his eyes focused on what he can see of the coastline ahead, so determined, so unflappable. Given a choice, I'm not sure I'd want to be standing up on that exposed platform with so much enemy fire coming our way.*

BAM!

A sudden explosion to our right brought my attention back to the ramp. Either one of our landing craft had struck a floating mine or had suffered a direct hit by enemy artillery. I squinted over the top of the ramp for a glimpse of the shoreline, but all I could see was white smoke that had been spread off-shore to mask our approach – a man-made fog rendered even more impenetrably brilliant by the rays of the rising sun. Yet our tiny craft kept plunging ahead into that fog, as though desperately seeking a shoreline that constantly receded, leaving us in isolation.

I looked about me, suddenly conscious of the verbal silence of my comrades. Gone was the wise-guy atmosphere that had characterized our squad's demeanor for the past several days. In its place a speechlessness that became more foreboding the closer we got to the beach that must be there. Garret, to my left, despite the constant jolting progress of our craft, stared straight ahead, his expression unreadable. To my right, Hensley gripped the machine-gun tripod so tightly that his knuckles shown white through his sun-baked skin. From time to time he attempted to adjust the cigarette dangling from his lips. In front of me, alongside Kilgore, Prescott had placed his two ammo boxes at his feet, his head bowed, his lips moving ever so slightly.

Okay, so Prescott's praying. Maybe I should be praying too. But who can say it would do any good? I'd be smarter to think about something else, something – anything– far removed from here.

Like Matty. At the last mail call just before we boarded our transport in Naples I had waited for a letter from her, but came up empty. Nothing. That makes it two months. Ever since I wrote her with questions about Garret. Even Prescott – who wrote his "old lady" about two months ago – even he had had a reply in two weeks. But maybe I'm allowing my imagination to run rampant. Is there a simple explanation for all my fears about Matty having had an affair with Garret? If so, that's something I need to hear from Matty herself. Am I going to live out my last days not knowing the –

KARUMPH!

Brilliant plumes of water erupted on either side of our craft, jarring me back to reality. I turned to look up at the pilot. His face grim, he accelerated the speed of our LCVP, reminding me that this seaman on his elevated platform occupied a position fully exposed to the –

KARUMPH!

A gigantic geyser of seawater exploded directly in front of our boat, pitching several of us to the deck. We scrambled to our feet and peered over the side. As our LCVP sped past the impact area, we could see debris and parts of human bodies floating in the surf. By now the noise of our motor had escalated to a new high, drowning out all else.

A sudden jolt brought our craft to an abrupt halt, indicating that we had struck a sandbar. Immediately the ramp dropped with a splash and there facing us in the surf was our squad leader, Geoffrey.

"Okay fellas!" He reached up to adjust his helmet, which had slipped sideways, exposing his short-cropped, mixed-gray hair. "Grab your gear and let's get outa here!"

In the next few minutes we scrambled off the ramp in a confusion of arms, legs, torsos and equipment, struggling through hip-high water onto the beach. Gasping, my uniform soaked, I could hear the sound of machine-gun fire, but Geoffrey kept us moving ahead toward the cover of the dunes with their stunted trees and other greenery. There we halted briefly to make certain all members of our squad had reached shore. We had to endure several scattered mortar rounds before we were ready to move up along a shallow trench leading to high ground. On either side of the ditch I recognized members of F Company pushing ahead across the open sunlit terrain toward the first small ridge. The chattering of machine-guns, now more intense, was punctuated by the clump of mortar shells that began to bracket us.

Kneeling by the entrance to the ditch, Geoffrey signaled to Kilgore. One by one we followed him up the gully – Hensley behind Kilgore, me behind Hensley, then Garret, then Prescott and two newer members of the squad. Anxious to get off the beach as soon as possible, I was annoyed by how slow Kilgore and Hensley were moving – until it was my turn to enter the gully. Then I discovered the reason for their snail-like pace: each foot of the waist-high trench was a tangle of booby-trap wire. Following Hensley's lead, I carefully stepped over and between trip wires, each having the thickness of a human hair, each threatening to set off a blast that would mean losing a leg, a foot, or –

BAM!

A sharp explosion around a curve in the ditch ahead. Along with the rest of the squad, Hensley and I halted. We waited several minutes for Geoffrey, who came up from behind in a crouch, following the shoulder of the ditch. Slowly, painstakingly he proceeded around the curve in the gully. After a few moments he returned, his face drawn.

"Medic!" he called out, then stopped next to us. "Kilgore's been hit." he said, nodding to Hensley. "You better go up and take over the barrel. Give the tripod to Fletcher."

Me? I straightened up. "I don't want it, Geoffrey," I said, my heart thumping. "Give it to someone else."

Our squad leader stared at me long and hard but said nothing. I suddenly realized that the sun was already heating things up. I could feel perspiration trickling down my back. Finally Geoffrey turned to Garret directly behind me. "Okay Wald. I guess you're it. Move up to assistant gunner."

Without hesitation, Garret took the heavy tripod from Hensley, who in turn proceeded cautiously around the bend to retrieve the gun barrel from Kilgore. Such was the snarl of trip-wires that several minutes passed before everyone was ready to resume moving up the ditch one careful step at a time.

Slowly I moved past the spot where Kilgore lay, bloody and unconscious, his helmet gone, his straggly hair askew. By this time a medic had hurried forward to check on his vital signs. Carefully stepping in Garret's tracks and now more than ever aware of the penalty awaiting a misstep, I felt my throat getting dry.

As I watched Garret, how carefully he placed each foot so as to avoid tripping the wires, how he struggled to keep his balance with the tripod on his shoulders, I wondered if I had made the right decision about remaining No. 3 in the squad.

Was that the right one, Matty? I know if ever I hope to return to you in one piece, I'd better stay away from any job more dangerous than the one I have now. If Garret wants to become corporal and assistant gunner, that's his funeral. I'm facing enough danger already. I don't need to stick my neck out any further.

From time to time in our progress up the ditch we paused to crouch whenever a mortar shell tore up the earth on either side of us. Also it quickly became evident (from a series of explosions off to our right) that F Company had wandered into a minefield. Nonetheless, our column pushed ahead, finally reaching a point where the gully met the headlands. By now the mortar fire had stopped and Geoffrey ordered a halt to await signaled instructions from F Company.

As we paused against the hillside, my heart still thumping, I struggled to get my breathing back to normal.

How have I made it this far? Is it because of Matty's prayers? Of the precious few letters I've received, most of them I still carry in my pack? Letters that usually with began with "Chad darling, each day I thank the Lord for protecting you and pray that he will continue to keep you safe."

I nudged Prescott. "With you praying and Matty praying – do you think it makes any difference?"

"Sure 'nuff," he nodded, fatigue slowing his response, his features more pinched than I had ever seen them.

But still I wondered. *No letters from Matty in the past week. Does that mean Matty has stopped caring, has stopped praying? But then, why should God care about what happens to Chad Fletcher?*

*　　　*　　　*

The unmerciful hot August sun bore down on us, just as it had all during the past week of fighting the Germans for the high ground over the beach. Now our squad and a platoon of G Company were enjoying the shade in a grove of trees alongside a small farmhouse somewhere south of Aix-en-Provence. Hensley and Garret had leaned their machine-gun against the side of the farmhouse. A couple of the others were matching pennies for smokes – all while we awaited truck transport.

The rest of us were clustered in small groups in among the trees, a few trying to get some shut-eye, others engaged in small talk. For myself, having scraped most of the mud off my pants and jacket, I was looking through my pack for one of the Government Issue chocolate bars given to us aboard ship and I was having trouble getting my mind off yesterday. Because now I realized that Garret's attitude toward me had undergone a big change. Even so, I appreciated the relaxing atmosphere of our present circumstance – far from the tension we all had experienced yesterday approaching this same farmhouse, now so freshly abandoned by the Krauts.

Our involvement with this farmhouse had begun quite unexpectedly after we pushed out of the beach area. The battalion had been gathered with full equipment in a small town north of the Durance River waiting to board trucks in pursuit of the retreating German 19th Army.

However, the sudden, noisy arrival of a reconnaissance jeep from the road north heralded a possible change in our mission. Carrying Sgt. Otis and his driver, the jeep came skidding to a stop in front of a small building temporarily serving as Battalion Headquarters. Otis disappeared inside.

Prescott and I were about to join the rest of our squad in the back of a 2½ -ton truck when Lt. Watson emerged from the building.

"First Squad off the truck," he shouted.

Ignoring our grumbling about the sudden change in plans, the lieutenant explained that E Company had run into stiff resistance several kilometers up the road. In light of this development, a platoon of G Company (with our machine-gun squad attached) would proceed on foot to help E Company overcome this newly discovered strongpoint. As planned, the rest of the Battalion would head north by truck on a parallel road bypassing the resistance.

It took about fifteen minutes to get our people sorted out. Then with a First Lieutenant from G Company in command, our little band finally set out along a road that wound between forested hills on its way north. A large man with a neatly trimmed mustache, the lieutenant formed us in two columns, proceeding along the gullies on each side of the road, everyone maintaining regulation intervals to minimize casualties.

During the fighting in Italy, as No. 3 man in the squad, I had grown accustomed to following the pale, blond Hensley through fields and forest, up trails and across rivers. However, because of Kilgore's elimination on the beach, the chain of command in our squad had abruptly changed. Now Hensley was No. 1 and Garret No. 2 (Assistant Gunner). He would henceforth be known as Corporal Garret Wald. So as I followed him up the road, I wondered how his new status would affect our relationship. Before the day ended, I would find out.

On the first half mile up the road our tactics were simple. At each bend our columns would halt and an uneasy quiet ensued while the point man in Company G explored what lay beyond the turn. Once it was found to be clear, we would proceed to the next curve. We moved cautiously past several curves without any sign of E Company, nor any evidence of the enemy. Each time we halted, I detected an uneasy muttering up and down the columns. And although the cool breeze brought us the sweet, cooling scent of the surrounding forest, I began an uneasy sweat. The mounting tension seemed to magnify the weight of the water-can and ammo box I carried. And with the uneven terrain it became harder to keep my carbine from slipping off my shoulder. Then around the fourth or fifth curve we came upon our first sign of the enemy: mortar shell craters every few feet along both ditches. A pattern so precise that it followed each twist and turn – a strong indication that the Germans had "zeroed in" the gullies on each side of the road. And almost as though to remove any doubts we might have had about the efficiency of the Kraut mortarmen, every few feet we began stepping over the bodies of E Company riflemen.

I had approached and passed eight such bodies on my side of the road – men sprawled like rag dolls in every sort of grotesque position – before the lieutenant called a halt while one of the riflemen crawled forward to scout the area. After about ten minutes the G Company scout signaled "all clear" and we moved on to the next curve.

Most of our squad had passed the latest curve – and I could see the farmhouse up ahead on the left when –

SEEOW! SEEOW! SEEOW!

Mortars began dropping on us! Blast after blast rocked the ditches, beginning at the head of each column and proceeding down the ditches, following each turn, wounding or killing several G Company riflemen, some as they crouched, others as they rose up and ran to a less exposed position. The pattern of the explosions continued to move swiftly and inexorably toward our end of the column.

Amid the continuing blasts and confusion, two mortar shells burst in rapid succession just ahead of Geoffrey. He quickly signaled for us to pull back. With the taste of fear in my mouth, I turned and scrambled down the ditch seeking the protection of the previous curve. At that point I followed the others up out of the trench and into the woods above. For the next five or ten minutes mortar fire continued to tear apart the ditches alongside the road. Though up and out of the gully and hunched over with Prescott at the base of a large tree, I could feel the earth shake as round after round came in. From the way we were being showered with earth even on the hillside, I suspected that the enemy had begun using some larger caliber mortars.

Finally, during a brief pause in the bombardment Prescott and I were able to look up. There, hunkered down next to us was Garret. He had dragged his heavy tripod all the way from the ditch around the curve to where we lay.

After signaling to let Geoffrey and Hensley know his whereabouts, Garret eyed me critically. "Where's your ammo and water-can?" he asked.

His question caught me off-guard. I suddenly realized I'd left the water-can and my single box of ammo behind. "They're back in the ditch," I replied, somewhat red-faced that I had taken off without my load.

Even as I scanned the hillside below and spotted my load, the Kraut mortars erupted once more, this time at our end of the line. "Back in the ditch?" Garret exclaimed, leaning toward me. "What the hell kind of a soldier are you anyway? Go back and get 'em!"

I turned to Prescott, who showed no expression that I could interpret. Both his ammo boxes lay at his feet. By now Garret was tugging his tripod into position so that he could swing it onto his shoulders.

I can't believe this! He's asking me to slide back down the hill through all that fire – just to retrieve one measly ammo box and a water-can!

With the tripod resting securely on his shoulders, Garret again focused his attention on me. "Geoffrey's signaling that he wants us up in the clearing ahead. That's where they're gonna set up the gun," Then he paused to look down at me. "Are you going after the stuff we need – or do I have to report that you refused to obey a direct order?"

Without waiting for my response, he began working his way up along the side of the hill through bramble and waist-high brush. Prescott followed.

Reluctantly I gripped the shoulder strap on my rifle and began a gradual descent toward the ditch, half-sliding on my back, not daring to stand up. As I drew closer to the gully, the mortar barrage intensified.

I waited until it appeared that the pattern of mortar blasts was moving up the road, further churning the trench and the dead GI's in it. Then I made my move, dropping into the ditch and hastily clambering over debris toward the water-can and ammo box, still intact and beckoning from the spot where I had abandoned them.

As I stumbled and crawled over bodies and debris in the ditch, it became obvious to me that the enemy must have positioned an observer high on the opposite slope directing the fire. For a cluster of mortar shells once more descended, a deadly barrage working its way back along the gully toward me. Twice I dove to the bottom of the ditch as rocks, shrapnel and all manner of fragments whirred and buzzed on every side. Lying in the putrescent wet and filth at the bottom of the trench, I could hear mortar shells chunk into the earth, some hitting wet soil and failing to explode, others bursting on impact with a terrific clatter. In a sudden surge of energy I plunged forward and seized my water-can and ammo box. Then I turned about, still keeping my head down, waiting a chance to make a break for the woods up the hill. Suddenly a wave of revulsion washed over me as I discovered that my head was resting upon a khaki pad, the lower half of someone's body. Trying to ignore the stench, I rose up and just as quickly ducked back in the identical spot as another mortar round slammed into soft earth a mere foot from me. It did not explode.

Head throbbing, I waited for the next salvo. Nothing came. I hesitated a few moments longer. Still nothing. In a frantic burst of energy, I shouldered my carbine, grabbed my equipment and turned back toward the hill. Struggling to keep my balance, I paused briefly at an opening in the woods. Now I could see that Hensley was already firing our machine gun. Apparently Geoffrey or someone with field glasses had discovered the location of the German mortarmen in the rear of the farmhouse. As Hensley kept pouring fire into the enemy position, I could see many of the Germans take off through a grove of trees in back of the farmhouse. Already a few of the G Company riflemen had reached a spot where they could begin firing directly into the German position as well. Once I had reached our gun crew and deposited my ammo and water-can, I fell back against a hillock, gasping for air, my heart hammering. I took a quiet swig of water from my canteen. From that position I was able to focus on Garret who was feeding the clattering machine-gun with what seemed like an endless belt of bullets. As I watched him, I realized how little I understood this complex individual.

Is he simply the epitome of the efficient soldier, well schooled in the art of war and intent on his task of destroying the enemy? Or does that cold, rough exterior mask a faithful, but unappreciated friend who had twice gone out of his way to save my life? Or is he merely a profligate, a consumer of women, who bristled at my challenging his past relationship with Matty? I dunno.

Nonetheless, I'd be smart to watch my back. It's quite possible that now I must contend with a Garret considerably more dangerous – one who is trying to get me killed.

XXIII

It had been an arduous, exhausting week of movement day and night as our battalion struggled to keep pace with the German 19th Army, now in full retreat. Sometimes we had ridden on the backs of tanks, other times we had quick-marched miles on end, despite our state of near-exhaustion. Always striving to keep the Krauts off-balance, often delayed when an enemy roadblock precipitated a bloody firefight.

Now our armored column had halted on a mountain road well north of Orange, a gap in the forest giving us a clear view of the bright, sun-splashed valley below. While the officers discussed the latest intelligence concerning the whereabouts of the German 19th Army, Prescott and I seized the opportunity to stretch out for some shut-eye along the roadside. However, I made it a point to keep my distance from Garret, who was splitting a "captured" bottle of cognac with Hensley.

Before long, my nap was interrupted by a heated exchange between Lt. Watson and one of the officers from E Company who was standing on a large stump sweeping the valley with his binoculars.

"...and I tell you, that's a German convoy down there!"

"Okay, okay!" Lt. Watson held up his hand. "If you're so sure of it, maybe we better get the captain over here!"

My attention aroused, I slowly got to my feet, squinting at the valley far below, now flooded with sunshine. Even without binoculars I could make out a string of trucks, half-tracks and other vehicles moving through a village. Admittedly at this range it was difficult to distinguish any vehicle markings, but I could only agree with the E Company lieutenant that this was indeed a column of enemy vehicles. I glanced down at Prescott still fast asleep and decided not to disturb him. Fascinated by the drama playing out next to me, I sat quietly, anxious to take it all in.

As soon as the captain arrived with his radioman, he conferred briefly with the two officers, and then called Battalion. Within minutes he had an answer. Battalion confirmed the sighting of a German column in the valley below and that it was okay for us to call in fire. I watched the captain and the lieutenants hurry past several vehicles in our column and engage the driver of a tank destroyer. After another brief exchange, the driver mounted his vehicle. Slowly the long barrel of the tank destroyer swiveled in the direction of the enemy convoy. Then a pause.

WHAM !

The sound of the projectile being fired was enough to wake Prescott.

"What's goin' on?" he asked as he slowly got back on his feet, zipped up his jacket and pushed his faded blond hair out of his face before donning his helmet.

"Looks like we've caught up to a German convoy along that road below us," I replied.

The two of us stood transfixed as another tank destroyer in our column joined in the shoot. At this close range the sound of cannon fire hurt our ears, but Prescott and I continued to watch as puffs of smoke blossomed all along the valley floor. Without letup shell after shell began to interdict the line of enemy vehicles. Soon several of the German trucks, half-tracks and other vehicles broke out of the column seeking shelter behind village buildings and various terrain features.

As we continued to listen, the officers' conversation over the next half hour filled in details we could not have guessed. Before long we learned that Division artillery, well back in our column, had begun to train their long-range guns on the enemy column. I could see that all this shelling was causing serious damage to the Krauts as they tried to move through the town so far below us.

Soon Geoffrey appeared and motioned for our squad to assemble. "Get your gear together," he said. "The captain wants our squad to reassemble down by that first tank."

There Lt. Watson informed us that we would be part of a special Battle Patrol that would go on ahead of our armored column. In typical Army fashion, we waited the better part of an hour while the officers juggled the personnel, equipment and vehicles needed for our task force. Once the changes were made and equipment located, two Platoons from F Company linked up with our squad on 2½ -ton trucks. Then, with the addition of a ¾-ton truck carrying several aid men and supplies, our Battle Patrol slowly worked its way around the other vehicles.

As we began moving down the mountain road, I looked back at Garret in time to see him poke Prescott.

"Okay choir boy, if that god of yours is so great, why does he have us going out in front of the whole damn army to intercept a bunch of Germans who have about three times our firepower? Does that make any kind of sense?"

"Mebbe not to you," Prescott replied, "but I believe God has a plan for each of us. He knows why we're here and He knows where we're goin'".

"Then how come he doesn't let some of us in on the secret?"

Prescott opened his mouth as though to reply, his brown eyes focused on Garret. Slowly his lips moved as though forming words. But after a protracted interval of silence, Prescott looked down at his boots, pulled a small rag from his jacket and began wiping off the stock of his rifle.

Garret has a point. Does God really know where we're going? And does he care one way or the other?

By the time our trucks reached the base of the mountain heavy black clouds shrouded the moon. We began off-loading amidst a cluster of abandoned homes. A sharp chill shook my body as we assembled by the side of the road.

With mixed feelings I watched the now-empty trucks maneuver in the dark and gradually realign themselves for the trip back up the mountain to rejoin the rest of the battalion. Obviously from this point forward we were on our own. The grinding sound of truck transmissions had barely faded away when Lt. Watson ordered us to bed down where we were, with guards posted. By dawn, he said, we would be striking out across open country.

However, as soon as the lieutenant had moved on, his orders were promptly ignored. For across the road stood a sprawling, evidently vacant, chateau. It proved to be too much of an attraction for several members of our group, including Garret and surprisingly, Prescott and Geoffrey. Joking and jostling one another, they disappeared into the darkness.

For myself, I was too exhausted to get interested in the looting expedition. I spread out my bedroll in the front yard of a smaller house nearby. The sweet smell of flowers hung in the air, indicating that we had reached an area quite recently vacated by the civilians and that, in the midst of all the carnage of war, there were still some people who believed in the importance of flowers. As I drifted off to sleep, I could hear the muffled sound of shellfire from the mountain pounding the German convoy still some distance ahead.

*   *   *

It seemed like I had barely closed my eyes when I felt someone shaking me. It was Prescott. "Wake up, Sleepin' Beauty," he said. "We're movin' out in about five minutes."

I peered into the blackness on every side." It can't be dawn yet," I said. "Where – "

"Y'all shouldn't complain. I never even had time to sleep." Prescott continued stuffing several articles in his pack. "Soon as I got back from that big ol' house yonder, Geoffrey put me on guard duty."

"I hope the trip across the road was worth it all."

"There sure was a mess of stuff over there. I picked up a couple souvenirs. Garret found hisself one of them Nazi swords." Prescott paused to bite into an apple, the dim light of dawn accenting his pinched features.

"Where'd you get the fruit?"

" 'Cross the road," he grinned. "That place musta been a German Headquarters or somethin'. Didn't look like them Nazi folks had been gone too long. They even left cooked sausage in the refrigerator."

"Better smell it before you eat it," I warned. When I looked up, Geoffrey was back.

"Okay Fletcher," he said, keeping his voice low. "Can the chatter. You two get up there in the column with the rest of the squad."

By now our column had formed up along the road and I was fully awake in the chill night air. Famished, but with no time to dig into my pack, I found it hard to keep my eyes off the sausage Garret was chewing. When he returned my gaze, I could read the contempt in those steel-gray eyes.

Once the order was passed down the line, we shouldered our gear and began what I felt certain would be an extended march.

How long? Anybody's guess. This much I do know: it'll be a monotonous, no-talking ordeal with the only sound a steady, rhythmic clomping of heavy combat boots and the muted clanking of equipment as we move down the road to who-knows-where. One thing's sure, I better not forget that out there ahead of us somewhere in the blackness are over one thousand enemy soldiers who are likely to discover us at any moment.

After all, what are we doing out here in the first place? What has happened to this world that Prescott's god has created? Why is it necessary for a bunch of grown American men to separate themselves from their families and travel some 5000 miles just so that they can march down a strange mountain road in the middle of the night trying to catch up to a bunch of Germans who hate all this marching and fighting as much as we do?

Must we follow them wherever they go? To the ends of the earth? When I think of all the strange roads I've traversed in the past year trying to catch Germans...Will we ever catch up to them? Will it make any difference when we do? If, as Prescott insists, we're all subject to an all-powerful god, how can he permit such idiotic behavior?

I could only shake my head.

Better I should concentrate on more mundane matters – such as keeping Garret's back in sight. To fix my gaze on the load he is carrying – one heavy leg of the tripod over each shoulder, the third extended down his back. That's what's important.

A sudden halt in the column up front interrupted my reverie and caused much cursing as many of us collided with the man ahead. At that point I recognized that for the past half hour I had been hearing many sounds of distress up and down our column. Abruptly Geoffrey returned from the head of the line, hushing everyone, then ordering Garret and Prescott to fall out. Both were groaning and holding their stomachs, When Garret began to vomit, Chaim was ordered to take over the tripod. As we began to move forward again, I caught a fleeting glimpse of Garret and Prescott staggering their way toward the rear.

Now that Garret was gone, I had to keep Chaim's back in view, a task somewhat more difficult because Chaim was smaller and the pace of march much faster. All of which led to more confusion, rattling of equipment, stumbling and cursing until we reached a grove of trees just short of an East – West road. Again Geoffrey came down the line.

"It's okay to relax, men," he said, "but don't rattle equipment. Remember, keep your voice down. A heavily-armed Kraut column could be less than a half-mile to our left. If they hear us – I don't need to tell you what will happen."

The abrupt halt gave me an opportunity to assess our present situation in the growing light of what promised to be another scorching-hot day. Apparently we had reached the edge of another village. Several homes were barely visible to our right and to our left. I could see the lieutenant and a first sergeant conferring in a ditch alongside the road.

Curious, I sidled up to Chaim who had put down the tripod and was rubbing his shoulder. "This damn thing weighs a ton!" he said, keeping his voice low.

"What happened to Garret and Prescott? " I whispered.

"Not sure, but it sounds like they ate some bad food. Geoffrey's at the rear of the column now, talking to them. I hope Garret comes back real soon. I sure don't want this job."

Before long Geoffrey reappeared, this time with Garret in tow. Fatigue etched in his face, Geoffrey spoke quietly to Chaim. "Okay, you can drop back to Number Four. Garret here will take over the tripod."

He looked at me. "Prescott's still pretty sick. One of the aid men will stay with him back in the woods. Meanwhile, the rest of you just wait here while I go forward to talk with the officers. Remember, no noise."

Exhausted, I stretched out on the ground, using my pack as a pillow, and closed my eyes.

*   *   *

I awoke with a start and sat up, bewildered. "Where am I? What –"

Heavy artillery was landing off to our left. I could hear Geoffrey talking, apparently to Hensley and Garret: "...not sure how long we'll be able to hold on, but I'm told the head of the German convoy has nearly reached the intersection just ahead. Battalion has ordered the F Company platoons to move as close to the intersection as possible and dig in. They've already started to move to a position that should block the German column. Get ready to follow them."

I watched in fascination as Garret and Hensley began to lug their gun down the road and started to dig an emplacement. *This is crazy! We'll never be able –*

Although the growing danger of our position certainly had my attention, my eye was caught by something that occurred just as Garret swung the tripod onto his shoulders in preparation for the move – two envelopes fell from his pack. I hurried to scoop them up, even in the faint light I recognized Matty's handwriting on each envelope. *Both these letters are addressed to me! Mail I've been waiting for all these weeks!*

I could feel my blood begin to boil. Quickly I stuffed the letters in my jacket as Geoffrey signaled for Chaim and me to begin digging a foxhole alongside the road. Even as I joined Chaim in digging, my insides were churning with questions about my discovery. Spurred on by the realization that at any moment an enemy tank could stick its 88mm neck around the intersection up ahead, Chaim and I lost no time in opening a hole alongside the road large enough for both of us. Although rivers of sweat were running down my back and I could hear Chaim talking to me, I was totally distracted by the discovery of the two letters.

That lousy sneak! Grabbing my letters! He better watch his back!

When I glanced down the road to assess the progress that Hensley and Garret were making on the machine-gun emplacement, I saw Garret say something to Hensley and toss his shovel into the hole. He then hurried toward a tree-choked ravine nearby – obviously a latrine break.

I quickly nodded to Chaim. "Be back in a few minutes," I said. Ignoring his look of surprise, I hustled across the road and down into the darkness of the ravine.

Garret was in the process of loosening his belt when I came upon him. "What's the idea of grabbing my mail?" I asked through clenched teeth.

Garret's response was interrupted by my knee to his groin. He tumbled backwards. In a moment I fell on him, clutching at his throat. With surprising agility Garret pushed me aside and scrambled to his feet. He attempted to kick me in the head, but I intercepted his leg and toppled him. Quickly I grabbed a fallen limb and swung at him, but he deflected the blow with both hands, then wrestled the heavy limb from my grip and threw me to the ground. I struggled to my knees in time to see the limb come hurtling toward me and – OBLIVION!

XXIV

Montelimar, France
August, 1944

Someone's shaking me, shaking me, shaking me, each movement an explosion of pain. A blurry image...a dark beard hovering over me. Who?

"Dammit Fletcher, wake up!"

Prescott? Are you – No...the dark beard ...Chaim? Are you Chaim?

It was Chaim. I struggled to rise, slipped back, then felt strong hands under my armpits, lifting. I rose to my knees, shaky, pain subsiding, head throbbing. "Where's – "I remembered Garret, but said nothing more, touching a large welt that ran across my cheekbone. My tongue explored the cut on my lip, savoring the taste of it.

"That's a nasty red mark on your face, Fletcher, but quit feeling it! Sergeant Geoffrey's already moved Hensley and Garret up ahead with the machine-gun. He's looking for you. Now hurry!"

"Thanks," I mumbled, following him up out of the ravine and across the road to our hole where, to my surprise, I found Prescott digging frantically.

"I'll go on up the road where I've got another one started," Chaim said.

Prescott glanced at me. "Y'all look a mess." He hardly paused in his digging. "Better git down in here and help me finish this hole. Things could get sorta mean 'round here in a hurry."

I looked in the direction of his nod, to where our East-West road crossed the North-South highway where the

German column was stalled. Although I could hear the steady chatter of small arms fire from the F Company riflemen who had taken up positions all along the intersection, the intensity of the shelling had abated. Not far from the intersecting roads, Hensley and Garret had hollowed out an emplacement for their gun, giving them a clear field of fire for anything or anyone approaching from the south.

I picked up my entrenching tool and began chopping at a large root protruding from one side of the hole Prescott was working on. I soon discovered I couldn't control my shaking – a condition that resulted as much from the morning chill as from the peril of our exposed position. "When did you get back?" I asked.

"Jist about the time y'all went down into that ravine." Prescott said. He paused to squint at me. "I reckon y'all been fightin' with Garret again."

Rubbing my hand over the welt on the side of my face, I looked down at my hand. *Blood.* "That dirty – "

"It might help if y'all stopped yer cussin'. Jist remember, Jesus went through far more than any of us. Yet He said cussin' won't do no good, that we should love one another and – "

"Leave Jesus outa this! Maybe if you would stop your almighty quoting, I'd be able to quit my cursing" I chopped through the large root and tossed it aside.

Before I could say anything further, Geoffrey came running up to us in a crouch. He slid into our hole. "You two better snap to it! Get this damned hole finished – and make it deep!" he said, gesturing toward the intersection. "I'm going up there to see what they need. I may want you to bring up some more ammo, so keep your eye peeled for my signal."

I watched as he rushed toward Hensley and Garret's gun emplacement, then turned my attention back to Prescott. "Hey, you don't exactly look like the picture of health – and you don't smell too good either."

"Blame them sausages. They sure 'nuf messed me up," he grunted.

"Didn't the medics back at the Aid Station give you any help?"

"Not much. I reckon their orders was to git me back to my unit as quick as possible." He continued digging, albeit much slower. "They gave me a little medicine and told me to go back to my squad. It was some funny-tastin' pink stuff that made me a mite dizzy, but it finally stopped the runs."

"Probably paregoric. Had some when I was in the hospi – "

WHAM! WHAM!

Two shells zipped over the intersection and exploded harmlessly further up the North-South road.

Prescott dropped his shovel and crouched down beside me. "I still feel kinda poorly."

"Same here." I nodded toward the intersection. "I guess the Krauts have discovered our roadblock."

"Which reminds me. Y'all are plain lucky Lt. Watson kept Geoffrey so busy he didn't have time to check up on you and Garret. The two of 'em had a real go-round."

"What happened?"

Prescott waited a full minute before replying, his eyes shifting back and forth as he listened for the next incoming salvo. Nothing materialized.

"Well sir," he said, "when I got back from the Aid Station, there was this captain with a big ol' mustache kneelin' next to Garret and Hensley, conferrin' with Geoffrey and a lieutenant from F Company. He was explainin' that this here German column is jammed up jist below that crossroads up ahead. He's the one who wanted our machine-gun up there with one of the rifle platoons to set up a roadblock that would keep the enemy convoy from goin' any further north."

"How long is the convoy?"

"The captain said he didn't know fer sure, but figgers it must go back for about ten miles." Prescott's lips curled into a smile. "When ol' mustache said that, Geoffrey like to blew a gasket. And he wasted no time straightenin' him out. 'Captain,' he says, 'I bin fightin' these same Germans ever since I was a two-bit private swimmin' the Volturno back in Italy. They's no way a few heavy weapons and a couple platoons of raw recruits is gonna hold up a big armored column.' "

"But ol' mustache said we shouldn't fret ourselves 'bout the German column. We're already bringin' fire on 'em from the rear and from the hills on their right. And since there's a big river on their left, them Kraut fellers is bottled up with no place to go. They're bad off."

WHAM! WHAM!

Two more shells landed short of the intersection.

I hunkered down. "Hey, somebody better explain to the Germans how bad off they are."

"It sure 'nuf looks like they're hankerin' to break out."

"I think I hear a tank."

WHAM!

We flattened ourselves against the side of the hole. Then I peeked over the rim of our foxhole. "Looks like that last shell hit one of the F Company positions."

Geoffrey was frantically waving his arms and shouting something I couldn't hear due to the din of the explosives.

I looked at Prescott. "The sergeant wants more ammo, so I guess that means me." Reluctantly I grabbed two ammo boxes and, crouching low, scrambled along the roadside ditch toward the intersection. Twice I hit the ground, and felt the earth move as tank shells crashed into the North-South intersection. When I reached our gun emplacement, I dropped down alongside the two gunners, holding the ammo boxes tightly. Garret was busy feeding the gun while Hensley fired several short bursts.

From this vantage point I got my first glimpse of the forward elements of the Kraut convoy. All I could see was a German flak-wagon up front with numerous trucks immobilized behind it. Apparently the Kraut flak-wagon was stalled in position, but an enemy soldier manning four unitized 20 mm guns kept directing fire at some of our troops that had moved into position on a hill overlooking the North-South road. In the field to the right of the flak-wagon a Tiger tank had become mired in the soft earth. I watched the turret of its long gun slowly pivot toward our gun emplacement.

At one end of the emplacement Geoffrey was scanning the enemy position with his binoculars. He turned briefly and jerked his head, indicating that I should get back to my hole. I wasted no time sprinting down the road and falling into the foxhole next to Prescott.

"This is absolutely nutty!" I shouted above the noise as an 81mm mortar shell burst in the Kraut column back of the tank. "We're about to get ourselves killed over a one-horse French town out in the middle of nowhere!"

WHAM!

That was close!

Prescott merely nodded. From the pale green cast of his complexion I figured he was still suffering from the French version of Montezuma. Again I peeked over the edge of our foxhole toward our forward gun emplacement.

"Medic!"

Someone up in our machine-gun emplacement was calling for help. After a few moments I could see Hensley crawl out of their dugout dragging something – *the barrel of our machine-gun!*

"The gun barrel? That doesn't make sense!"

With obvious difficulty Hensley continued crawling and sliding the gun barrel along the ground toward us, frequently pausing to shout, "Medic!"

I scanned the lush green fields on either side of our East-West road. No medics in sight. Prescott joined me at the edge of our foxhole. "Mebbe we should go help him," he said.

"Don't be screwy. Any minute that Kraut tank is likely to stick his nose around the corner of the intersection."

"We can't just leave him out there!"

Prescott tried to climb out of our hole, but I stopped him. "You want to get yourself killed?" I pulled Prescott back into the hole.

He struggled to regain a foothold, his breathing labored. "Y'know, the Bible tells me I ought to love my brother enough to – "

"Okay, love 'em!" I shouted, grabbing his collar, "but just don't get your head blown off doing it!"

"And don't y'all git yerself 'tween me and the Lord, Fletcher. I know I should be willin' to go out there for my brethern."

"Well, he's not *my* brethren! " I released my hold on Prescott. "Hey, if pleasing Jesus means that much to you – "

Prescott crawled out of the foxhole, sweat rolling down his face.

WHAM!

Another shell screamed over the gun emplacement. Slowly, but surely Prescott inched his way up to where Hensley lay, trying to pull the gun barrel over an obstruction. Together they yanked it loose and resumed a slow, methodical crawl back to where I was crouching, salty rivers of sweat running down into my eyes, my mouth so dry I could hardly utter a word.

As soon as Hensley slid down into our hole, I could see blood seeping through a ragged tear in his pants above the knee.

Garret's been hit bad," he gasped. "Geoffrey's dead...the tripod..." His voice trailed off. Then looking directly at me, he added: "We gotta get it back here!"

Prescott helped me move Hensley to a more comfortable position in the hole. Then I looked up to see Kennedy, one of the aid men, staring down on us. "Gimme some room," he said. "I'll put a tourniquet on that leg."

I crawled out the rear of the foxhole. Down the road another medic was coming with a litter, Chaim helping him. Several minutes passed before Kennedy and the others were able to move Hensley down the road toward the trees.

Back in the hole, I looked at Prescott. Obviously he was preparing to go out again.

"You can't be serious!"

"We need the tripod, so we can use the machine-gun," he said, his breathing troubled. "Besides, I gotta save Garret!"

"Save Garret? After all he's done to you?"

"That's all bin fergiven. Now y'all listen to me."

"I'm listening."

"If God knows when even a tiny sparrow falls to earth, He sure 'nuf figgers any of us is far more precious than a mess of sparrows."

"Will you *stop* it?"

" 'He that hateth his brother is in darkness ...and knoweth not whither he goeth.' ... Fletcher, I'm goin' to git Garret! "

When Prescott started to crawl out of the hole, I grabbed his arm and jerked him back. As he wheeled around, I punched him hard in the jaw. He collapsed against the back of the hole. Nearly out of breath, I slid into a sitting position in the hole.

What do I do now? I looked over at Prescott, his head canted to the right, blood trickling from his mouth. *Great. I just did the Krauts a favor.* I contemplated the barrel of our machine-gun, lying there in the muck *Not much good for anything now. Not without the tripod. What have you done, Fletcher? You trying to earn an Iron Cross?* I looked up at the sky – a cobalt blue, not a cloud to be seen. *Hey God, are you hiding up there somewhere? Can't say I'd blame you. What with everything that's going on down here, I know you have a lot to do. But could you take a minute to tell me, what do I do now?*

Maybe I should ask Hensley, but he's gone. They took him away. But not his words: "The tripod – we've got to get it back here!"

Before I realized what was happening, I found myself out of the foxhole, slowly crawling toward the intersection.

WHAM!

I buried my face in the dirt for what seemed like several minutes, then slowly resumed my crawling. The tank shells continued to land among the F Company riflemen. I finished the remaining distance at a snail's pace, expecting another shell at any moment, but there was none.

When I finally reached the crossroads, I avoided looking toward the German convoy, but kept my focus on the edge of the ditch where the tripod had fallen. I noted that Garret was still half-sitting up against the back of the emplacement, one eye watching me, one hand holding a blood-soaked rag to his face, the smell of nitro everywhere.

I slipped down into the ditch and tried to maneuver the tripod into position so that I could swing it onto my shoulders. After several failed attempts, I shook my head in desperation. *If I ever hope to get the tripod up and onto my shoulders I'll have to stand up!*

A grunting noise behind me. I turned for another look at Garret. Plainly he had suffered a devastating facial wound. He moved the bloody rag aside and tried to say something, but what with the noise of all the shellfire, I couldn't understand him. I continued dragging the tripod down the ditch toward our foxhole. When I finally reached the end of the shallow trench, I turned for a last look at Garret. He was still watching me, his left hand extended.

Well, what's it gonna be, Fletcher? Do I try to bring him out, or leave him to rot?

I let go of the tripod and turned back toward Garret.

WHAM!

A tank shell whooshed over the ditch and exploded on the hillside. Without waiting for the next one, I rose and ran for the emplacement in a crouch. I dove into the hole, landing next to Garret. Promptly I tried to get my arm under his shoulder, but when he screamed in pain, I paused and leaned over to catch his words, barely audible.

"Go. Leave me."

I looked down the North-South road toward the enemy. Several Kraut soldiers had dismounted from their vehicles and were making their way toward us. *Garret's right. If I stay here, I only get myself killed.*

Moving to the far edge of the emplacement, I waited my chance, then sprinted back to where the tripod lay, all the while conscious of Garret's eyes following me. When I stooped over and rotated the tripod onto my shoulders, the weight almost buckled my knees. I staggered away from the ditch, regained my balance and, crouching as best I could, headed for the foxhole where I had left Prescott.

As I approached, I saw that Prescott had regained his feet and, hunched at the edge of the foxhole, had sighted his rifle down the road past me. At last I could hear him: "Hurry Chad! The tank's already reached the corner! It's turnin' the turret!"

I tried to run with the tripod on my shoulders, but nearly fell.

"Hurry Chad! They're gonna fire agin. Y'all better – "

WHAM!

XXV

A jarring thump against the side of the foxhole scrambled my senses. *Where Am I?* Then a geyser of pain erupted and I looked down at my left foot. Bloody. Crushed beneath one of the tripod's heavy legs.

Prescott crawled to my side, grabbed one leg of the tripod and lifted it off my foot. When I screamed, he tossed me a look of scorn. "It may hurt, but y'all better hunker down in the bottom of this hole with me. That tank is fixin' to fire another one at us any minute."

Despite the excruciating pain, I eased down into the hole. As we huddled in the bottom, I noted Prescott's grimace. Then he pulled his right pant leg out of his combat boot.

Although I could plainly see a reddish rivulet running down his leg and into his boot, the intense throbbing in my own foot made it difficult for me to focus on his problem. I looked down at my foot and shivered. A pulsing mass of blood saturating everything...flesh and leather intermingled... the smell of nitro *Everything fuzzy...Prescott moving...the rim of the foxhole...light fading...*

WHAM!

*   *   *

"Never thought I'd turn down food that tastes like this, " I said, "but my stomach's too upset."

The young nurse nodded and picked up my tray. "I'll be back in a few minutes," she said. "That dressing needs work."

Her remark reminded me about the large bulge at the other end of my cot. Gingerly I lifted the thin, olive drab blanket, then paused while a bolt of pain surged up my leg. A heavy bandage covered my left foot and ankle. Although I couldn't reach down far enough to touch the dressing, a large, crimson blotch and a pervasive antiseptic odor bore witness that something serious was going on down there.

Looking about me in the mounting heat of the tent, I recognized things I must have seen earlier: my cot snugged against the wall of the tent, a nurse hovering over a bed halfway down the row, changing the dressing for a GI with a buttocks wound. The long row of cots on my side of the center aisle interrupted midway by a black potbelly stove. Across the aisle another row of beds. A male nurse was helping another GI back to his cot. The soldier, who wore only Government Issue undershirt and shorts, emitted a series of barely audible groans.

Then I realized that my "uniform" was no better – olive drab undershirt, olive drab shorts. After a limited search, I discovered my ragged, muddy o.d.'s jammed onto the bottom "shelf" of a wooden box that stood upright between my cot and the next one – a sort of "nightstand". On top lay something leather, and bulky – my wallet. Quickly I grabbed it and inspected the contents.

Not much money. Snapshots – several of Matty, one of my mother – a stick of gum, a few personal papers. Nothing missing. I stuffed the wallet under my pillow, then noticed two envelopes. *The letters from Matty! The very ones that had caused all the trouble between me and Garret. Have I read them? I can't remember, although I see they have been opened.*

I reopened them. One was dated May 5, the other June 12. *Both written before she could have received my questions about Garret. Damn!*

May 5, 1944

Dearest Chad:

You must be on the move again. I haven't had a letter from you in over a week.

I believe I told you before that my folks urged me to stay in school rather than quit Wellington University and get a defense job. At the moment, however, that matter is somewhat "academic" since summer break is coming up. Which means that I'll soon be pounding the pavement looking for some kind of summer job.

Despite what I said in my letter last month, I'm having second thoughts about the importance of serenity in this time of such turbulence. It still bothers me that while you're overseas fighting a war, and while my brother, Eddie, (he's in the Navy) is off somewhere in the south Pacific, and while my Dad's putting in tons of overtime at the plant, I spend so much of my time studying Schubert *lieder* and the poetry of Wordsworth. (Although I do enjoy reading Alphonse Daudet's plays in the original French.) What good are those subjects in this kind of a world?

One of my girlfriends is Italian. Sometimes we have lunch on the same stairs in the back hall where you and I used to go. Her folks were born over there. She says that northern Italy is absolutely gorgeous! Picturesque rolling hills – all in green! I hope the Army is giving you some time off to visit places like Rome and Florence. If you do get to visit some of these cities, be sure to send me a card.

I'm going to a party tomorrow night and I dread it. A wedding shower for another of my girlfriends who's getting married next month. I'm happy for her, of course, but events like that only

172

remind me of our own wedding – the one we never had.

When, oh when, will this terrible war ever end? How much longer must we be separated? Please forgive me for being such an old grouch, darling. I pray for you every day, so I know the Lord is protecting you and will bring you back to me soon.

Love, Matty

*　　*　　*

I stared at the letter for several minutes, not knowing how to react, oblivious of the heat and the buzz of conversation around me.

Such a sweet girl. How could I think evil of her? And what about Garret? Did he ever make it out of the gun emplacement? And Prescott? I don't imagine they held him at the Aid Station. As soon as I can get around, I'll check the hospital bulletin board. There are likely other men from my outfit in this hospital. Maybe one of them will know.

I picked up the other letter.

*　　*　　*

June 12, 1944

Dear Chad:

I wandered lonely as a cloud
That floats on high o'er vales and hills
When all at once I saw a crowd,
A host of golden daffodils;

I can almost smell those daffodils! Wordsworth's lines mean so much more to me now that we're finally beginning to get good news about the war: Rome has been captured! And, Lord be praised, our troops have come ashore in Normandy!

Maybe now all of us can sleep better at night, knowing that the war can't last much longer. Wouldn't it be wonderful if you could be home by Christmas! Write and tell me all the news from your side of the Atlantic.

Well, I finally landed a job for the summer. I was hired last week by an auto dealer. Although the dealer has only a few used cars to sell, the company has landed a Defense contract to make parts that will be used in tanks. I haven't yet learned all the details, but part of my job will be to keep books for the company. Now, at last, I feel like I'm contributing something to the war effort.

Meanwhile, I hope you'll keep my parents in your prayers. As I've said before, Dad works too much overtime. He comes home dog-tired and has had to resign several projects at church. Believe me, I know how much his church work means to him. Besides that, I've heard Mom and Dad discussing whether they'll have to drop their Bible Study group.

Sorry to hear that you injured your arm in a fall. Please be more careful! I'm glad you didn't have to stay too long in the hospital. Also, I thank the Lord that you've got a safe job where a little arm injury is the worst that can happen to you. As soon as your arm improves, please write me a nice, long letter. It's been quite some time since I heard much about what –

*   *   *

Someone poked my letter.

"Y'all better lay off readin' them love letters and git back to work, soldier. They's a war goin' on!"

There stood Prescott in fresh O.D.'s, but still wearing his helmet.

174

"Seems like no matter where I hide, you always manage to find me," I grinned.

"Have to admit it took me a few days. Thank the Lord; I'm back at this here provisional hospital with y'all, seein' as my leg wound didn't amount to much." He looked around then wiped his brow. "It's gittin' mighty warm in here. Then he removed his helmet, placed it on the floor and sat on it. "I'm shippin' back to our outfit in the mornin' "

"So soon?"

"Yessir. A major from the Medical Detachment came through our ward late yesterday, markin' them that's fit fer duty and them with wounds that ain't quite healed."

"That's rotten! You shouldn't have to go back so quick, although I'm glad you didn't get wounded any worse. How about Garret? I don't remember much after that last tank shell. Did someone get him out?"

Prescott looked down at his boots, his color rising. "Nope. I understand he died before anyone could git to him." Prescott looked up again, a half-smile lighting his face. "I heard tell them Kraut fellers ended up bein' trapped and we wiped out hundreds of 'em. Over 2000 prisoners. A real mess!"

Somehow that news doesn't elate me. What hits me the hardest is the news that Garret is dead! Should I feel relieved that I no longer have him to contend with? Maybe so, but I'm not. His death only strengthens my feeling that by their silence over the past year, he and Matty have been hiding the truth about their former relationship. Repeatedly I had expected Garret to explain it – and always he refused. Now he'll never be able to tell me.

As for Matty, I asked her for an explanation more than two months ago. So far I haven't had a response. No matter how much I love her, I can't plan a future with someone who won't level with me – even though the thought of losing her gnaws at my insides so much I feel sick.

I suddenly realized Prescott was staring at me. "Y'all okay?" he asked.

"Yeah. Just my foot. Starting to hurt again." I pulled back the cover, exposing my bandage, the red spot much larger.

Prescott rose quickly. "Lemme git the nurse."

I waved him back. "Don't worry about it. She's working her way down the row."

Prescott leaned over to look at the bandage more closely. "Y'all got a bad one there. My guess is that they'll probably ship y'all back to Naples where they got more doctors."

"And how about you? Going back to where they've got more burp guns and tank fire?"

"I figger it sounds crazy, but I guess that's where the Lord wants me."

"You gotta be kidding."

"Mebbe they's somethin' more He wants me to accomplish. He's protected me so far."

"Look, you've already been through enough. Why doesn't that god of yours send up some of these rear-echelon Johnnies to take your place, give them a chance to get within smelling distance of the Krauts? Nobody's luck lasts forever."

"I'm not trustin' in luck. I'm trustin' in the Lord."

"And it doesn't bother you that this god of yours keeps sending you back into the thick of the fighting?"

"They's a Bible verse I remember that says: "Thou wilt keep him in perfect peace whose mind is stayed on Thee.""

"That may be okay for you, but the only kinda peace I understand is what you find in places like this – beaucoup miles behind the lines. And the further behind I get, the better I like it." I looked at the big, red blotch on my bandage and decided to pull the cover over my leg again. "When I think back over the past year, I wonder how you and I have lasted even this long."

"The Lord chooses whom He will." Prescott glanced toward the nurse, now working a few beds away. Abruptly he rose and donned his helmet. " I reckon He had good reasons why He decided to take Garrret."

"I'd say he had plenty."

"Whatever the reason, it's a cryin' shame that Garret died before I could – "

I felt a surge of pain ride up my leg. "You're better off forgetting Garret."

Prescott gripped my shoulder. 'Fraid I can't do that. I just wish I had spent more time with Garret – more time talking with him 'bout the Lord." He reached for my hand. "The nurse is gonna be lookin' at you next, so I best be on my way." I grasped his hand tightly, surprised that I found it so difficult to let go.

"I'll try to git over to see y'all agin before I head back," he said, eyes misting. "We need to talk a little more." He turned away.

I watched him walk back toward the exit door. *He's going back to the* real *hot spot. Will I ever see him again?* I looked away. *So okay Fletcher, count your blessings! That means you won't be going back with him, either!"*

As another wave of pain broke over my foot, my attention shifted to the bulge at the end of my cot. *You're looking at a million-dollar wound, Fletcher. That's your ticket back to Naples, maybe all the way back to the States! All sorts of exciting prospects ahead!*

But I feel no heart-pounding excitement. Because my future's got a big hole in it. There's no Matty.

XXVI

"Hey, if you expect to see my hand, I better smell your money first."

Sgt. Herb Ison squirmed in his wheelchair, hesitated for a few moments, then tossed five pennies onto the card table.

Five? He's that confident? Once again I squinted at what I had: three Kings, two sevens. *But the way Herb is playing, God knows if that's enough to beat him. Oh, what the hell.* I matched his bet.

Next I shifted my attention to Velletri, the only one in our trio with any mobility. "Okay Lou, you stayin'?"

Lou slowly drew an index finger the length of his small, dark mustache, then abruptly abandoned his cards.

Herb's normally ruddy complexion took on a deeper hue. He spread his hand: two Queens, two Aces, watching grimly as I slowly peeled off my cards. "Damn you, Chad!" I could taste this coming!" He slammed the arm of his wheelchair. "For the second time, today, I've been wooed, skewed and tattooed!"

I couldn't hold back my grin. "Looks like I win the battle of the pushcarts." I nodded for Lou to gather in the pot and shove it across the table to a place close enough that I could reach it.

"You're not getting off that easy," Herb grumbled. "Anybody who'd take advantage of a one-legged poker player ought to be made to dig latrines wearing nothing but his combat boots (This loud enough to be heard by most of the other soldier-patients in the day-room.)

178

"Alright," I said, "I'll go another hand. But remember, this is only a game. The pot goes to the best player, not the one with the most stripes."

"Uh-oh." Lou's smile faded. His eyes told me he had spotted the Medical T-5 making his way through the crowded room toward our table.

The orderly stopped behind my wheelchair, careful not to bump the cast on my left leg, which rested on a support arm extended parallel to the floor. "You're Fletcher, right?" he asked.

"Yes."

"Major Adams wants to talk with you. I can wheel you over there."

As I gathered in my winnings, trying to ignore the look on Herb's face. Pvt. Lou Velletri emitted a quiet laugh that soon brought on a spasm of violent coughing. *The bullet that pierced his lung at Omaha Beach is acting up again.* Then the orderly began pushing my chair across the room, careful to circumvent other groups of soldiers gathered to play games and talk. I wondered what kind of news Major Adams would have for me.

*   *   *

Neatly arrayed in Army khakis complete with a row of ribbons denoting Stateside service, Major Roy Adams looked up from a file as I was wheeled into his office. He nodded and the T-5 left me facing his desk and the antiseptic odor that went with it.

"Fletcher?"

"Yessir."

"Excuse the dress uniform and all these gaudy decorations. Fact is, I've just returned from a weekend pass to visit my wife and our young son in Chicago. Haven't had time to get into my doctor clothes."

Think nothing of it. Not often I get to meet a veteran of the Battle of Chicago.

The major's eyes shifted to the file before him. "I see by your record that you suffered a serious injury to the left foot during service in France." He lifted an X-ray negative from an envelope and held it up to the light. "Your ankle was only sprained, no broken bones. You're a pretty lucky guy."

I'm lucky alright. My best friend double-crossed me. But now he's dead. And my girl friend turned out to be a tramp. Lucky me.

I couldn't think of anything to say, so I just grinned back.

"As for the foot, it appears that you've torn several tendons. However, the prognosis is good. I believe that we can soon get you walking again."

"No bones broken?"

The major smiled and repeated the words slowly. "For a more detailed explanation, we'll only be moving a few tendons to compensate for the torn – "

"Sounds like a lot of work."

"Not all that difficult. I've performed this operation enough that I could probably do it in my sleep."

"How about 'wide awake' on this one, sir."

The major laughed." Of course, of course."

At this point the major buzzed someone and before long a corporal brought in coffee for both of us. I savored the smell of freshly brewed coffee, but obviously the major could see that I was puzzled by this sudden departure from official procedure.

Officers don't have coffee with mere privates. Why am I here?

"Before we were so pleasantly interrupted," the major said, "I was about to tell you that this operation may limit the lateral flexibility of your foot, but it shouldn't take you long to get used to it. Earlier I had noticed something on the second page of your file." He took a slow drag on his meerschaum. "I see you were wounded once before."

I nearly spilled my coffee. "Yes sir. In Italy."

Major Adams shoved the file aside. "Italy? That's interesting."

I watched as he went through the ritual of stoking and relighting his pipe, then leaned back in his chair.

"Maybe you can give me a little information," he said. "Our oldest son's with some unit in Italy, but he doesn't write very often, so I don't know too much about what he's doing over there. Frankly, my wife's worried sick that he may be in great danger."

"What outfit's he with, sir?"

"Not too sure." The major opened a drawer and withdrew an envelope. "Here's one of his few letters. Look it over. Maybe you can tell me."

I scanned the air mail envelope and repeated the return address aloud: "A.P.O. 88, c/o N.Y., N.Y." Inside, I glanced at the heading of the letter, then handed it back. "From the look of the return address, I'd say that he has a pretty safe job at Division Headquarters. A job, generally miles from where the actual fighting is going on."

I watched Major Adams close his eyes, his lips moving soundlessly. Then he turned to me. "And thank you, Pvt. Fletcher! That lifts a burden off my shoulders. I'm sure my wife will be relieved to get that kind of news."

As the orderly returned to wheel me back to the day-room a feeling of emptiness slowly came over me. *Besides Herb and Lou, who would be interested in my good news? And by the way, who was the major thanking?*

*   *   *

...The dimly lit USO dance floor is crowded with GI's and gals swaying slowly to the pulsating melody of "That Old Black Magic" played by an aggregation of white-jacketed musicians seated on a gaudy bandstand. Light flashes intermittently from the brass section. The bandleader's back is turned, but I'm certain he must be Harry James or Tommy Dorsey.

With Matty's head nestled against my shoulder, my arm around her narrow waist, I willingly surrender to her disarming fragrance. We seem to be gliding mere inches above the surface of the floor, oblivious of the heat, of the other dancers, aware only of our closeness.

"Chad," she whispers in my ear, "It's so wonderful to feel you near me again, to know that the Lord has brought us together again for the rest of our lives."

I kiss her softly on the cheek.

A tap on my shoulder. It is another GI asking to cut in. Reluctantly I start to surrender my partner, then realize that the soldier cutting in is Garret – Garret Wald. His brown hair so thick and lustrous, his dark eyes so intense, so focused on Matty. The two of them exchange smiles, instantaneously creating a channel connecting them, one I cannot penetrate. An abrupt comment from me quickly escalates the tension and I lash out at him. Garret goes down and I stand over him. But now the Garret I see is sprawled against the bandstand, his lips moving, one hand clutching his cheek as blood stains his khaki uniform, his eyes pleading, yet tracking my every move. I turn to Matty, but there is no Matty. She is gone! And when I look back to Garret, he too is gone. In his place I see the gray uniform of a German soldier, his face hideously crushed, eyes watching...

I awoke with a start, then realized that I was back in the day-room. Lou lay back in one of the large, plush chairs regarding me with some amusement.

"Wow!" he said. "The way you were jerking around, it must have been *some* dream!"

I nodded absently, my mind still focused on the dance scene, unable to wrest myself free.

"I was about to slap you awake," Lou said. "There's a lady asking for you. I'll tell the T-5 you're awake."

*   *   *

I rubbed out my half-smoked cigarette as I watched her make her way through the buzz and confusion of the day-

182

room to the bay window area where Lou had left my wheelchair. Although she was dressed smartly and smiling, her dark suit reflected little of the cheery mood so radiant a year ago.

Before Mrs. Seagrave settled herself on the window seat, she gave me a hug, leaving a wet kiss on my cheek. "How absolutely miraculous to have you back here with us!" She glanced at the heavy cast on my leg. "Even with that, your coming home answers my prayer." The voice soft with a slight tremor.

"Thanks. I appreciate your – " I stopped abruptly. "Where's Matty?"

"She's at home," Mrs. Seagrave clasped her slim hands together, leaned forward and cast a vacant stare at the scene outside the window. "Chad, when I learned you had been returned to the Battle Creek hospital, I knew I must drive out here to see you by myself."

"But what about Matty?"

She reached over to touch my hand. "Please bear with me. Right now there's something else I need to talk to you about."

"And that is …"

"Your letter. That one asking about Garret." She paused to look out the window at the steadily darkening sky. "I came across it several weeks ago while I was straightening up Matty's room."

"And you *read* it?"

"Yes. That's why I'm here."

I couldn't hide my look of surprise. "But why – "

"Let me finish." She paused to clear her throat. "For reasons I'll explain later, I read your letter through." Mrs. Seagrave nodded. "I must say, it was carefully written and showed little of the bitterness you likely were feeling at the time you wrote it." Another pause. "I'm afraid my throat has gone dry. Let me find a drinking fountain and I'll be right back."

My heart began to pound as I watched her thread her way through various groups of GI's and the mix of furniture in the day-room. In a few minutes she returned, carrying a small paper cup which she carefully placed on the window seat before resuming.

"Matty never told you how she and Garret first met?"

"Never once mentioned Garret." All at once I got a whiff of her perfume. *Too heavy. So unlike my first impression of her.*

"It was during the winter of 1941- 42," she continued. "Right after Pearl Harbor. Leonard wanted us to go to a Homecoming Dinner at a Baptist church we had attended regularly before moving to another part of town. It had been over ten years since we had been back. Because Leonard and Garret's father were such good friends all through high school, our two families arranged for a table large enough that we could all sit together."

I could sense that Mrs. Seagrave felt ill at ease. She spoke with a voice so soft that I asked her to move a little closer.

"This all must have happened long before I first encountered Matty at St. Francis Hospital – right?" Now *my* voice was trembling. To hide my expression, I deliberately turned my head as though eavesdropping on the nearest group of GI's.

"Yes," she continued, "At the time Matty was a high school senior and Garret was attending Wellington University." She paused to look directly into my eyes as though searching the blueness for some sign of my soul. "Did you by any chance know Garret? He would have been in your class."

"We were acquainted," I replied, perhaps a little too quickly. Fighting the temptation to say more, I tried reaching for a smoke, but soon gave up. *This is too good an opportunity!* "This fellow Garret and I weren't exactly chums, but I knew him. We had first met when I was writing sports for the college paper and he had established some thing of a record in Cross Country. From time to time he would show up in our gang of sports buffs who palled around together. Among the guys, however, he was known as a womanizer. He bragged a lot, but he never talked about individuals, never named names."

Mrs. Seagrave waited while a voice on the PA system asked Pvt. Somebody to return to his ward. I lit my cigarette and motioned to Mrs. Seagrave." Please go on."

After an awkward silence, she resumed, a noticeable amount of sheepishness in her voice. "I'm afraid Leonard and I weren't too observant during that church dinner. While we failed to notice that Matty and Garret had taken an instant liking for one another, who could have guessed that they would begin a close, secret relationship?"

"Secret?" My throat dry again. *Why am I asking the question and dreading the answer?*

"It seems our little girl could be quite devious once she set her mind to it. Somehow she enlisted several of her friends to pretend she was paying them a visit."

I nodded, increasingly aware that my shirt felt wet, that my heart had begun to pound.

"Nonetheless, by the spring of '42 Leonard and I began to suspect that Matty's frequent so-called 'visits' to her friends' homes were actually masking something else."

"You mean – "

"Before long, Matty couldn't hide the truth: she was pregnant."

I closed my eyes and gripped the arms of my wheelchair as a thunderbolt of pain struck my injured leg.

Mrs. Seagrave reached over to pat my arm. "I know how unpleasant all this news must be for you. Likewise, I hope you realize that for Leonard and me, reliving this experience has been a nightmare."

She paused for a sip of water before continuing: "Once Leonard and I recovered from the original jolt, we recognized the need to sit down and talk with Matty. We had to find our way out of this mess. Unfortunately, even after endless sessions with Matty and much time on our knees seeking the Lord's guidance, there seemed no clear path laid out for us."

"What about Garret?"

"That turned out to be another surprise. Evidently, he and Matty had been keeping in touch by phone. Sometime after our discovery, Garret came to us with news that he and Matty had decided to get married. Plainly he was seeking our blessing. However, Leonard would have none of it. He practically threw Garret out of the house and forbade Matty to see him ever again!"

At that point I could no longer restrain myself. I gripped the wheels of my chair, swung it about and with some effort, moved it a few feet away. I remained there for some time, staring straight ahead, seeing nothing but the cold rain on the window.

Before long, a gentle hand caressed my shoulder. "I'm sorry to have to tell you all this when you have so many other problems to deal with."

"That sounds like there's more." I couldn't bring myself to look at her.

"Yes, there is." Mrs. Seagrave shifted my chair around, then resumed her seat. "And I don't know exactly how to – "

By this time it wasn't necessary for the building to fall on me. "Let me save you the trouble of describing the next episode," I said, struggling to keep my voice under control. "You and your husband made a high and mighty decision that Matty should have an abortion."

She turned away quickly, but not before I caught her look of surprise. After an awkward silence, she regained her composure. "Yes, we took her to Toledo for the procedure. St. Francis Hospital came later when Matty developed complications. "

Mrs. Seagrave hesitated again, reading the scorn in my eyes. "Unfortunately, it took Leonard and me quite some time to recognize the mistake we'd made. Compelling Matty to undergo an abortion was a bad decision, not something the Lord wanted us to do. Consequently, the past months have been a torment. But now that we've taken the matter up with the Lord and He has forgiven us – "

"Forgiven you?" I banged my fist on the arm of my wheelchair. "And has he also forgiven you for ordering Matty not to tell me all this?"

Mrs. Seagrave flinched. "Chad, we never did such a thing! We felt she would tell you all about it when the right time – "

"Well, I guess the 'right time' never came, did it? Even now Matty doesn't have the guts to tell me herself!"

"I'm sure she would if she could."

"What do you mean by that?"

"Last July, just before Matty got your letter asking about Garret, we received a telegram from the War Department informing us that our son, Edward, had been killed in the south Pacific."

I saw Mrs. Seagrave's eyes rapidly filling. Several moments passed before she could continue. It was raining heavier now.

"You can understand that Eddie's death struck us all pretty hard," she said. "We're still not over it. But even so, I *had* to come out here today – to talk to you, to let you know that Leonard and I are truly sorry for the way we handled this entire matter. We want you and Matty back together again. I only wish Leonard could be here to tell you himself. As happens so often, he'll be in Washington for the next several days."

"You still haven't answered the first question I asked: where's Matty?"

"She's not well. It's clear now that it took much too long for Matty to respond to the questions in your original letter. She should have answered you right away, instead of allowing the whole mess to fester. As you can expect, all this has had a terrible effect on her health."

"In what way?"

"Matty's gravely ill. She's lost considerable weight and running a fever. Yet when she was in the hospital for several days last week, the doctor couldn't find anything to account for her weakened condition. I think she's getting worse."

Matty gravely ill? My head was spinning.

Mrs. Seagrave abruptly turned her head to gaze out the window, toward the distant woods, her brow furrowed as though studying the wind-swept landscape.

Suddenly, as though emerging from a trance, I became conscious of my surroundings, aware of the other GI's in the room, some reading, some talking together, some engaged in a raucous card game against the far wall. Once again I regarded Eva Seagrave. Despite everything, I was struck by her disarmingly candid manner. I wanted to like her.

Now she seemed to have reached some threshold in her thought process and she turned again to me.

"As you might expect," she said, "I've spent countless hours praying about Matty, repeatedly asking the Lord to show me what to do."

"And the answer?"

"It's always been the same: *Go to Chad. Bring him to Matty*. Mrs. Seagrave rose and fixed her eyes on me. "Chad, Matty *needs* you!" There was no mistaking the fiery determination in her voice. "You've *got to* help her pull through this crisis!"

Help Matty? I looked down at my leg. *How could I do that – even if I wanted to? And I no longer want to.*

XXVII

Battle Creek, Michigan
September, 1944

I met her gaze and our eyes locked for a long moment. Then I reached over and slid my hand along the rough surface of the cast on my leg. "Mrs. Seagrave, the only thing I've **got** to do is to get my ankle healed so I can walk normal again."

"But don't you want *Matty* to walk normal again?" She brushed back a few strands of her black-streaked hair.

"I'm afraid you're omitting something. The three of you have spent much of the past year ignoring my questions about Matty's past. Now it's time for the three of you to get yourselves out of the putrid mess you've created."

I felt my heart thumping against my chest.

"That's a cruel way of looking at it, Chad. We don't want to lose our Matty. And my heart tells me that you don't want to lose her either, that you *want* to help her."

"*Me* – help? You're a very optimistic person, Mrs. Seagrave. After all the time you, your husband and Matty have spent hoodwinking me – you expect *me* to help *you?*"

An almost child-like optimism quickly surfaced in Mrs. Seagrave's small eyes.

"Yes, I do," she said. Once again she took a seat in the window facing me. "I know it sounds crazy, but I'm convinced *that's* the reason the Lord brought me out here to see you." She flinched when a sudden gust of wind spattered a few raindrops against the window.

189

"Hey, your god is a little confused," I said. "Even if I wanted to help, which I don't," I gestured toward the cast on my leg." This soldier is in no condition to – "

"Remember Chad, Christ the Lord isn't held back by human limitations. Let me tell you something. From Matty's very first day on this earth, God has had his hand upon her. She was a frail, premature baby. From a human standpoint neither Leonard nor I had any reason to expect that she would live past her first birthday. But God answered our prayers and chose to raise her up."

"I'm certainly glad she made it, but those successful early years didn't translate into much of a success in later life."

"Maybe Matty's life doesn't look like much of a success story to you, young man, but to see our weak little baby grow up to become a beautiful God-fearing young lady certainly was a success story for us."

I shifted my gaze to the chandelier in the center of the day room. "Oh, she was a success alright. She certainly succeeded in fooling me."

Mrs. Seagrave turned her head aside before replying. "I admit Matty has made her share of mistakes along the way. But God isn't through with any of us yet. And He's not through with you either. Frankly, I believe He wants you to have a part in helping Matty."

"And you believe this god of yours told you to come out here and hassle me about – "

"Please don't use the word 'hassle'. In fact, Chad, the Lord has spoken to me about you, so I'm just doing my job as a prayer warrior – something I've done throughout my life."

"A prayer warrior? What's that?"

"It's someone who talks with God in prayer most every day, asking for help, seeking guidance. And because I've had this close relationship with Him, I've learned to respond promptly whenever I feel Him nudging me."

"Nudging?"

"It's difficult to explain, but there are times when I have felt an overwhelming urge to pray for a specific person or to contact him." She pulled her velour jacket closer around her neck. "Usually later I discover that my prayer, or my contact, came at a critical time in that person's life."

She must have noticed that I was getting restless.

Abruptly Mrs. Seagrave began fumbling in her purse. "There's something here that I want to show you." She withdrew a small notebook. "I call it 'My Daily Prayer Log'."

Her hand shook as she handed it to me.

"You mean you keep track of everything you pray for?"

"I've only been keeping a log since Pearl Harbor. There's not an entry for every day, but only for those dates when I felt something prodding me to pray for someone in particular, or to contact them personally. The notebook you're holding is just the latest. I've filled several since the war began."

This is all getting pretty sticky. Maybe if I had another cigarette. I glanced at my watch. *Lou will be down here pretty soon to take me to lunch. So in the meantime, what more can I say to this woman? She and the rest of her confederates have already destroyed my life. The Matty I fell in love with apparently never actually existed. So what's the point of talking any further? Maybe Lou will come early and get me out of this.*

To escape the pleading so evident in Mrs. Seagrave's eyes, I pretended to scan her little book, feigning interest in some of the most recent entries:

"Jan. 17, 1944 – Called Charlotte. Her son coming home on emergency leave.

"Feb. 29, 1944 – Prayer for Chad. Special danger?

"Mar. 5, 1944 – Visited Mrs. Johnson. Learned that her daughter joined WACS yesterday.

"June 19, 1944 – Prayer for Richard. Something urgent?

"July 7, 1944 – Called on Edith. She and Jim decided on divorce yesterday.

"July 8, 1944 – Prayer for strength. Telegram: Richard has been killed.

"July 10, 1944 – Prayer for Matty. She came home ill, has taken to bed.

"Aug. 15, 1944–Prayer for Chad. Keep him safe!

"Aug. 18, 1944 – Prayer for Matty. Chad's letter asks about Garret.

"Aug. 20, 1944 – Prayer for Agnes' son in Army Hospital.

"Aug. 31,1944 –Prayer for Chad. Has something happened?"

"Sept. – "

My eyes were clouding. "That's quite a list," I stammered, then looked away "I'm not so sure why you prayed for me so many times, but I do thank you."

"And *I* thank the Lord," she replied. "Keep in mind, Chad, that each time I prayed for you specifically – I see there are three entries – I felt you were in special danger. And here's something even stranger. That first entry – February 29. On that date I remember feeling the need to pray for you as so strong that the next morning I mentioned it to Matty. And would you believe, *she* had awakened in the middle of the night, her heart pounding, convinced that you were in grave danger – and she didn't understand why you should be. You see, even when we had little definite information to go on, we were praying for you to be spared."

I took another look at the list, conscious of the rain against the window, then handed the notebook back to her. "I have to admit that on the first two dates I was spared. On the third one I got wounded. Two out of three – not bad."

A smile momentarily brightened Mrs. Seagrave's expression. She fingered her simple silver necklace for a moment before she responded. "Just consider the fact that you're here today – and that you're *alive.* So I'd say we're talking three out of three." Again she leaned toward me, her fragrance stifling. "Now Leonard and I are praying that *Matty* will be spared. And you can help. Your presence could – "

My throat dry, I shook my head. "Look, Mrs. Seagrave, I appreciate your concern for me, but like I told you before, by lying to me, Matty destroyed whatever relationship we had. Sorry, but I can't help you."

Mrs. Seagrave carefully tucked the notebook back in her purse, closed it with a snap, then looked up, her eyes taking on a cold, penetrating hue, more the color of slate. "I haven't wanted to say anything about this previously because Leonard and I realized why you did it."

"Did what?" My heart began to thump.

"You know what I mean, young man. From the outset of your overseas service you fabricated a story about the type of unit you were assigned to. Time and again when Matty mentioned you in our family prayers, she rejoiced about your assignment to a so-called service unit well behind the front lines and away from any great danger."

I could feel a burning redness creep across my face. "I was just trying to – "

"It's not hard for any of us to find some way to justify a lie." Mrs. Seagrave reached over to touch my arm. "Matty frequently shared your letters with us. But the first time Leonard saw the address and heading, he suspected the truth. Later on, after he had confirmed his assumption with other more knowledgeable persons with loved ones overseas, he let me in on the secret: that you were serving with a front-line outfit."

I looked toward the entrance to the day-room. *Where is Lou?* "Did you tell Matty?"

"No. We realized you were trying to shield her, to keep her from worrying about you. Maybe we were wrong to support you in that lie, but we did you that favor. Now we're asking you for a favor in return."

I glanced at my watch. "Hey, I'd love to spend more time with you, but I can already smell lunch. I expect my buddy will be down here in a few minutes to take me – " I reached for my smokes, but my appetite had already disappeared.

*   *   *

Through the large bay window I watched activity in the parking lot below. I could see Mrs. Seagrave hurrying toward her car, her coat billowing, her collar upturned against a sharp wind that drove the leaves before it.

I leaned forward, but could not touch the window, frustrated that it was not possible for me to halt her flight, to bring her back, to make her explain the unexplainable. *Those entries in her prayer log: Feb. 29...Aug. 14...Aug 31. Why did she and Matty pray for me on those particular dates?*

How did they even know about February 29?...

...Our regiment had moved up into the Ponte Rocco sector of the Anzio beachhead two days ago in a desperate attempt to help stem the tide of the German counterattack. All day it had been bedlam for Kilgore and Hensley manning our machinegun, firing at anything that moved. It seemed like the waves of Kraut infantry throwing themselves at our gun position would never end. Now in the gloom of early evening our gun lay silent, but we knew the enemy was still out there. From time to time we could hear the sound of shovels digging, digging. Geoffrey chose this moment to crawl back to the foxhole Garret and I shared. He wanted to remind us that it was our turn to take over the machinegun so that Kilgore and Hensley could get some rest for a few hours. That transfer took almost a half hour due to the necessity of being so careful about making any sound.

Once Geoffrey had us in position, he prepared to move back to his hole. Even in the dim light, I could read the exhaustion in our squad leader's eyes – and also the warning. He knew of the tension between Garret and me. He didn't want any more friction. I sensed that he would shoot the first one of us to cause any more trouble.

As I looked out across the barren, shadowy field commanded by our machinegun, I pointed to several mounds some fifty feet in front of our gun pit and nudged Geoffrey. "Shouldn't we get rid of them? With mounds like that in front of us, we don't have a clear field of fire. They just make it easier for the Krauts to infiltrate our position."

Geoffrey bit into his ration of Army chocolate. I flinched as I got a whiff of his breath. "Don't worry about those mounds," he grunted. "Before the night's over, there'll probably be a few more of 'em. Those mounds are actually the bodies of Germans who tried to reach our position and never made it."

Or a date like August 15…

…Off the coast of sunny southern France the smoke of battle and the height of the ramp on our LCVP limited my view of the shore. I could barely make out the beach where we would be landing. I figured we must be about a half-mile offshore. Soon our landing craft would be hitting the beach. Even though the sound of the boat's powerful motor clashed with the noise of shells exploding around us, a pall of silence hung over our crowded group of infantrymen, each of us struggling with thoughts of our loved ones – and with the uncertainty about what would happen in the next few minutes as we stormed the enemy beach.

And just what had prompted Mrs. Seagrave to pray for me on August 31?

…Nothing focuses the mind so well as the realization that the next few minutes might be the last ones you spend on this earth. We were a few short miles north of Montelimar, France. Our machinegun had played its part in trapping the German column on the main highway leading north. Now a Kraut tank had broken loose from the German column and kept firing shell after shell as it moved up the road toward our hastily-dug foxhole. The first shell tore up our emplacement, badly wounding Garret and forcing Hensley, with shrapnel in his leg, to dismantle our gun and drag the barrel back to a more secure position. It had become my job to rescue the rest of the gun. So there I was, with the heavy machinegun tripod on my shoulders, my mouth dry as sand, kneeling in a shallow defilade, scanning the last few yards of open terrain, wondering: would I make it to the relative safety of a new position before the tank fired again?…

What had brought me through those episodes alive? How could Matty and her mother, both so far removed from the carnage of battle, have sensed my desperate need at that moment? Why had they felt an immediate, urgent need to pray for me? The answers to those questions had to lie in a region beyond my ken – something I could not comprehend.

I lit a cigarette as I watched Mrs. Seagrave pull out of the parking lot in her aging Ford, conscious that after all the back and forth, I was still torn with a sudden aching loneliness, conscious of a bottomless silence in the midst of a noisy room, and yet with those nagging doubts about Matty and her mother. *Haven't they been loyal and supportive during all those months I was fighting in Europe? Now when they need me – is it right for me to refuse them help? Or are they both merely a couple of liars and deceivers who don't deserve my help?*

XXVIII

Detroit, Michigan

February, 1945

It's only been a month or so since my medical discharge and already my Army separation pay is running dry – and they'll be playing ice hockey in Hell before my disability pension is approved. Sure, I'm a civilian again. But now it looks like I better get a job.

Of course, initially the daily newspapers attracted a good deal of my attention. But only after reading the latest on the fighting in Europe (We're banging on Germany's front door!), did I turn to the want ads.

Let me tell you something, it's not that easy finding a position suitable for a person with my training and experience – someone who's carried a gun the past few years, walks with a limp, and – let's be realistic, Fletcher! Job openings in the underworld aren't usually listed in the "Help Wanted" section.

Nonetheless, I began searching the classifieds more carefully for other avenues of employment. That's when I noticed an ad for a "Jobs Conference" now being held in Ann Arbor. It stated that "key officials from nearly fifty area firms would be on hand to interview prospective employees." *Sounds great – a cinch for Chad Fletcher – right? Wrong.*

After that verbal bout I had with Mrs. Seagrave last month I better stay away from any events in Ann Arbor or Plymouth. I might meet up with somebody from Matty's family. I don't need Bible quotations and aggravation. I need a job.

Thus it was on a cold but sunny Thursday morning while I was enjoying a quiet cigarette in my tiny Detroit apartment, who should phone but Norm Weingarden, Stella's old flame, the guy who used to pal around with me and Garret during our undergraduate days at Wellington University.

"Chad? This is Norm. You know, that lucky 4-F. Right now I'm involved in a Jobs Conference in Ann Arbor and I just read in the Alumni Newsletter that a certain Chad Fletcher has once more become a tax-paying member of society."

"You're right on the 'society' part, but wrong on the 'tax-paying' part. I understand you don't have to pay taxes if you don't have a job."

"Right you are my fine-feathered hero, but that means you and I have a big chance to catch up on old times. How about you coming out to the Ann Arbor Conference? I have to work the Wellington Booth out there but won't have much to do late Friday. I'm anxious to see my old buddy again."

"Same here, but the weather – " I tried to make some excuse, but Norm continued to play hard of hearing.

"Let me pick you up at your room at noon tomorrow and we'll run out to the Conference. Friday's the final day. That'll give you a chance to check out a few of the companies while I put in a couple hours at the University booth. Might give you some – "

"Look, Norm. I'd love to, but – "

"Chad, you know you can't 'out-but' me. I promise we'll be away from Ann Arbor by 4 p.m. Then it's back to my place in Plymouth – snug, warm and ready for a party weekend …"

This is beginning to smell like an interesting bash. From his description, I figure that Norm has a pretty swank apartment. And the babes he'll be lining up–Hey, it sounds better than another weekend of crossword puzzles in this crappy place I'm renting in Detroit. I need to start mixing with the human race again – if only to get my mind off Matty.

At noon Friday Norm picked me up as planned. Although during the rain-and-sleet ride out to Ann Arbor I had intended to fill him in on what I had been through during the years I spent overseas, I only managed to get in a condensed version of Garret's death. For several minutes following that news Norm said nothing. Although Garret had always needled Norm, I could see that my condensed story of Garret's passing hit Norm pretty hard.

Of course, there's nothing 'condensed' about Norm himself. Somehow he's managed to cram his 210 lbs. into a 5 ft -8 in. frame – a bit more hefty than the Norm I had known when we were locker-mates at Wellington. What hasn't changed is the humorous Norm, the generous Norm, the Norm I've always liked.

"Lighten up Chad," he said as we pulled into the parking lot of the hotel where the "Job Fair" was being held. "You're home now, so put the war behind you." A light rain had begun falling. Norm paused to stare at me before turning off the ignition. "By the way," he said, "whatever happened to those marriage plans I had heard so much about many moons ago?"

I turned my head, but said nothing.

"Don't tell me you two have broken up."

"Okay, so I won't tell you." *I can see that Norm and I still have some catching up to do. But right now I don't want to talk about it.*

Once Norm had guided me to the Exhibition Hall and we'd agreed to meet again in two hours, he was off to his booth while I began wandering among the various exhibits of companies looking for special employees in a growing labor market.

It wasn't long, however, before I was reminded of why I had had such strong misgivings about attending this Job Fair in the first place. For there, resplendent in a Navy blue suit and red tie, seated in the Ford Motor Co. booth talking with a student wearing a U of M jersey, was none other than Leonard Seagrave, Matty's father.

I tried to hurry past his booth. *When you've got a bad leg, your top speed isn't much to brag about.*

Abruptly Seagrave rose from his chair and waved. Pretending not to notice, I quickened my pace, guessing that he wouldn't leave his booth. *Okay Fletcher, let's get out of this stuffy atmosphere. Let's head for the anonymous atmosphere of the hotel coffee shop where I can wait for Norm to get off duty.*

*   *   *

"Hope you came up with some good leads," Norm said as he turned on his window wipers, maneuvered his beat-up Dodge out of the hotel parking lot and headed for downtown Plymouth. "All I need is one more accident and I'm back walking to work." At the first traffic light he turned to me. "How would it be if I drop you at the grocery store while I run over to the post office to check my box? I need to have you pick up a couple items for the party."

"No problem," I said, "as long as this weather doesn't get any worse." The rain we had encountered earlier in the day now had turned to sleet.

Inside the store I had no difficulty locating the garlic pods and the olives Norm needed for his pasta extravaganza. As I shopped, however, I did notice a few folks giving me the eye. *Okay, so I limp. The Army doctors said I'll walk this way for the rest of my life. Better a live gimp than a dead GI with two good legs.*

Outside, bag in hand, I shifted back and forth trying to find a dry spot under the ragged store awning, the thin veneer of ice crackling underfoot. All I found was an icy section that sent me sprawling onto the sidewalk. I watched my jar of olives slowly roll out into the parking lot.

Feeling like a fool, I looked up to see who was reaching down to help me regain my feet. *Is that Matty's father wearing a slicker?*

"A nasty fall", he said.

"Wha – " I stammered, still mystified by his sudden appearance.

"I saw you and Norm leave the hotel," he said. "He and I spent some time together yesterday. I hadn't realized you had just been released from the hospital."

I tried to wipe the sleet from my pantlegs, all the while wondering about this guy Norm. *He's a lot more devious than I remember.* Bewildered, I watched Seagrave retrieve the jar of olives and rejoin me under the so-called protection of the awning.

"You mean you followed us here? " I asked.

Seagrave nodded, shaking out his raincoat.

"But why?"

"Two reasons," he said, scanning the parking lot, apparently watching for Norm. Up close, I can see the guy's losing his hair. Seagrave doffed his hat, shaking off some of the raindrops. "I tried to catch up with you at the Job Fair, but you disappeared on me."

I stuffed the olive jar down in my jacket pocket along with the garlic pods, tossing the fetid, sodden bag into a container. *These Seagrave people aren't easily discouraged.*

"First of all, I figured you showed up at the 'Job Fair' because you needed work."

"You're right about that. Now that I'm out of the Army it's time I started supporting myself, so – " I paused, as suddenly everything became clear. "You said there were two reasons."

"Yes." He adjusted the collar on his raincoat. " I need a favor from you."

"Look, I already told Mrs. Seagrave two months ago – "

Seagrave eyes widened. "You never heard what happened?" He gave me a stern appraisal.

"Happened?"

"Yes, to Eva – Mrs. Seagrave. You must have known that after she visited you in Battle Creek she was pretty upset. Driving home in the rain, she had an accident. Cracked her hip."

I shook my head. "This is all news to me. Is she okay?"

"Not so good. She's had an operation, but the hip's still giving her trouble. I've had to arrange considerable care for her."

After an awkward pause, I shook my head. "I appreciate your predicament, but – "

"I was hoping you'd come over to see her. She's asked for you several times." With the light fading, Seagrave peered into the lot, apparently watching for Norm.

I was beginning to shiver. "Let's wait inside," I said. "Norm should be here any day now."

During the next several minutes as I adjusted to the odiferous atmosphere inside the store, Seagrave recounted the events of the past few months, pausing frequently to watch for Norm.

"When Eva left after visiting you in the hospital, she was greatly agitated. Unfortunately at one of the intersections on her drive home, she made a hasty left turn, swinging her car directly into the path of a pickup truck. The crash knocked her unconscious. She was rushed to the hospital where she was held for several hours. Next came a series of X-rays, but the doctors found nothing. When Matty and I got her home, she took to her bed, still complaining of much pain. Our family doctor recommended another series of X-rays and found a hairline crack in her thighbone. Now he wants her to return to the hospital for further treatment, but so far she's refused to go."

My heart began to pound again.

What do you say after a story like that? All this has turned out so much worse than I had ever imagined!

I looked down at my shoes, now thoroughly soaked. "I'm really sorry about all the trouble you're having," I said, "but I guess there's not much – "

"Hold on, son. Maybe there is. Eva's asked for you several times. Maybe, if you visited her – "

"I can't see that it would make any difference. Even you haven't been able to convince her – "

"Neither has Matty." The lines in his face deepened.

"Matty?" *His eyes tell me that he knows what I'm thinking.*

"Yes, Matty. She's finishing up her junior year at Wellington. Tonight Matty's staying with one of her sorority sisters in Novi, so she won't be home *at all* tomorrow." His countenance brightened. "Might be a good opportunity for you to drop in on Eva."

I found it hard to say anything while I mulled over his suggestion. Then, finally, with a sigh: "Okay, I'll talk to Norm about driving me over to your place in the morning. It'll just be a brief visit, since we're – " A car in the parking lot was blinking its lights. "That must be Norm."

"Good. You'll be helping Eva immensely, and you'll still have time for your weekend plans."

*   *   *

Although Norm's apartment in downtown Plymouth proved to be a gem, I spent a fitful night, my sleep interrupted by a series of crazy, fleeting images:

Mrs. Seagrave shouting: "You lied, young man! You lied to all of us!"…Prescott and I holding off a counterattack…Alabam, his face, a mass of purple and blue, horribly disfigured, his eyes following me down endless corridors…Matty surrendering herself in my arms…

The next morning as Norm drove up the long circular approach to the majestic, two-story Seagrave home on the outskirts of Plymouth, his eyes widened. Although I had visited the Seagraves many times before, my lips still formed a soundless "Wow!"

Matty's home appeared every bit as impressive as when I had first seen it three years ago: broad eaves extending over the tall, rectangular windows on the upper floor, sheltering a wide, ground-level entrance, rough timbers set amongst massive stonework. Truly a castle.

Shaking his head in disbelief, Norm pulled his aging Dodge to a stop at the doorway. "Chad," he said. "If you marry this gal, you'll be lapping up the good times for the rest of your life." His layers of corpulence rocked with laughter.

"Dammit Norm!" I cast him a menacing look. "I told you before that Matty and I are no longer – "

"Now, now." Norm waggled a finger at me. "You said you were gonna drop the Army talk."

"Yeah, you're right." I turned to stare at my chubby friend, hardly able to hold back a laugh of my own. I closed my eyes and extended my hands, feeling my way along the dashboard to the door.

Merriment faded from Norm's beady eyes. "Something wrong?"

"Just making sure of where I am." I opened my eyes. "You sounded so much like one of my buddies overseas."

"You mean the Bible-quoting guy?"

"That was Prescott alright."

How about it, Rev. Prescott? Still over there trying to get the rest of the U.S. Army to do what the Bible says? You always had a lot of 'don't', but not much 'why'.

Norm deposited me at the entrance to the Seagrave home with a promise to return at noon, then waited in the car until the bell was answered.

When the door opened, there stood a short, stout, middle-aged woman complete with a starched white apron and the aroma of kitchen cleanser.

"You must be Mrs. Quigley," I grinned, waving a farewell to Norm. "I'm Chad Fletcher, here to see Mrs. Seagrave."

"Come in, young man," she said, an Irish brogue coloring her words. "The mister will be down shortly."

She took my jacket and ushered me through the heavy glass doors into the library, an expansive, thickly carpeted room just off the entrance hall. *Not the best room for me. Matty and I spent too much time here.*

Try as I might, I couldn't keep my eyes from drifting over to the far corner of the room, between two rows of bookshelves. There atop a small table sat a wind-up record player. The bookshelves, giving off a musty smell, were mostly devoted to technical volumes on management and automotive subjects, plus a sprinkling of books with Christian themes. I recalled Matty telling me that her father had served as an instructor at a trade school prior to joining Ford Motor Co.

Finally I moved over to the grand piano by the window, tapped out a few notes, then casually picked up a book lying face down on the bench. I sat down on the bench, noting that the book was a hymnal open to – I hastily replaced it and tried to think of something else, anything else. All that came to mind was a series of questions:

What am I doing here? Why do I drift into a situation like this – one that can only dredge up memories, some painful, some indigestible, some –

Leonard Seagrave's sudden appearance in slacks and sweater interrupted my reflection, the air redolent with the fresh smell of shave cream, surprising me with his cheerful demeanor

"Sorry, I wasn't downstairs to greet you. When I saw the car coming, I thought it best to let Eva know you'd be up to see her. You two can have a nice visit while I'm away."

"Away? You're going – "

"Won't be for long. Our housekeeper's been wanting a day off, but I couldn't leave Eva alone. So I'd planned to drive Mrs. Quigley home late this afternoon when Matty gets back. But now that you're here, I can run her home earlier."

Hey Seagrave. Kinda short notice, wouldn't you say? If I didn't need this job, I'd tell you to –

Reading my surprise, Seagrave sat down beside me. "Don't go worrying. Eva will be okay. The two of you should have so much to talk about that you won't notice that

I'm gone." He rose. "Eva's in the master bedroom at the far end of the upstairs hallway. Let me take you up there."

Negotiating the stairway to the next level proved to be a slow, somewhat painful exercise for me. But it did afford a chance to talk with Seagrave a little more.

"What about Matty?" I asked. "I thought she was sick."

"Not any more. Took about a month, but she finally shook off her illness." We paused at the landing. "Eva and I never did agree what was wrong with that girl. I figured it was all in her head – and I was right!"

As we approached the Second Floor, a medicinal odor gradually tainted the air.

"You mean something was bothering her?"

"Something she had to come to terms with."

"And now she's changed?"

"Quite a change, I'd say. But only after much prayer. Matty's become a very serious young lady. Been a big help to her mother – and I'm proud of her."

I gripped the rail tightly, my knuckles showing white. As we resumed climbing the steps, a question began nagging me. "Did you say that Matty's gone for the day?"

"She took her mother's car and drove over to Novi to visit a friend. I expect her home in time to warm up the dinner Mrs. Quigley has in the refrigerator. I tell you. Mrs. Q has a knack for making ordinary food taste like a banquet out of Heaven" Seagrave placed a hand on my shoulder. "But don't go worrying. I expect you'll be long gone before Matty returns. I know how you must feel."

"Norm should have me out of here by noon."

"Good. If we don't get any more rain, I'll be back by then,"

As we continued down the hall toward the master bedroom, I still felt uncomfortable. *Something Matty's come to terms with? It all sounds so final. And what's crazier still, I feel so left out.*

We passed several plaques and framed citations mounted on the wall, apparently testimonies to Leonard Seagrave's industrial achievements. When we reached the door to the bedroom, he turned to me. "I should warn you that Eva has undergone a radical change in the past month. Right after her accident she was extremely optimistic about how quickly she would recover – 'just as long as we don't let any doctors interfere. I know the Lord will heal me.'

"Matty and I appreciated her upbeat outlook, but once we learned of the cracked thighbone, we both tried to caution her about the long period of treatment and convalescence that lay ahead."

"Now wait a minute," I said. "In the past Matty herself has bragged to me about the 'Lord being the Great Physician' and – "

Seagrave shook his head slowly. "Oh we still believe that, mind you. The Lord is a miraculous healer. But maybe our faith falls a little short of instantaneous New Testament healing. In the meantime, you can imagine what a challenge Eva's ranting was for Mrs. Quigley. On top of everything else, Eva kept trying to make plans that were way beyond her capability."

"Like what?"

"Like planning a trip out West – just the two of us – hiking in the San Gorgonio mountains. Something we'd done twenty years ago. And her with a broken hip? There was no end to her optimism, her impractical ideas. I couldn't reason with her."

"Sounds like she's become a very optimistic individual."

"Not exactly. On our last visit to the doctor he told us that surgery is absolutely necessary for the bone to heal properly. That's considerably dampened Eva's enthusiasm."

Seagrave reached for the doorknob, but I tugged his arm. "About Matty. You didn't tell her I was coming?"

"No," he replied. "And I made certain not to tell Eva till this morning."

Following him, I saw Mrs. Seagrave in a hospital bed at the far end of the room, I was immediately struck by the overwhelming medicinal odor and then by the brightness of the yellow-green furnishings and decorations, how the high windows allowed light to bounce off the pale wallpaper and drapes creating a cheery atmosphere. *Far different from the dark, miserable mornings Prescott, Garret and I endured in the foxholes of Italy and France. But then, this is civilian life. A high-flown version of it, but civilian, nonetheless.*

With only her head exposed, Mrs. Seagrave lay under a bundle of covers. All smiles, Leonard hastened to her side, leaned over and gave her a kiss on the forehead. She made no response, no sound.

"Chad Fletcher is here," he said, rubbing her forehead. "I'm going to leave you two to get reacquainted. Have a good chat while I drive Mrs. Quigley home." With that he turned and left.

Now with her eyes open and her brow troubled, Mrs. Seagrave seemed deep in thought, unaware of my presence. I pulled a chair over to the bed. "Really sorry to hear about your accident," I said. "Hope there's something I can do to help."

"Not much anyone can do," she murmured without turning her head nor changing her expression, her voice barely audible. "I just need to be left alone."

While I watched a few errant leaves blow along the street below, I let that statement stand for a long minute. "It's kinda cold, but beautiful out there today. I bet you're looking forward to the time when you can sit outside and enjoy the bright sunshine."

At this she finally turned to me, her eye searing. "Whatever gave you the idea I'd look forward to that?"

Her response surprised me. "I imagine that fresh air, some of Mrs. Quigley's good home cooking and a little movement would make you feel better, closer to the day when you'll be able to exercise again."

"Obviously you have no appreciation of how much all this foolish home care is costing." She shook her head. "I worry about that every day. That's my exercise."

Another period of silence enveloped us like a heavy cloud while I fumbled about trying to come up with some alternative, neutral subject.

Suddenly Mrs. Seagrave half-raised her head. "Matty – did you talk to her?"

"Well, uh…no. I haven't seen her."

"She's due back. I just talked to her on the telephone. She went to see one of her girlfriends." A pause, then: "She's not well, you know."

"I'm surprised to hear that. Your husband said she had recovered."

"Fat lot he knows about it." Again a pause. "You men don't appreciate what that young girl's been going through."

I made no immediate reply, choosing instead to review what had been said, still searching for an acceptable topic, something to cut through the silence. "Have you been eating and sleeping alright?"

"No. I lie awake most every night, listening to the howling wind. And as for that Quigley woman, I've given up on her. By the time she gets up her with the food, it's cold and inedible." Again she turned to face the window.

Obviously something has this woman by the throat. "Hey, I know you're hurting. Can't say I blame you. All this hospital business is bound to leave you discouraged, Mrs. Seagrave. But I hate to see worry eat you up like this. Tell me how I can help."

"Help? You want to help? You had your chance to help months ago – and you turned it down. Now you come crawling back. I'll tell you this: Matty knows you're here – and she's terribly upset. And you've certainly got me upset. I just can't cope with your nagging!"

She began to sob.

Without further ado, I retired to the bathroom and brought her a glass of water. "Here, please sit up and drink this."

But her mood hadn't changed. "I don't want it. Put it on the tray."

"Okay, but isn't there *something* I can do?"

"There's nothing. You've already done enough. And now you've even made me cry. I can't stand it anymore." She groaned and turned her head away.

I eased out of my chair, hurried across the room and closed the door behind me. *Hey, this is way beyond what I had expected. These Christians have all the answers – right?*

Yeah, tell me about it. I glanced at my watch. *Eleven! Matty's father and Norm will be here before long. I need to get back on track.*

Flipping the light switch in the hallway, I decided to leave Eva alone briefly while I tried to concentrate on the various plaques and framed testimonials from government and industry leaders praising Leonard Seagrave for his outstanding contributions to the war effort. But I soon discovered that reading about Seagrave's successes was not having the calming effect I had hoped for. I moved over to a section of the hallway devoted to family photos. In among portraits and snapshots of grandparents and other notable members of the Seagrave family tree, a clutch of more recent photos attracted my attention.

And even though noises from downstairs indicated that Leonard Seagrave had returned, nothing could draw my eyes away from the Seagrave family photos. For there in the midst of the entire display was a large color portrait of Matty. One that must have been taken about the time she and I met. Once again I was captivated by the curly, blond hair, the green eyes, the pert little nose.

Okay, so it's been ages since I last saw Matty, yet this simple picture brings her rushing back. Once again I can hear her singing, the gossamer timbre of her voice caressing each note:

"Amazing grace! How sweet the sound,
That saved a wretch – "

Angelic, bell-like tones resonating in my head, haunting, ethereal –

A wild scream! *Mrs. Seagrave!*

I turned and, trying to ignore the extreme pain from my ankle, burst into her bedroom, hobbled to her bedside and grabbed one flailing hand that gripped a jagged shard of glass. As I struggled to wrest it loose amid repeated screams, I became conscious of blood spattering the bedding, of someone opposite me locked in a battle to hold onto the other arm. It was Matty!

XXIX

Plymouth, Michigan
February, 1945

Matty slowly closed the front door and leaned back against it, her face ashen, her voice a harsh whisper. "Thank you, Lord," she murmured. "Thank you for helping...for helping us." Her eyes were full.

I peered through the window, watching the ambulance, with Mrs. Seagrave aboard, head down the driveway through a sparse snowfall toward the main road on its way to the State University Hospital. A blustery wind promised to complicate the drive to Ann Arbor.

Trying to ignore the throbbing in my ankle, I turned my attention to the improvised handkerchief-bandage on my left hand. The red stain was growing in size and the tremors had increased. Yet even so, I could not keep my gaze from shifting back to Matty.

Here she is right in the room with me – the Matty I dreamed about so much during all those long, dark months overseas. I want to reach out to her. But I cannot. There is something different about this Matty.

It's not just the dark, autumn-leaf skirt and the pale orange turtleneck that she's wearing. (So different from the teenage colors she had worn when last I saw her.) The difference is not in her clothes. It's something else.

Yes, I remember noticing a strangeness, a certain aloofness, sometime earlier when the two of us were struggling to get Mrs. Seagrave under control. And later while we awaited the ambulance. Something distant, something off-putting in Matty's behavior. The simple, smiling acknowledgement of my presence, her almost off-hand recognition of my help – all so impersonal, so detached. Sure, she expressed relief that finally I had been shipped home from the danger and carnage of the war. But not the 'Darling, you're home again!' greeting I had expected.

Tugging at my bandage, I tried to keep it from unraveling, then nodded to Matty. "If we're going to follow your mother to the hospital, we'd better get on our way!"

"Yes, of course." She passed one hand across her face as though recovering from a bad dream. "You'll need to have someone look at that hand. Let me fix your bandage, then I'll get my car keys."

She disappeared into the hallway, leaving me to sort out the frenzied sequence of events of the past half-hour. *What had happened?*

I remember that after visiting with Mrs. Seagrave, greatly troubled by her negative attitude, I had brought her a glass of water. Then returning to the hallway to give her time to settle down, and to give me some relief from the antiseptic smell of the room, I had –

Hey Fletcher, you goofed! When you've got someone like Eva Seagrave in a crazy state of mind – you don't give her a glass of anything! All she needs is a piece of broken glass – a golden opportunity to end her torment!

And that scream! If I'd been downstairs, I never could have stopped Mrs. Seagrave in time. And then to have Matty – my Matty – so close at hand. The two of us struggling as a team to bring her mother under control. And after all that thrashing about, her mother, the color of death, ending up with nothing more than a few deep cuts on her forearm? Whew! And these people claim to be followers of Jesus?

Within minutes Matty returned, carrying a first aid kit. Her hands were shaking, yet without a word she set about unwrapping my bandage and cleaning the wound area.

"You realize that none of this would have happened," she said, "if you hadn't brought that glass into the room." *No smile, no warmth in her tone.*

212

"How was I to –?" My heart renewed its thumping.

"Never mind now," she said.

I watched in silence as she wiped the wound clean with warm gauze, then selected a pad and began taping it over my palm. *Okay, maybe now isn't the time or place to expect Matty's customary ebullience to show through. But what has happened to the radiance so evident in that hallway portrait upstairs?*

Even so, I could not keep my eyes away from her. *Why is it that after all the news about her and Garret, and her reluctance to answer any of my questions – why is it that I want so much to gather her in my arms, to let her sob on my shoulder, to comfort her, to dry her tears?* I had tried to comfort her while the emergency crew was here, but she had pulled away.

Something has happened to the Matty I have been dreaming about the past two years. Something has dropped a curtain between us. Or am I making too much of this? Should I expect Matty to wax romantic when she has just witnessed her mother's attempt at suicide? Wake up, Fletcher! Although Matty and I have come through a long separation, and we have much to share – this is not the moment for it. Not until we've worked our way through this emergency.

In the pervasive silence that still cloaked the room, I was thankful for any thought – or anything – that would lift me out of this morass of gloom.

I looked at the clock in the hallway. *Hey Fletcher, if you expect to salvage what's left of that big weekend you and Norm have planned, you had better call him right away!*

I reached for the phone.

"No calls," Matty said. "Sorry, but we're running late." With that she was out the door. And I was left to limp along behind.

No sooner had I slid into the seat beside her and slammed the car door, than Matty kicked the accelerator and we were off. Cutting in and out of noonday Plymouth traffic, her foot heavy on the pedal, Matty quickly reached the main highway to Ann Arbor, only to find it heavily congested as well. She slapped the steering wheel, muttering to herself.

"Matty, I know you're anxious to get to the hospital," I said, "but let's show up at the Emergency Room as visitors, not patients."

She turned to me with a wry smile, quickly interrupted when she spotted a gap in the lineup and darted around the car ahead.

I took a moment to catch my breath, my heart still pounding. "Okay, so you're worried about your Mom. Well. I am too. I can't forget how often she prayed for me while I was overseas. I still don't understand it." Matty nodded assent. "But face it Matty, You're not just worrying about your Mom. Something else is bothering you."

"There is?"

"Yes, and you need to tell me about it."

No response.

It soon became obvious that we were never going to get anywhere in this traffic. The highway was becoming more clogged by the minute.

"So many cars!" Matty sighed. "Where are they all going?"

"Probably some kind of sporting event at U of M today."

"Whatever it is, we do have gas rationing. And about half of these people have no right to be out here!"

With that she jerked her wheel hard right, then left rolling us onto the thin, unpaved shoulder. From that point we slithered along, passing several cars at a dangerous speed, their horns blasting us. We skidded onto an intersecting, muddy, unpaved road – an alternate, little-used route to the hospital, Matty quickly informed me.

As we jounced along this narrow, deeply-rutted lane, I began to question whether we would make it to the hospital in one piece. "Matty!" I shouted, my throat dry. "Slow down! Otherwise – "

"No need to worry," she exclaimed. "The Lord will protect us. I've learned that He sometimes puts obstructions in our path – " She paused, gasping for air. "just to show us when it's time to change direction."

I tried to ignore the implication of her remark. "Do you have any idea how often I dreamed about coming home?" By this time I cold smell my own perspiration. "But Matty, it wasn't at all like this!"

"I know – and I'm sorry. But things do change."

"Not – " We struck a deep rut and I banged my head against the windshield. "Not my love for you, Matty." *Why did I say that? Are these blows jarring my words loose?*

"That's sweet of you, but – " Matty said. Jamming on the brakes as we skidded up to a "Y" in the road. With little hesitation she opted for the left-hand route, which, unpaved but less used, proved to be much smoother.

As Matty promptly ratcheted up her speed and I realized we were encountering fewer ruts and holes, my confidence began to return.

"This morning has been so crazy!" I said. "Before all this confusion started, when I was in the upstairs hallway admiring your family photos, I felt as though I could actually hear you singing!"

"You probably *did* hear me singing. I came home early from visiting Janice. She'd developed a cold, so I couldn't take a chance – not when I've got a solo coming up tomorrow at church."

"A solo? That's a surprise. What will you be singing?"

" 'Amazing Grace.' "

"Great!" I shook my head, remembering. "Do you recall the first time I heard you sing that song? We were in church and – Wait a minute! –You mean you came home early today? How long had you been home?"

"Not long. When I returned and saw Dad's car gone, I figured you must still be upstairs with Mom. So I decided to wait downstairs where I could practice my hymn in the library."

"Why didn't you come upstairs right away?"

"It would have been too awkward," she replied.

"Awkward?"

"Because – " She threw me a glance I couldn't interpret, but said nothing further.

"Hey, if you're gonna be singing in church tomorrow," I said, "maybe I'll be able to snag a ride and – "

Matty swerved to avoid a large rut. "Don't get your hopes up." Her tone was crisp and cutting. "I may have to cancel."

With that she floored the accelerator and we hurtled down this new road which, it developed, was a much-neglected artery that boasted frequent, extended breaks in its formerly macadamized surface.

Even though my repeated attempts at conversation proved futile, I could detect in Matty's voice a coldness, a reckless determination to get to the hospital regardless of the danger.

Hey Matty, you're upset. Who wouldn't be under the circumstances? Your mother nearly killing herself, and before that, my letter asking about Garret. But the picture's changing, Matty – and I want to tell you about it. You see, when I saw you today (for the first time in nearly a year), something happened. Something great. Something altogether unexpected and unexplainable. Despite all the doubts and torment of the past several months, I fell in love with you all over again and –

I grabbed hold of the dashboard as the car slipped off the roadway, then Matty immediately brought it back.

Matty, I've got so much I want to tell you. But first, you've got to stop this crazy driving! Let's grind to a halt somewhere – anywhere – and let's talk this thing out. I know it's crazy and I don't understand it, but Matty I still love you!

So now, as we raced along this country road, I studied her profile, her gaze so focused on the congestion up ahead of us – and I took a deep breath. "Matty," I said," let's talk about what's bothering you."

"Nothing's bothering me."

"Matty, don't tell me that you're still in a stew over my letter asking about Garret. I'm sorry now that I ever wrote the damned thing! That episode in our past is something we'll both be better off forgetting."

That remark prompted a quick, sidelong glance from Matty, but no change in her demeanor. In fact, as we approached a Model T that was lagging behind the cars up ahead, her only response was to rev up the engine, propelling us past the Model T.

Suddenly, Matty turned to me, her features stern. "Bury the past," she said," is that what you want me to do?"

"Hey, whatever the problem, we can't change the past. There's no sense in getting ourselves so worked up."

"Easy for you to say."

A cutting remark, but let it pass. Keeping a wary eye on the traffic situation, I found it harder to ignore Matty's belligerent behavior. *Where is that sweet, young Christian Matty I left behind a couple years back?*

At this point I suddenly realized that Matty was staring at me – not watching the road! When I shouted a warning, her attention shifted back to the line of cars halted dead ahead. Color drained from her face. She frantically applied the brakes and swerved right. The car wobbled, nearly overturning, and with a terrible screeching noise, vaulted off the shoulder into a shallow ditch, tearing up gravel, ripping through brush, streaking along the gully, finally slamming up against a small culvert.

As my head struck the side window, I momentarily blacked out. When I came to, my eyes immediately sought out Matty–and my stomach contracted into a tight ball. Matty was slumped over the wheel, unaware of a terrible, ear-splitting roar and the crimson rivulet trickling down the side of her face and onto the collar of her coat.

XXX

Ann Arbor, Michigan

February, 1945

After shaking my head several times to clear away the fog, I let my fingers gingerly inspect the hairline above my right ear. *A lump, but no matting, no blood. But what is this dark veil over my eyes? This mist that cloaks everything? What is – the windshield – cracked, the radiator spewing a cloud!* Cautiously I tried moving my legs. *An explosion of pain from my ankle, yet everything seems so –*

Matty! Where's Matty?

I leaned over, gripped her shoulder. "Matty! Matty!" I shouted. "Wake up!"

No response.

"Wake up!"

But why am I shouting? Why is everything so noisy? The accelerator – it's jammed, the motor roaring! Can I reach the pedal? What's that smell? Antifreeze? Gasoline? It's getting stronger, the smell's everywhere! We've got to get out of this car!

I grasped the handle on my door. It refused to budge. I pulled the handle again. Some movement.. I put my shoulder against the door and shoved. Nothing happened. Then I noticed the door lock – still closed. *Dummkopf!* I raised the door-lock pin, pushed the door open and with some effort, clambered out. To keep my balance, I held onto the door. Once I had let go and endeavored to walk, pain again erupted in my ankle. I leaned against the car, casting about for some means of reaching Matty's door.

Fletcher, if you ever expect to get there, you'd better find some kind of a crutch.

Spotting a stout tree branch lying on the edge of the ditch, I dropped to my knees in the muck and reached out. *Still beyond my fingers!* I crawled through the glop, grasped a feathery offshoot and dragged the branch closer to where I could gain a tight grip on it. Using it as a crutch, I pulled myself upright and began a slow, laborious trek out of the muck to the other side of the car.

At the driver's side window it chilled my blood to see Matty still slumped over the wheel. *This close and yet I can't reach her!* Although fortunately the door lock-pin was still in the "open" position, when I tried the handle, nothing happened. Steadying myself with the branch and with the smell of gasoline flooding my nostrils, I yanked the handle repeatedly, only to lose my balance and fall backwards. Once more I slowly regained my feet and tugged on the door handle, concentrating my weight on the crutch. With a sharp "crack" the tree branch splintered, sending me reeling to the ground. I felt a sharp pain as one of the splinters gouged my left side.

Again I struggled to get back on my feet only to be bowled over by a loud "WHUMP"! The hood had burst into flames! *If those flames creep any further –*

Scooting along on my back, I edged closer to the car. Then raising my right leg, I kicked the side of Matty's door with all my strength. Something clicked. I scrambled to my knees and yanked at the door once more.

CRACK! It opened!

With a firm hold on the door handle, I regained a standing position, leaned against the door, reached in, clutched Matty's arm and at a snail-pace I pulled her free of the car. Then I made a final lunge that propelled both of us backwards onto firmer ground. Getting to my knees, I began dragging Matty away from the car. *This is slow. Much too slow. Faster, Fletcher, faster!* I kept at it and after what seemed like several minutes, I began shouting for someone to help us. Then –

WHAM! The car exploded! Fiery debris flew in all directions! A small piece struck Matty's arm, but I brushed it away, then shifted my attention toward the road and someone came running toward us – then BLACKNESS!

*   *   *

The next few hours passed in a series of blurred episodes during which I was barely conscious of someone helping us, of white-coated attendants...of a stop-and-start ambulance ride that seemed to last forever...of a nurse and a doctor inspecting cuts and abrasions on my body...of new x-rays of my ankle.

As I became more aware of events around me, I realized that, having suffered only minor injuries, I was being released from the Emergency Room.

Immediately I asked about Matty and learned that she had been transferred to the Third Floor of the University Hospital and was now in the Operating Room. Now as I studied the wall clock outside her room, I noted it had been well over an hour since she had been taken to the Operating Room.

While I waited, I ran my fingers along the old incision on my ankle, inspected the two bandages on my side, then checked the abrasion on my knee. The tattered condition of my trousers and jacket reminded me to try one more time to reach Norm. Again no success. Before long, Al, a short, stocky U of M student, dropped by inquiring about Matty's condition.

One of Matty's classmates, he had been on his way to the U of M basketball game, had seen us veer off the road and crash into the culvert. Because of the heavy traffic he experienced considerable difficulty working his car over to the shoulder so that he could help. As luck would have it, he had to leave his car alongside a large thicket that made it extremely difficult for him to reach the ditch where our car lay wedged against the culvert, the fire still limited to our radiator. As he pushed his way through the heavy brush, he kept looking over his shoulder to see if any other help was coming. Although he saw no one, some driver must have turned in a report on the accident since an ambulance soon arrived, amid the confusion of traffic, much shouting and honking of horns.

Before Al left I shook his hand and thanked him for what he had done. Then as I watched him head down the busy corridor for the elevator, I felt confused by the turn of events. *How did Al just 'happen' to turn up at the accident scene when he did? It's a cinch Matty (and Prescott too) would probably try to convince me that someone was praying for us at the time.*

Yeah, sure.

Now as I awaited Matty's return from the Operating Room, I learned from the nurse that Mrs. Seagrave had been treated and assigned to a bed in the Intensive Care Unit where Matty's father stood by to monitor her progress.

I was about to head down the hall to try calling Norm again when an orderly wheeled Matty into the room on a gurney. I squeezed her hand. *How great to see her conscious again and trying to smile!* But before I could do anything further, the nurse asked me to step outside while she and the orderly settled Matty in her bed.

Fortunately I put the time to good use, reaching Norm on the phone to explain the crazy chain of events that had thoroughly disrupted our original plan for him to pick me up at the Seagrave's home. He agreed to call for me at the hospital later in the day with whatever clothes he could scrounge from the meager wardrobe in my apartment.

When I returned to Matty's room, I was surprised to find her asleep and Seagrave, dressed in a smart brown suit, bending over to give her a kiss.

"Good to see you again," he said, extending a hand. "Thought I'd drop down here while Eva's undergoing a few tests."

"How's she doing?"

He loosened his collar. "Reasonably well. I think Eva'll be released after a week or so." Seagrave paused, shifting his feet a little. "There was a fellow named 'Al' who dropped by while you were phoning. Apparently he witnessed your accident. From what he told me, you had a lot to do with Matty surviving." Seagrave briefly felt Matty's forehead. "What have you learned about her condition?"

"A few stitches on her forehead. The burns on her arm aren't serious, but they'll leave a scar."

Seagrave grinned. "It looks like your wardrobe's not long for this world."

"You'll have to excuse the muddy pants, jacket and shoes. My friend Norm should come by later with whatever clothes he can find." I raised one arm. "Come to think of it, I probably don't smell too good, either."

I slumped onto the window seat and Seagrave leaned on his chair. "You haven't told me much about your condition."

I looked out the window. It was beginning to rain. "The doc advised me to keep off my feet as much as possible. The ankle's throbbing some, so I'll be using my cane a little."

"This fellow, Al, said you and Matty were unconscious when he reached you."

"I guess the explosion knocked out both of us, but the people in Emergency weren't able to find anything terribly wrong with me." I paused while the PA system called for a Dr. Rutledge to report to the Emergency Room. "A few patches here and there and they turned me loose. Thank goodness."

"Thank the Lord."

"Yeah, sure."

Abruptly Seagrave looked at his watch. "I guess it's about time I get back to see how Eva's coming. Meanwhile – " Seagrave's cheeks colored slightly, "I want to thank you for what you did." He clasped my hand. "When I realize that today my family could have been wiped out – " He looked directly at me, his eyes tearing, his expression unflinching. "Lord be praised, it wasn't – thanks to you." The timbre of his voice fluctuating as he fought to maintain his composure. "Chad, I'll never be able to thank you enough!"

"Hey, you must know how much Matty and her mother mean to me."

Seagrave patted my shoulder. "You'll be here for a while?"

"It'll be an hour or so before Norm arrives. But I won't leave until I can change clothes and until I'm certain Matty's okay."

Seagrave paused at the door, fingering a button on his jacket. "Good. Maybe I'll be able to take you back by the house so you can pick out a few items from my closet. Give us a chance to talk about something for you at Ford's. Would you be able to stay at the house for a few days after Matty gets home? I'm sure the two of you have plenty of catching up to do."

I nodded and he was gone. *I don't know, Seagrave. Dredging up the past isn't likely to be all that much fun.*

*   *   *

"There you be!" Mrs. Quigley said. "I'm hopin' that beastly bandage feels a wee bit more comfortable now."

"Oh, it does!" Matty said, easing back in her chair. She smiled at me. "I know the sun's shining, but will you be warm enough out in the gazebo with only that light jacket? I'm sure we can find something else for you in Dad's closet."

"Come to think of it," I nodded, "could you rustle up another one of those capes – say something in chartreuse?"

Mrs. Quigley laughed.

Matty merely crinkled her nose. "Don't you go making fun of Mom's cape. It may be slightly oversize for me, but with my arm in a sling, it certainly makes it easier to keep everything covered."

Just to see Matty smile like that! Hey, maybe the climate has improved. With a little more 'limping', I might even get her to help me make it out to the gazebo.

Sure enough, after watching me "struggle" to keep up with her, Matty put her free arm around my waist – and I was awash in her fragrance. Together we hobbled along the stone walkway toward the gazebo.

Even in the stark February sunlight the Seagrave backyard resembled something out of a landscaping magazine. Although many times Matty had told me the names of the various plants that bordered the stone pathway, at the moment I couldn't remember one of them. All I could think of was: *Hey, Matty! We're back together!*

We followed the stone walkway bordered with low shrubbery and groundcover (now somewhat gray) – past a rock garden and an elaborate birdhouse – to Matty's beloved gazebo with its quaint cupola– a sanctuary she and I had visited so many times during the fall and winter before I left for the Army.

Once we had settled ourselves on the built-in bench that lined the inside perimeter of the gazebo, she squeezed my arm. "I'm sure you must love this place as much as I do. I specially remember weekends when I was home and the weather wasn't too hot or too cold. Many of my letters to you were written right here."

Oh, what a thrill to hear her voice regaining its former softness! Those green eyes sparkling – yet there's something in those eyes I don't recognize –

"Every one of those letters meant a lot to me," I said. *True enough, but now I feel awkward. There are questions I want to ask, but I can't allow anything to spoil this moment.*

Then, even as I watched, Matty's smile hardened. "Of course," she said, "there were some letters that never – "

My throat tightened, suddenly grew dry. "Don't, Matty! Don't go there! Forget about the explanation I asked for. I already know what happened. Let's wipe the slate clean and start over – right here, right – "

"No, let me finish." She placed her hand over mine, her expression grim. "I know it's hard, Chad, but there are some things we need to talk about. You know, those letters we never mailed."

I shivered a little as the sun went behind a cloud. "Never mailed?"

"Yes." She looked away from me, back across the walkway toward the house, her lips quivering. "We need to talk about these things, Chad." Again she paused. "Like the letter I should have sent you long ago. A letter confessing my relationship with Garret, my pregnancy and – " She stopped, suddenly voiceless, her lips moving tentatively, forming unspoken words. " – and the abortion."

I put my arm around her and kissed her cheek. "Don't beat yourself like that, Matty. I realize now how tough it must be for you to remember all that."

She closed her eyes and nodded. "Certainly it hasn't been fun, but don't make a heroine out of me. I can talk about it only because I asked the Lord to forgive me and grant me strength to deal with that whole mess." Once more she turned to face me. "Now I want to talk about a letter you never sent me."

"I was overseas, remember?" My heart began pounding. "I didn't get a chance to write every day."

"Yes, I know. But I realize now that in your letters you weren't telling me – everything."

"I wasn't?" I squinted at her. "What are you talking about?"

"It's something I sort of stumbled on." She reached out to caress my cheek with her free hand. "One day, while you were still overseas, I was reading Mother one of your letters, happy that in the midst of all the bloody carnage of war you had a safe job, well behind the lines. But suddenly in the midst of my reading, one of the stories in your letter must have disturbed mother. She interrupted me, took my hand and explained something she and Dad had figured out some while back. Apparently by discussing your return address with a friend in the military, they had learned that you were in a frontline outfit – and though terribly concerned about you, they had decided not to tell me – at least not then. When they finally did, however, I was first shocked, then angry. Angry that you had never told me the truth about the danger you were in over there."

"Matty, please understand," I said. "I simply did not want to worry you."

"But all the time you weren't telling me the truth!"

I could feel my face coloring, my underarms getting wet.

"That hurt, Chad. Hurt me deeply." Once again the sun broke through as she paused to look away towards the low stone wall barely visible through the evergreens. "But my folks had always taught me to forgive others – even as Christ forgave me."

"Then you've forgiven me for–for lying to you?" My mouth so dry.

"Yes, I have." She leaned over and kissed me. "But it took a while. The Lord had to deal with me first, reminding me how many times He had forgiven me, how many times He must have spared you."

"Matty, now you sound so much like Prescott," I grinned. "He was one of the guys in my squad. You remember him?"

I expected a smile, but none appeared.

Finally she responded. "Yes, I do. You mentioned him several times in your letters. But you know Chad, I may sound like Prescott for a reason. Sometimes Christians fall into speech habits that tend to make us sound alike." Inexplicably, she began shaking her head. "I had a letter from him not so long ago."

Despite the chill February breeze, my face felt hot. "You had...a letter...from Prescott?"

"Yes. He told me that you had been wounded – and Garrett had been killed!" She paused to draw a handkerchief from her cape. "Chad, that letter jolted me so much that I nearly fainted. To hear how you had been living in so much danger – and to get that kind of news from a stranger!"

I felt savaged. "Did he also tell you how long I had been waiting for an answer from you – the letter about you and Garret?"

She pulled her cape more tightly about her. "Yes Chad, he did, but I knew exactly how long it had been."

"So that, my dear, was the letter you never wrote."

"Oh, but I did write that letter. A long letter, explaining all about Garret, about my folks, about what had happened. I'm so sorry, Chad. I just couldn't bring myself to mail that letter."

I got to my feet and stared down at her, anger tempting me. *Do you have any idea what that delay put me through? Do you realize* – but I could not bring myself to say anything to hurt her. My gaze shifted to the small, faded-white cement pond at the center of the garden. I felt the chill wind as a few oak leaves scudded across its barren emptiness. "Why didn't you mail it?" I asked.

"Because about the time I was ready, something strange arrived from overseas." With her free hand Matty reached inside her cape and withdrew an envelope. She handed it to me, her eyes shining with tears. "Please read this."

Uncomfortable, a brackish taste in my mouth, I drifted to the other side of the gazebo before I could look at the letter she had given me, my hand unsteady, my eyes moving swiftly down the page, yet my mind bewildered by its content. *I cannot believe what I am reading.*

XXXI

I slumped onto the bench, my ankle throbbing, my lips moving slowly and silently going over the words again:

*   *   *

Dear Miss Seagrave:

You don't know me, but I'm a member of Chad's squad and damned glad he made it back home with a million-dollar wound. Because Chad was always bragging about "his blond" (I've seen your picture many times) I figgered anybody that gorgeous ought to be told the facts about the guy she may end up marrying.

Lemme tell you about something that took place back in North Africa a few years ago. Back when most of us were fresh out of the States not assigned to any unit and full of vim and vinegar.

At our first camp in Morocco it didn't take us long to find out that a large group of Arabs made it a habit to gather in the dark on a hillside just outside camp most every evening. They just wanted to do a little business with some of us rich GI's.

As you might expect, the Army command didn't want us to fraternize with those filthy, smelly Arabs, so they built a tall, barbwire fence around our camp.

It didn't take very long for a bunch of us lonely GI's (including Chad) to climb over that lousy fence so we could get to the Arabs. Naturally, during the time of our moonlight visit practically every one of us managed to spend some enjoyable time with the Arab girls, engaging in a little "personal exercise", if you know what I mean.

Maybe Chad has already told you about this incident. Maybe not. But anyway, I figgered you ought to know about it.

*   *   *

The letter was unsigned.

I rose, walked over to where Matty was seated and eased down onto the bench beside her. Wordless, I handed her the letter. *This is a pack of lies! All of it! But what can I say that will convince her?* Finally, I summoned enough courage to speak.

"Matty, none of this is true! I just don't know what to – "

"Never mind," she said. "I want to believe you, Chad, but at this point it really makes no difference."

"No difference?"

Matty placed her free hand on mine. "Please understand how much I appreciate everything you've done for me – as well as what you've been through. I'll never forget any of it. But the two of us need to face facts. Our relationship has literally been a house of cards – one shaky layer after another. Blame it on the war. Blame it on our long separation – whatever." She looked up at me, her green eyes filling. "Chad, don't you see where all this is leading?"

"I hope it's not leading you to believe that this letter is true."

"For the moment, let's forget the letter. Whether it's true or whether it's not true, let's recognize that the Lord is trying to tell us something."

"And what is that message, O Great Swami?"

"Chad, please!" She paused to get her breath as the sun suddenly broke through. "The Lord's trying to remind us that marriage is a serious matter. For it to last, each party must respect the other."

"And we don't?" I stood up.

"Not when we lie to one another. Not when one refuses to take the other seriously." Matty bit her lip and turned away. "Let's face it, Chad, so far our relationship has been based on lies that – "

"Now wait a minute!" I felt a bolt of pain go through my ankle.

Matty raised her hand. "Let me finish – please." Her voice was breaking. "I'm afraid I began it all when I failed to level with you about my former relationship with Garret – and about the..." Her lips struggled to form the words... "about the abortion."

I shook my head. "Surely, Matty, you must have known that I suspected the truth. What hurt most was that when I finally got the full story, I had to get it from Prescott."

"Prescott?"

"Yes, Prescott. I was surprised too. But apparently, when our unit left Italy to invade southern France, Garret began to worry that he might not survive the war – and decided to tell the whole story to Prescott." I looked back at the walkway, trying to count the number of patio blocks leading out to the gazebo. "Like you said, it is tough when you have to get the whole story from a third party."

Matty nodded. "As you can imagine, the job of keeping the truth about my life, keeping it away from you, that whole mess became a living hell for me. And, mind you, all that fallout came from just the *first* lie." She paused again. "Then you began the next lie about the danger you were facing every day as a – "

"I told you my reason for – "

"I know you did, Chad. But just as I had a reason for not telling you about Garret, you had a reason for not telling me about your dangerous Army job. And undoubtedly, you had some special reason for not telling me about the Arabs back in Africa." She carefully folded the letter and slipped it into the pocket of her cape. Then she turned her head toward the house, but I could see the tears streaking her cheek.

At this point I couldn't think of anything to say. Somewhere a dove began his slow, methodical, repetitive call.

When Matty had recovered enough to speak, her voice was much softer. "I've been praying about this whole problem ever since I learned you were in so much danger, resentful that you had never told me. But the Lord has made it clear to me that I was as much at fault as you were. You should have heard about Garret from me. And I should have – "

"Yeah, and you should have heard about my combat job from me."

Matty slowly shook her head. "There you are, Chad. Is that any way to begin a marriage?" A whiff of her perfume came my way.

Despite the cool breeze, I could feel myself perspiring under my jacket. *This is all so crazy! Why am I agreeing with her? After all the blood, the sweat, the terror, the cold, the loneliness! For everything to end this way!*

I leaned on my cane and looked into those luscious green eyes "Now listen to me, Matty! All this is so unnecessary. I'm perfectly willing to forgive you for what you failed to tell me about your past."

"You are?" Her look reflected a mixture of surprise and incredulity.

"All I ask is that you believe me when I tell you that everything in that mysterious letter is untrue. And that you try to be more understanding about my reason for hiding the facts of my Army service." I turned and walked to the center of the gazebo before facing her once more.

Matty rose and slowly prepared herself for the walk back to the house. "From my earliest days," she said, "I remember learning about Christ and his reference to the man who built his house upon sand. And the sky darkened and the storm came and battered the house, and it fell with a great crash."

I shook my head. "And because of your lie and my lie, you believe this god of yours is telling us not to get married?"

She pulled her cape closer about her. "And that's something even more important, Chad. Just think of how many times I've spoken to you about Christ, about reading the Bible, about – " She hesitated, rearranging the folds in her sling. "Always, – always you made light of what I was saying – as though it wasn't – "

"I know, Matty. And I've tried. But frankly, I find all those claims about Christ so difficult to accept, so – "

"Well Chad, there's your answer. You and I have reached the point where it makes more sense for us to remain friends. I'd love that. Getting married could turn out to be a big mistake."

Glumly, I moved to follow her, wincing at the effect of her words, my cane making a clacking sound as I moved along the patio walkway, my spirit flagging with each step. I looked up at the high, dark-edged cirrus clouds. They harbored a hint that snow was on its way. I shivered as again a bolt of pain surged through my ankle. *I feel so rotten that not even a cup of Mrs. Quigley's hot chocolate would do me any good now.*

Matty, I've told you the truth! What more can I say? Where else can I go? Now, if Prescott were here ... He always knew what to do ... If I remember right, when he was on patrol that time when we first landed on Anzio, how the tank caught them out in the open –no trenches, no foxholes, no nothing. And I asked him later where could he turn to get away from the tank fire in a situation like that. And all he said was: "I jest turn to God. He's my refuge."

Yeah, God.– and what else is new?

My brain still numbed by the shock of my exchange with Matty, I watched her walk along ahead of me.

Okay Fletcher, so now where do you turn – to Prescott? To – yeah, Prescott! That's who!

I called out to Matty as she reached the steps leading back into the house. "Prescott!"

She halted and turned back toward me, her expression questioning.

"Prescott," I said. "Write him. He'll tell you the truth. He was with me all the way." I waited for Matty's expression to brighten, but it did not.

"The more I hear about that man," she said, "the more I realize what a wonderful – "

"He's a Christian too. Straight up and down. Ask him about the Arab girls. He'll tell you the truth."

"Yes, I'm sure he would. And believe me, I've wanted to ask him – but I can't."

"You can't?" My throat tightened. "Why?"

Again Matty went to her cape. After a few moments she handed me an envelope, her handwriting plainly visible. The envelope was addressed to Pvt. James Prescott. It had been returned, unopened. It was stamped "KIA".

XXXII

Plymouth, Michigan
February, 1945

The two of us slowly continued toward the house, my mind still in shock after learning that Prescott was dead. This news only confirmed what I had contended all along. *Prescott's god doesn't give a damn what happens to men. You could pray all you wanted. His god would still do what he pleased.*

I hobbled on ahead of Matty and opened the sliding door. As she passed, I detected a glistening in her eyes. *Is it regret? Disappointment? Who can tell? All I do know is that I'm losing the one girl I've yearned for all these years. And all because of some damn-fool letter full of lies!* And only one thought kept running through my head: *Okay God, if you're so great with the miracles, show me what you can do with this one!*

Once inside, Matty dropped back on the sofa as though she were exhausted and gestured for me to take the large upholstered chair across from her. "Sit down for a bit," she said. "Did you say Norm's coming for you?"

I stood there, uncertain. "Yeah," I said finally. "He should be here any time." I slumped into the chair.

Actually I had called Norm's apartment earlier and left a message with his landlady: "I won't need Norm to come for me until late Sunday. The Seagraves have asked me to stay for the weekend."

But now, as I watched Matty, expressionless, slip out of her cape, I could see that my staying the weekend would be too much of an ordeal for both of us.

Abruptly an effusion of pleasant cooking odors swept into the room as Mrs. Quigley poked her red head of hair out of the kitchen doorway. "Mr. Chad, it's high time ye got out of that heavy jacket. Let me bring ye both some hot chocolate."

Matty nodded agreement. "Come on, Chad. No need for those heavy clothes in here. Mrs. Quigley has the right idea."

There was an emptiness in her tone that caused each word to cut into me like a knife. I settled back in the big chair and slowly shook my head. "This news about Prescott – what a shock! Why, I had a letter from him not too – Damn!" I looked away.

"He must have had a tremendous witness for the Lord," Matty said.

"Yeah, sure." The words came out slowly, mechanically. *Despite all the love I had for Prescott, I guess the guy was pretty stupid. All that prayer and sanctimonious Bible-quoting. What did it get him? One line in the Company Clerk's list of KIA's for the day.*

For the next several minutes of intermittent sunshine Matty and I engaged in an awkward session of small talk, energized by Mrs. Quigley and the strength of her hot chocolate. Nonetheless, I was actually grateful when I heard a car pull up in the driveway.

This has to be Norm. He probably never got my message. Just as well. The sooner I'm out of here the better.

Matty started to answer the door, but Mrs. Quigley waved her away. "Ye had better sit right there, young lady. I'll take care of greetin' our visitors."

Despite all the times I had kidded Norm Weingarden about his appetite and his girth, when Mrs. Quigley ushered him into the room, he looked absolutely handsome to me.

"Greetings and frosty salutations, my friends!" he said. Then, turning to Matty, he said: "I'm here, my dear, to take full custody of your – " He stopped in the middle of the room and squinted at Matty. "What in the world happened to you?"

"Just a little mishap," Matty replied. "Nothing too serious."

Norm shifted his attention back to me. "I hope you have a satisfactory explanation for all this."

His attempt at humor caught me off-guard. "Like the lady said, nothing serious," I stammered. Rising, I nodded to Norm. "I'm ready to leave whenever you are."

"Not so fast, my fine-feathered former foot-soldier." Again he turned to Matty. "Would you care to guess why in this world of scarce gasoline, this time of nationwide rationing, this era of – "

"Norm! For goodness sake!" Matty was growing a bit testy.

Long accustomed to his pronouncements being challenged, Norm was already heading back for the door. "Let me bring in a friend I'm sure you'll recognize." He paused awkwardly. "Someone, I venture to say, you'll both be happy to see."

While Norm eased out the front door, leaving it ajar, Matty and I exchanged glances. Her expression indicated she was as bewildered as I.

In a few moments Norm returned, guiding someone dressed in a long, heavy Army coat, smelling of mothballs

After some hesitation, the stranger said: "Hello to both of you," the tone familiar, but delivered in a weakened, halting voice.

It took me a few moments to recognize the identity of Norm's passenger, a process that shook me up more than any experience I had had in the past several months. As for Matty, she had risen, her eyes expressing shock, her face suddenly ashen. She slumped back onto the sofa and covered her face.

No one – not even Norm – said anything further, the ensuing silence punctuated by the tolling of the grandfather clock in the corner of the living room.

As for our mysterious visitor, a sizable bandage on his left cheek, a reddened area surrounded his right eye, indicative of facial surgery recently completed. Like a thunderbolt, the truth suddenly struck me: this was *Garret Wald!*

"Need a little help here," he said finally, gesturing for Norm. After the two of them succeeded in removing his long Army coat, Garret settled back ever so slowly onto the wingback chair next to mine. Norm, smiling broadly, sat down on the sofa next to Matty.

"Garret", I said, still recovering from the shock of seeing him again. "I never expected – "

"That makes two of us," he nodded. "I'm on a weekend pass from the hospital in Battle Creek." Brown eyes flashing, he turned to glare at Norm. "You never said one thing about Chad being here."

"I wanted it to be a surprise," Norm said, his face crimson.

Meanwhile, Matty had regained her composure. "Let's not blame Norm for anything. He's been a big help for all of us." She focused on Garret. "I – I guess we're all a little confused at this point. It's been such a long – " She closed her eyes and shook her head. "Actually, I'm so glad to see you! I'd heard that – " She turned her head away.

"In the past few months you've probably heard all sorts of stories about me," Garret said. "Fortunately, for me at least, a lot of what you've heard is untrue."

I leaned over to shake his hand. "Don't stand up," I said. "You've had enough exertion just getting here." As I resumed my seat, the strong odor of medication reminded me of the considerable effort it must have taken for Garret to make the trip from the hospital. *If I know Garret, he probably realized he would never get a pass, so he just walked out without one.*

As Garret continued to talk about his treatment at the hospital, my eyes kept searching him closely. I recognized the sandy, close-cropped hair, the blotchy skin. Yet – *This is not the Garret that I last saw. Aside from the bandages, the weaker voice, there's something different. Something has changed.*

Then I looked over at Matty for her reaction, but by now she had retreated to the picture window, looking out across the garden. Meanwhile Norm had got hold of a chair from the dining room. He sat down closer to Garret and me.

"Garret," he said, "when I picked you up, your tale about how you got here was enough to make my hair (all three of 'em) stand on end. I'm sure Matty and Chad are as anxious as I am to hear the full story."

At this point when Matty turned to face us all. I could see that she had been crying. She avoided looking directly at Garret. Then, awkwardly, a cloak of silence descended on our little group.

Finally Garret spoke, his voice a quavering remnant. He went on with a quick recounting of what he and I had experienced that fateful day in southern France last August, the day when our unit came head to head with a heavily armed column of the German 19th Army seeking to flee north to Germany.

Garret told how in the fighting at Montelimar he was badly wounded, how he watched as I retrieved part of our heavy machine gun and tried to carry it to our fall-back position under murderous fire, how the Germans swarmed over our former position and took Garret prisoner, how he passed out from the pain of his wound and awakened sometime later in the care of a German medical unit on the move.

A sudden clatter of pots and pans interrupted Garret's tale and Matty looked up with concern. But from the kitchen door Mrs. Quigley promptly assured us that all was well. I suspected that she had been listening to Garret's account all along.

As Garret continued, we learned that after his capture he was kept on the move almost continually with little time for treatment. Eventually he arrived at a hospital inside Germany where in the passing months he underwent several operations before the whole area was captured by American troops. That led to his transfer back to the States and the U.S. Army hospital in Battle Creek, Michigan.

Garret reached up to adjust his bandage, then pulled his sweater closer about him. "Obviously they're still working on me. Right now I've got a one-day pass. I expect there'll be more operations coming up"

"It's a miracle you're still alive," I said.

"Yeah, I was lucky. But more about that later."

"Garret, we want you to know that we're so glad you made it back to the States," Matty said, "Now tell me, do you need a fresh bandage?"

"No, this one's okay for now. I'll be back at the hospital by nightfall."

I remembered that he had always spoken so highly of his widowed mother. "Have you had a chance to visit your mom?" I asked.

"Before my last operation I was able to see her. She's in a home and her health's bad, but she's got a spirit that won't quit."

"How about the rest of the story?" Norm asked. "Want me to tell 'em how you got here?"

Garret turned briefly to stare at Norm.

"Let him go on with the story," I said.

Garret gave me an appreciative nod and continued. "Once I got a pass from the doctor, hitching a ride over here wasn't much of a problem. My roommate's father was driving to Detroit. He offered to drop me at your house, Matty, but since I wanted my visit to be a surprise, I had him let me off at the highway entrance to your subdivision."

I watched Matty's reaction. She slowly shook her head, obviously puzzled.

A delicious aroma drifting in from the kitchen told me that Mrs. Quigley had decided to prepare some treats for our visitors.

"As it turned out," Garret continued, "I had reached a point about halfway down the block, when I spotted a car in your drive. From the make and model, Matty, I figured it was your father's car." Again he reached up to adjust his bandage." So I decided this was not the best time to show up at your door."

"But why not?" I asked.

When Garret's only response was to stare at me, I realized that *dummkopf* had touched a nerve. Embarrassed, I looked out the window as a heavy bank of dark clouds suddenly eclipsed the sun.

Norm was quick to chime in. "I asked him the same question when I picked him up," he said. "I had just driven into the subdivision when I came across Garret walking back toward the highway. I stopped, took him aboard, we talked and – "

"Norm! Will you shut up!" Garret said. "I'm fully capable of telling my own story."

"Please Garret," Matty's tone was firm. "Let's be patient."

"Sorry." Garret ran his fingers through his hair, his face somewhat flushed. "I'd just like to speak my piece and be on my way. It wasn't easy, but I made the trip over here today for a reason – a tough reason." He cleared his throat and looked directly at me. "And the fact that you're here makes the whole damn situation that much tougher."

The sight of Garret with tears in his eyes surprised me.

After a moment Garret resumed his narration in a voice choked with emotion. "Chad, that day back at Montelimar, when in the midst of all the blasting, the dangers…and the confusion of the battle, you dropped the machine gun tripod and came back to help me – " He turned his head away for a few moments before resuming. "Even though you finally had to break off and go back to retrieve the tripod. I'll never forget what you tried to do that day." He reached out and took my hand.

I tried to say something, but nothing seemed right.

"For that I thank you." Garret said. Then he turned back to Matty. "As for you young lady, I have an apology to make."

Matty's expression of perplexity quickly metamorphosed into one of embarrassment. "No need to – " she began.

"Sorry, my dear, but there's a need alright. A need – my need – to straighten out a few matters." He paused,

240

obviously having difficulty, then glanced at me. "Obviously Chad, I had no idea that you'd be here – thanks to our mutual friend, Pinocchio."

Norm began another grin, then apparently thought better of it.

At this point Garret turned to Matty. "Some while back, I believe you received an anonymous letter from someone in Chad's squad – right?"

Matty nodded, her brow furrowed.

"Well, that letter came from me and not all of it was true – especially the part about Chad!"

There was no mistaking the shock in Matty's reaction.

"In fact," Garret continued. "I want to apologize to both of you. That letter was written last summer shortly after we landed in southern France. It was written, I must confess, out of meanness – and desperation."

Again he turned to Norm, who, for once, seemed nonplussed. "And now, my friend, if you would be so kind, I still have a chance to catch the west-bound train out of Ann Arbor. It should get me back to Battle Creek in plenty of time."

As Garret and Norm turned for the door, I followed close behind. Matty was still having trouble recovering from what Garret had said. When they reached the door, I found I could resist no longer. I reached out and placed one hand on Garret's shoulder. He turned and we managed a momentary, awkward embrace.

"Chad," he whispered. "It's all over now. It's all behind us." Then he was gone.

After Norm and Garret had left, Matty sank back on the sofa, speechless. She made no effort to resist as I bent over and kissed her. And no effort to stem the flow of tears that coursed down her cheeks.

XXXIII

The rooftop lights on the restaurant blinked off and on, off and on, announcing that "Jim's Coffee Shop" offered passersby a pleasant haven from the biting, late-spring wind and the threat of rain.

I pushed through the door into the brightly lit interior and limped toward a booth in the far corner, savoring the cooking odors drifting in from the kitchen. *Not many here tonight, but I'm not surprised.* I signaled the waitress to bring me a coffee, then doffed my topcoat and hat. Through the window I could still see my new Ford company car shining in the half-light of early evening.

This is crazy! I can't believe how things have changed! Seagrave snagging me an administrative job at Ford. Then, deciding I'd need a car to get me from my Detroit apartment out to Dearborn every day. Hey, I was so glad to get that job I would have been willing to limp all the way to Dearborn!

A quick glance at my watch. *Only 5:45. Matty should be here in a few minutes. I hope she understands why tonight's meeting is so critical.*

I opened my copy of the evening newspaper and, glad that I was out of it, I smiled at the glamorous treatment the press was giving the war:

AMERICAN TROOPS HAMMER GERMANY;
NAZIS CONTINUE TO GIVE GROUND

Hey God, thanks in advance if you can finish this lousy war against Germany in the next few months. And thanks also for pulling me out of it before the last act. I guess I'll always remember what Prescott said: "Give God credit for saving you." And Eva Seagrave, what she said. But God, I'm still confused about who gets awarded a 'Survivor Button' and who doesn't. What about Benicek, Geoffrey, and the others? They never got a 'Survivor Button'. Neither did the Seagrave's son. And remember Prescott? One of your star supporters. Yet you still shut him down. Doesn't make sense to me. And now you've even put Eva Seagrave in the hospital – Eva, the 'Prayer Warrior'. Frankly, from what I've seen of her in the past few weeks, it looks like she'll never get out of the hospital. That looks like a second-class 'Survivor Button' to me. But thanks again God for bringing Matty and me through it all in one piece. But I'm afraid your Awards System confuses me and –

"Greetings, mysterious person!"

I looked up to find Matty in a long, red coat and a small stocking cap, also red, her expression a playful smirk. She shed her coat and settled into the booth opposite me.

"You realize, I hope, that this is only Tuesday," she said. "I thought Friday was the evening when you were planning to take me out to dinner to celebrate your new job –" She stopped to look around. "at some high-class restaurant."

"I admit this isn't Longchamps. And I am sorry to break up your evening again after last night in your pastor's study, but – " I stammered, unable to find the words.

"But what, Chad?" Amusement still danced in her eyes.

'Well, for one thing, back in college my Philosophy prof always emphasized that there are no absolutes. Everything is relative. Yet, last night the pastor kept quoting Jesus so much. And there was nothing wishy-washy about what Jesus had to say. All of it was absolute!"

"Would it help if we went over some of those verses again?" Matty withdrew a New Testament from her bag.

My cheeks coloring, I fished for words. "Guess it would." After a little hesitation, the words came: "Last night

243

when the pastor went over the scripture with us, I realized just how much pre-marital counseling I need."

"I hope you also realize that our May wedding date is coming up pretty fast."

"That's the reason I called you this morning before you left for classes. I didn't want your pastor – "

"Keep in mind that now he's *our* pastor."

"Okay, *our* pastor." I paused for the noise of a bus arriving and departing from the stop outside the window. "Anyway, I realize now how much we need – I need – these pre-marital sessions. I just don't want to keep asking the pastor so many questions. Makes it look like you're marrying a dope."

We paused while the waitress came by to take our order.

"Don't beat on yourself so much, Chad," Matty said. "You did a good job on the first part of the session."

"You mean – ?"

"When he asked whether you were uncertain about whether God exists."

"Well, I had had some serious doubts."

"And I think I know what changed your mind," Matty said.

"Yeah. Your mother had a lot to do with it. I think I told you before that several times during the war I was in extreme danger – and yet each time I survived. Why? Later when I talked with your mother, I discovered that on those very days she had felt a strong urge to pray for me."

"That's a powerful story," Matty said as she removed her stocking cap. "I hope you're ready to acknowledge that when we pray, God does pay attention."

"Oh, He pays attention alright, but He doesn't always do something about it."

"That's because He's our heavenly Father, not our heavenly Genie."

"Hey, I guess I'll never understand His system, but He sure as h –, He sure saved my bacon more times than I can remember."

"And Chad, here's the beauty of it all: He isn't just a yesterday-God. He's working today!"

"I guess you're right."

"I know I'm right!" Matty paused to take another sip of coffee. "Remember that bitter cold day last February when we were walking back to the house from the gazebo – and you called for me to wait?"

"Yeah, and all you did was wave me away – why?"

"Because at that moment I was praying – praying that somehow that terrible anonymous letter I showed you would turn out to be untrue."

"And it did! Chalk up another one for God."

After the waitress had brought our order, Matty took a sip of coffee, then studied her cup for a few moments. "So tell me, does that incident settle the 'God' part of the problem for you?"

I started to reply, then paused. "Yeah, but –".

Matty's eyebrows arched. "You mean to tell me that now after all the time we spent together in the past few months – there's still something we haven't settled?"

"It's just that during all that time I hadn't been hearing the word 'God' so much as I'd been hearing the name 'Jesus'. Then at our first pre-marital session last night, the pastor started out asking how much I know about Jesus, do I believe that He's God's son and do I believe He can forgive sins? Whew!"

Matty shook her head. "Is that why when the pastor questioned you last night, you suddenly clammed up?"

I nodded. "I realized then, my dear, that I didn't really know much about Jesus at all. So now I'm hoping that you and I can meet a time or two before the next session with the pastor. Away from everyone – so you can help me better understand what I'm getting myself into." I reached across the table and covered her hand. "Do you mind helping a 'cripple'?"

"Chad, you're not a cripple." Matty looked down at my boot. "That ankle – it isn't getting worse is it?"

"No. Nothing like that. The 'cripple' I'm talking about just needs to get a better picture of what Jesus did during his lifetime and why he did it." I paused. "Sorry, but last night I just felt so stupid."

At that point Matty began rummaging through her purse.

"I hope you're not looking for a hankie," I said. "I wasn't trying to make you cry."

Matty shook her head, then blushed as she realized she had already retrieved her New Testament. It was sitting on the table right in front of her. She began thumbing through it. "If understanding Christ is the problem," she said," then that's where we need to get started." She handed the Testament to me. "I've opened it to the gospel of John. Starting with the third chapter, try reading each verse aloud and stop whenever there's something you don't understand. Then after we've discussed that verse, go on till you reach another verse that gives you trouble – and we'll discuss it. In that way each time we meet with the pastor, we will have already focused on verses where we need his help. Do you think that's a good idea?"

I saluted. "Yes, Commander."

"Chad, stop that grinning! Are you making fun of me again?"

"My dear, if we only spend half the time it takes to cover all the verses that I don't understand, we're going to have a long and happy marriage."

She took my hand. "What with all the obstacles we've faced, did you ever imagine we'd reach this point?"

I could only shake my head. "It's hard to believe that we're actually planning for a wedding day I never thought would happen."

Matty tried to make a face, but somehow it ended up in a grin. "And Chad, have you thanked the Lord for how He's helped it all to happen?"

I nodded. "Yes, my dear, I thanked Him." Then I brought her fingers up to my lips and kissed them.

Matty gripped my hand, an expectant look in her eyes. "And – ?"

"And –?"

"Is there something more?"

I could feel color rushing to my cheeks.

I see what you're getting at, Matty, but let's not make a big deal of it.

After a brief period of silence, I found courage to speak. "Yes, there is more. But I figured by this time you would have guessed."

"Guessed?" Her expression wide-eyed and playful. "What would I guess?"

I closed my eyes and winced, my heart hammering. "That this beat-up remnant of what used to be Chad finally got down on his knees and accepted Jesus – or better yet, He accepted me."

"It works both ways, Chad." Now even Matty was blushing. "All of us need forgiving."

"And by the way, my dear, while Jesus and I were having this conversation, He suggested two people who should be named Honorary Members of our wedding party."

"And who might that be, Mysterious Person?" The wide grin that suddenly brightened Matty's face told me that she already knew the answer.

"Jimmy Prescott and Eva Seagrave," I replied.

"And do you believe that's a good suggestion?"

I leaned across the table and kissed her. "Absolutely, my dear. Absolutely!"